LORINDA'S LEGACY

LORINDA'S LEGACY

Clarissa Thomasson

Clarissa Thomasson

s M p

Salt Marsh Publications

Published by:

Salt Marsh Publications

P. O. Box 1978

Nags Head, NC 27959

ISBN 1-929202-02-4

Cover Design by:

Carol M. Trotman
102 Azalea Court
Kitty Hawk, NC 27949

Library of Congress Catalog Card Number: 00-090647

The paper used in this publication meets the minimum requirements of
the American National Standard for Information Sciences—Permanence
of Paper for Printed Library Materials, ANSIZ39,48-1984.

Printed in the United States of America
10 9 8 7 6 5 4 3 2 1

For Lane and Amie, my severest critics, most painstaking editors, unfailing sounding boards, and staunchest supporters. This book would not have been possible without the two of you.

PART ONE

CHAPTER ONE

IT JUST AIN'T FAIR

CLINT'S BEND, NORTH CAROLINA—OCTOBER, 1919

LORI! LORI BETH! GIT in here! Mamma, I can't find Lori Beth nowhere!" fifteen-year-old Leah Belle Causey screamed. Her thin, brown hair streamed out behind her as she ran across the muddy chicken yard. Storming up the two wooden steps of the old Victorian frame house, she dutifully stomped the mud from her shoes on the weathered wood porch before opening the door. Then, slamming the screen behind her, she entered the small, dark kitchen and turned to face her mother.

"Leah Belle, fer God's sake, calm down," Malene Causey called, looking up from the scarred wooden table where she was busy popping late summer pole beans into an oversized tin pot. Turning to her eldest daughter, she blew absently at a stray wisp of brittle, brown hair—flecked with gray—and lifted a red, calloused hand to tuck the strand back into the tight bun at the base of her neck.

"Lori Beth disappearin' ain't no cause to go breakin' up the only house we got!" she scolded. "Lord knows your pappy works hard enough tryin' to keep up with what breaks around here without you helpin' it all along. Now, what's got you so all-fired riled-up about Lori Beth?" she sighed, continuing to break the beans.

"Seems to me the best thing you two can do nowadays is stay out o' each other's way. Never could git along any better'n a room full o' wild cats, nohow!" Malene added as a slight smile appeared in the wrinkles around her striking gold-flecked, green eyes.

Those eyes were the only feature on Malene's weathered face which still hinted of the beauty she had been when Clint Causey had first offered to carry her lunch pail home from school when she was thirteen. Fighting off all the other boys in town for the next two years, Clint had finally taken her as his bride in the tiny white church on the hill overlooking the muddy Roanoke River that day in May when she was the same age as her daughter was now.

"But, Mamma, it just ain't fair! Lori Beth don't do no work around here," Leah Belle wailed. Jerking a ladder-back chair around to face her mother across the table, she flipped her faded, brown calico skirt to one side and plopped herself unceremoniously into the chair. Uttering an exaggerated sigh, she stared at her mother with watery blue eyes—waiting to gain the attention she craved.

"Just how do you figure that?" Malene Causey asked calmly, throwing another handful of beans into the pot—while peering at Leah Belle from beneath her slightly-arched brows.

She did feel sorry for the girl. It must've been hard enough growin' up plain as mud, she thought as she looked at Leah Belle's nondescript, thin, straight, brown hair, which hung limply down her back, and noticed her pale face flecked with faded freckles, which framed two lashless, pale-blue eyes. But the fact that her younger sister Lorinda—with her thick honey-colored hair and gold-green eyes—had suddenly blossomed like the tall sunflowers in their side garden that summer of 1919 had to be the crowning blow.

She knew Leah Belle felt it—although her anger at her sister always seemed to have a valid underlying reason, which had nothing at all to do with her looks. "What's Lori Beth gone an' done to you now?" Malene sighed.

"Just run off again—as usual," Leah Belle seethed. "Like this mornin'. You know she's supposed to feed the chickens afore she leaves fer school?" she asked, waiting for her mother's absent nod before continuing. "Well, when I went out to gather the eggs after she left, there weren't a speck o' seed on the ground—an' them pesky hens peckin' aroun' in the dirt waitin' fer their breakfast. I ain't said nothin' then, 'cause you an' Pa was both busy. But I had to feed them chickens, too.

"Then, now," she went on, "it's Lori Beth's turn to milk the cows. Jake's gone to bring 'em in, an' Pa's yellin' at me to git out the milkin' stool. It just ain't fair, Mamma. She runs away every time there's work to do. Pa don't never seem to blame her, neither—just yells at me fer the work she don't do!" Leah Belle concluded, drawing a deep breath as she looked at her mother for understanding.

It was a relief just to get it off her chest. Summer had been hard enough, with Lori Beth runnin' off each chance she got—down to the river, like as not, to watch those hands from the lumber mill skinny-dippin'. But, now, since school had started up again, Lori Beth was gone most of the day. That meant Leah Belle, who had finished her schooling at the one-room schoolhouse last spring, now had to do most of Lori Beth's chores as well as her own.

"Hey, Ma, got any more o' that blackberry pie we had last night?" Leah Belle's older brother, Jake, yelled—slamming the screen door and stomping his worn boots off on the wooden floor.

"Jake Causey!" Malene screamed, forgetting her daughter and turning around suddenly at his approach, "Fer God's sake, I ain't deaf. Stop yellin'. An' don't wipe yer feet off inside the house when I just finished sweepin' this floor. Land sakes, does this look like the barn?"

"Aw, Ma, you gonna fuss at me when I done gone an' brung ya flowers?" Jake grinned, his hazel eyes atwinkle as he pulled a wilted bouquet of late daisies from behind his back. "They done sprung up all over the pasture since the rains, an' I thought how purty they'd look on the supper table," he added. Pausing to wipe a grimy hand over his perspiring face and push a dark-gold lock of hair out of his eyes, he handed them ceremoniously to his mother.

"Well, now. It's been years since a fellow brung me flowers." Obviously pleased, Malene smiled at her eldest son, took the bouquet, and rose from the table. "Leah Belle, Honey, run fill that old vase on the counter from the well, will you? Need to git these daisies in water afore they wilt," she added, turning to her daughter.

Rising angrily, Leah Belle gritted her teeth and glared at her brother. Pausing to kick at the chair leg in passing, she pushed past him, grabbed the vase from the counter, and ran from the room—accompanied by the crash of the high-backed chair as it hit the floor.

"When you're finished, better git out that milking stool," Jake yelled through the door. "I just brung the cows in, an' Pa's gonna skin some hide if they ain't milked afore supper.

"What's eatin' her?" he asked, then, turning to his mother as he righted Leah Belle's chair and sat down—his long, lean legs in worn denim overalls stretched under the table to rest on the chair opposite.

"Oh, Lori Beth's run off again, an' Leah Belle says it's her turn to milk the cows," Malene added, exasperated. Laying the daisies in the center of the table, she opened the ice box and pulled the last piece of blackberry pie from it.

"I swear, it's hard enough keepin' up with all o' you without fighting yer battles fer you, too," she added, as she pushed the pie in front of Jake and handed him a fork from the chest on the mahogany sideboard.

"But Leah Belle's right," she sighed, sitting down to her pot of beans again and gazing at her favorite child. At seventeen, Jake was as tall, lean, and handsome as they came in Eastern North Carolina—with his bronzed skin, hazel eyes, and wavy gold hair. She'd outdone herself on that one. Just, maybe, though, she should've saved a little bit for her next child. Poor, plain little Leah Belle—to be sandwiched between Jake and Lori Beth!

"Lori Beth does seem to be gone every time there's work to be done," Malene continued. "An' yer Pa dotin' on her so. It really ain't fair. But I ain't got enough energy right now to run after her."

"Want me to go find her?" Jake offered, showing a row of perfect teeth—now stained purple from the blackberry pie—as he smiled, rose, carried his plate to the sink, and paused to give his mother a hug. Being as smart as he was handsome, Malene's favoritism had never been lost on Jake. And he played it for all it was worth. It never seemed to fail, he smiled to himself, licking the remnants of the last piece of pie from his lips.

"Would ya, Son?" Malene asked, her eyes pleading with him. "I'd be right grateful, an' it'd sure help make peace aroun' here again."

She must've been beautiful once, Jake thought as he met his mother's gaze. Maybe that was what Pa'd seen so long ago. But to Jake, Ma was just Ma—a thin, hot, tired, aging woman in a stained calico dress and apron. But she did love him. He knew that. And he guessed he loved her, too,—although he had never given the matter any real thought. He just knew he couldn't stand the hurt in her eyes right now. Darn those sisters! What with Leah Bell's temper and Lori Beth always running off . . .

"Don't worry," he called over his shoulder as the screen door banged behind him. "I'll find her!"

• • •

HEY, NATE?" JAKE yelled as he stepped around two battered wicker chairs and rounded the wide wraparound porch with its peeling gingerbread trim. He stopped at the front door and looked around in the scattered leaves beneath the spreading oak tree, which hung over the far side of the house.

"Gonna bust my eardrums, sure as shootin'," his younger brother called from a cleared space beneath him. Crouched beside the wooden front steps, Nate never took his eyes from his target as he aimed and shot a shiny, white marble into a crude circle he had drawn in the damp earth.

"What's yer big hurry?" Nate asked at last, brushing his hands off on the seat of his denim overalls and leaning back on his heels to peer upward at his older brother—his damp, sandy hair standing on end giving him the appearance of a wary porcupine. At seven, Nate idolized Jake, but he was wise enough not to let it show. To survive as the youngest child, he had carefully cultivated his indifferent attitude until it had become a part of him.

"Seen Lori Beth this afternoon?" Jake asked, running down the stairs two at a time and crouching down in the damp leaves beside Nate.

"Maybe I has, an' maybe I hasn't," Nate taunted, his clear blue eyes—so like Pa's—coming to rest on Jake's face as he paused to retrieve his marble, wipe it off on his overalls, and slip it into his pocket.

"Who wants to know?" he asked at last, grinning up at Jake. His gap-toothed smile showed four permanent teeth, which were much too large for his small face, and several large gaps where his new teeth were yet to appear.

"Ma wants her. So, if you've seen her, you'd better tell," Jake continued, catching and holding Nate's unblinking stare. Two could play this game.

"Ain't seen her since school let out," Nate mused slowly, enjoying having the upper hand.

"Did she come home?" Jake asked. Nate could be so annoying. He was losing valuable time, he thought, looking in the distance at the sun as it sank behind the tree-line beside the Roanoke River.

He'd promised to meet Carrie Sue Phelps at the big tree by the river right about now. He'd thought the excuse of looking for Lori Beth would give him an hour free of chores—at least. He could envision Carrie Sue's clear-blue eyes gazing into his right now. And he could almost feel the warmth of her body through her thin summer dress as he wrapped his arms around her slim waist.

"She started this way," Nate began, nodding.

"An'. . . ," Jake prodded, returning to reality.

"Well . . . , Lori Beth wouldn't like me tellin' you this. . . ," Nate hesitated.

"Come on, Squirt, out with it," Jake threatened, grabbing a handful of Nate's spiky hair and pulling straight up on it.

"Ow! You're hurtin'!" Nate gasped, wrapping his own fingers over his brother's in an attempt to free them from his hair. "Let go, an' I'll tell you!" he shouted at last, breathing a sigh as Jake finally released his hold.

"Now, give!" Jake threatened again, his hand just in front of Nate's face—fingers splayed. "I ain't got all day."

"Well, she sorta walked past the lumber yard—like she done every day since school started," Nate continued. "But I don't think old man Phelps likes it none," he added, shaking his head. "Seems every time she walks by, he has to yell at all them hands to git back to work.

"Me and Bobby Joe was on the other side of the street, and old man Phelps was a yellin' at Willie again. Then Willie near to cut his hand off—lookin' at Lori Beth an' swinging that ax at the same time," Nate added.

"How badly was he hurt?" Jake gasped, wincing.

"Oh, it weren't that bad really," Nate hedged, shrugging his shoulders. "Only Lori Beth took on so. Then, old man Phelps got really angry an' ordered Willie home to bandage it up. Said he couldn't sell bloody lumber . . . ."

"Did Lori Beth go home with him?" Jake asked, incredulous. "You know how Pa feels about the Phelpses," he added, remembering his father's undisguised anger each time he saw Joe Phelps or heard his name.

Seemed both Pa an' Joe had courted Ma. He'd heard that from Willie—along with something about a fight at a dance just before Pa an' Ma were married. He hadn't really wanted to listen, especially when Willie had lewdly suggested that he an' Jake might be related. 'Course there weren't no truth to that! But, then, old Joe Phelps didn't seem any more disposed to bury the past than Pa.

"Pa's feelings don't bother you none," Nate added, looking at his brother defiantly.

"He don't mind us bein' friendly," Jake added in defense. "So me an' Will talkin' in town ain't gonna bother him none."

"That ain't what I'm talkin' about," Nate teased. "I seen the way you been lookin' at Carrie Sue when we pass her in town."

"Hey, just leave Carrie Sue out o' this!" Jake ordered. He could feel the red creeping up his neck. "I'm just askin' if you know where Lori Beth is."

"Probably where you'd like to be," Nate announced triumphantly.

"An' just where's that?" Jake asked.

"Down by the river with Willie—under them old oak trees—huggin' an' a-kissin'—like I seen you an' Carrie Sue all summer,"

Nate concluded, sitting back on his heels with a satisfied grin on his face. It was nice to have the last word.

"I wasn't . . . ," Jake began, then colored again as he looked at Nate's grinning face. "An' Lori Beth sure as shootin' better not be down there!" he yelled, jumping up and beginning to run toward the distant river bank. "Pa'll skin her alive if he finds out!"

"Ain't no skin off my nose," Nate called after him. Then, receiving no reply, he shrugged, removed the marble from his pocket, and took aim once again at his makeshift ring.

CHAPTER TWO

TOO YOUNG FER BARN DANCIN'

WILLIE PHELPS JUMPED TO his feet from behind the woodpile at the sound of crunching leaves in the woods behind him. His long, flaxen hair brushed the tops of his pale eyebrows as he shaded his eyes with a bandaged hand to look more closely into the copse of gnarled, gray-green oak trees, which bordered the rapidly-flowing Roanoke River below him.

Crimson and pink rays streaked the pale-blue horizon, and the late afternoon sun created a halo around the slender, tanned young woman running toward him in a billowing, white summer dress—her long, honey-blond hair flying around her.

Willie blinked and looked again. Then, hurrying forward—his face breaking into a wide grin—he called out, "Hey, Lori Beth! Been waitin' fer you."

Breathlessly drawing up beside Willie, Lori Beth paused to brush the loose strands of hair from her eyes—while not failing to notice the direction of Willie's gaze as the lace on her deep-cut bodice rose and fell from her exertion. "I had some chores to do first, Willie," she smiled. "An' I gotta do the milkin' today, too, so I can't stay . . . ."

"Did you remember to ask about the barn dance?" Willie interrupted—searching her face.

"I tried," she answered sadly—her wide-set green eyes with the golden flecks suddenly downcast beneath long, gold lashes.

"What did yer pa say?" Willie asked, tipping her chin toward him with one hand and tentatively reaching out his other hand to twine his fingers in her luxuriant hair.

Lori Beth made no attempt to stop him—rolling her head backwards in obvious enjoyment and murmuring as he caressed her neck. "I asked, 'What'd he say?'" Willie persisted after a moment, wadding her hair up in a fist and playfully holding her head immobile.

"Stop, Willie!" she ordered, laughing nervously and looking away from him—embarrassed—searching the nearby riverbank for any unknown spectators.

"I want to know what yer pa said," Willie persisted—refusing to release his grip.

"He said just what I knew he'd say," Lori Beth sighed. "He thinks fourteen is too young to go to barn dances—even though I reminded him that Mamma had gone to lots of dances when she was my age, an' then they got married when she was only a year older than I am."

"What'd he say then?" Willie asked, releasing his hold on her hair, but still holding her with his eyes.

"He said that was just what he was afraid of an' he wasn't about to let me end up like Mamma—birthin' babies an' tied to a stove before I was even outa school," Lori Beth added sadly. "He's gonna let Leah Belle go to the dance with Jake. But he says I gotta stay home with Nate.

"It ain't fair, Willie. It just ain't fair," she continued, her full lips drawn down in a well-practiced pout.

"Too young, huh?" Willie began. "Little does he know!" he added impishly. "You're not too young fer this, are you?" he whispered in her ear as he wrapped his arms around her waist and pulled her to him. He could feel her heart beating through the thin fabric as he bent her head backwards and buried his face in her neck.

Lori Beth felt herself grow limp. Willie smelled delicious—of harsh lye soap and wood shavings tinged with perspiration. The stubble on his lips and chin sent chills through Lori Beth's body as they brushed her skin. As Willie's mouth at last pressed hers and forced her lips apart, she opened her mouth, inviting his tongue inside.

"Or this," Willie continued. Releasing her mouth at last, he raised one hand to slip the thin organdy fabric from her shoulder—just as a quivering gray squirrel dropped to the ground from a tree beside them.

"Willie, no!" Lori Beth gasped, her eyes flying open at the noise while she grabbed the fabric from his hands, pulled the sleeve back into place, and glanced quickly down the path. "Suppose somebody comes?"

"Come on, Lori Beth," Willie continued, pulling her to him again. "Ain't nobody out here but us. You been teasing all sum-mer—struttin' around town in them thin dresses an' prancin' past all o' us at the lumber yard. I seen you lots of times sneakin' up over by the water hole when the guys an' me was swimming. I know you want this, too. It's what you come out here fer, ain't it?" Willie asked.

"I come to see you, Willie. But it's gettin' late now, an' Papa'll be looking fer me," Lori Beth replied, her eyes downcast. "If he ever finds me out here with you . . ."

"He thinks he's too good fer us, don't he? Just like yer mamma was too good fer my pa all those years ago. Oh, I know all about it. Now, us loggers ain't good enough fer his little girls neither? That what he thinks?" Willie asked, angrily, grasping Lori Beth's chin in his hand and forcing her to look at him.

"I . . . I don't know what he thinks, Willie. Please, you're scaring me," Lori Beth added, wriggling from his grasp and adjusting the neckline of her dress as her eyes quickly roamed the nearby riverbank and the wooded path behind her.

"Worried somebody seen us, ain't you?" Willie asked, noticing the direction of her glance. "What're you gonna tell Papa if somebody does see us an' tells him where his sweet little girl spends her afternoons?" he went on, as footsteps thudded on the path behind them—causing them both to turn.

"Lori Beth! Lori Beth! I been searchin' the whole county fer you!" Jake called, out of breath, as he ran down the leaf-covered path toward his sister. He stopped short as he rounded the woodpile and glimpsed her companion.

"Willie!" he called angrily, as Nate's words came back to him. "What're you doing here?"

"Probably the same thing you been doing down here all summer with my sister," Willie replied with a smirk.

"I . . . I don't know what you're talking about," Jake hesitated.

"Don't mind him," Lori Beth interrupted, laying her hand on Jake's arm. "I seen him hurt his hand today as I was walking home from school. When I seen him out here just now, I only wanted to see if he was all right. Is Papa real mad at me fer not being there to do the milkin'?" she inquired, her luminous eyes searching Jake's face.

"Pa don't know yet. But Leah Belle's on the warpath. I wouldn't put it past her to tell him if he makes her do the milkin'. Mamma sent me to find you an' tell you to git home fast," Jake answered.

"I was just comin', anyway," Lori Beth shrugged. "Bye, Willie. Hope your hand gets better," she added, running down the path.

"See ya, Willie," Jake offered, as he turned and made his way down the bank. He hoped Carrie Sue was still waiting . . . .

● ● ●

THIS THE SHARPEST ax you got?" Joe Phelps demanded, running his finger gingerly across the blade of the new ax as he leaned against the scarred counter in the general store.

"Same brand you always get," Elliott Kingsley laughed. Taking a final draw before laying his pipe in the ash tray he kept behind the counter, he wiped his grizzled brown beard and adjusted his red suspenders across his extensive mid section before taking the ax from Joe. "Never had a complaint before," he added casually.

"Well, you got one now. Think I'm due a refund. Darn kid o' mine nearly cut his hand off with the last one I got here," Joe grumbled angrily, stretching to his burly, six-foot-three inch height and glaring from under a shock of faded yellow hair at the short, balding Elliott. Moving to Clint's Bend as a kid with no money and no family background, Joe had learned early the only respect he was likely to get was through intimidation. His size and his strength—built up by many years of lumbering—had given him the weapon. It had seldom failed him.

"Weren't the ax's fault," Elliott smiled knowingly, ignoring Joe's pose as he turned to the cash register to ring up the sale. "Have to take it up with the company if you want a refund. I just sell 'em," he added, turning back to the counter and waiting as Joe grudgingly reached into his overall pocket, drew out a roll of wrinkled bills, and laid his money on the counter.

"Think yer answer might be to put blinders on that young 'un so he'll tend to business," Elliott added, his head still bent over the cash drawer. "Maybe it runs in the family. Don't think I haven't seen that little Causey gal walk by here on her way home from school. Just as pretty as her mamma was, isn't she? I seem to remember a barn dance my daddy threw not so very many years ago when you and Clint . . ."

"Got nothin' to do with it," Joe interrupted angrily as he reached for his change and stuffed it into his pocket. "My boy wouldn't be caught dead with any kid belongin' to Clint Causey."

Turning with a sack of chicken feed in his hand as he heard his name, Clint Causey strode around a nearby display rack—his face beneath his wiry brown hair flushed with anger. "Got some problem with my family?" he asked, heaving the bag of feed onto the counter as his deep-blue eyes met the startled gray ones of Joe Phelps.

"Now, Clint," Elliott called nervously as he pulled a long piece of brown paper off a roll beside him and carefully arranged it on the counter between the two men. "We was just talkin'. No need takin' offense. I was just remarkin' how much that young 'un o' yers looks like Malene used to. She sure was a looker. Had every boy in town wantin' to do battle with you just to get her to notice him.

"You remember that barn dance when my daddy had to separate you two fellas? I tell you, you was a sight—hoppin' around on that broken foot o' yours tryin' to lay Joe flat, and the whole party takin' sides and cheerin' you on. Still got the blood stains on the barn floor," he laughed.

"Wouldn't nothin' have happened if Joe'd kept his hands to himself on that hay ride," Clint snorted, slamming a handful of change on the counter.

"Wouldn't nothin' have happened if Malene had stayed behind with you an' yer crutches neither," Joe countered. "She made her own decision. Believe me, she didn't do nothin' she didn't want to that night. Ask anybody else who was there, an' they'll tell you," he laughed.

"Speakin' o' barn dances, Clint," Elliott added quickly—hoping to end the unpleasant encounter, "are you comin' to the one the missus an' I are throwin' next week? We haven't heard from you an' Malene yet."

"Got a horse that'll probably be foalin'," Clint answered sullenly. If he never attended another barn dance, it would be too soon.

"But you oughta at least send Malene an' the kids," Elliott prodded as he wrapped Joe's ax in the paper and laid it on the counter. "Got three fiddlers set to play. An' Alice has been cookin' fer weeks. She'll be awful upset if some o' you don't come."

"Think Clint had his fill o' barn dances years ago," Joe laughed, picking up his package. "But if Malene wants to go, let me know," he added over his shoulder as he turned to leave. "Since you'll be tied up, I could show her a right good time."

"Sorry, Clint. Guess I shouldn't have brought the dance up. Didn't know that little incident still ran so deep after all these years," Elliott commented with a shrug as Joe disappeared through the doorway.

"Married eighteen years, but that damned Joe Phelps never lets it die," Clint muttered as he took the change Elliott handed him and picked up his bag of feed. "Been a thorn in my side all my life," he added.

● ● ●

YOU DONE OPENED yer mouth one too many times, Joe Phelps. Ain't no way you're gonna get away with that last statement you made in there," Clint yelled as he dragged the bag of feed through the open doorway and approached the back of Joe's wagon, which was parked at the curb.

"You got a bone to pick with my dad?" Willie asked, raising his head from the bundle he was tying down on the far side of the wagon.

"I sure as hell have," Clint answered, fuming as he looked about for Joe.

"Well, he ain't here right now, but maybe I'll do," Willie continued, flipping the ends of the rope across the bundle and brushing his hands off on his overalls before turning defiantly to Clint.

"You can give him a message from me. Just tell him to keep his damned mouth shut—if he knows what's good fer him," Clint exploded.

"Maybe you better take a dose o' yer own medicine," Willie answered, nonchalantly. "Seems you been opening yer mouth right much lately. Don't think I ain't heard what you been sayin' in town 'bout my family.

"Oh, I know the story—how yer big-shot granddaddy, Jake Clinton, owned this town when my granddaddy was just an out-o'-luck railroad worker lookin' fer a job on his big spread. But yer daddy weren't the businessman his father-in-law was. And that spread ain't so big since the '94 depression, either—is it? Now all them kids o' yers ain't no better'n my granddaddy was—milkin' cows an' sloppin' pigs fer a livin'—while you still go struttin' 'round town like you owned it.

"Still think you Causeys are too good fer us Phelpses, though, don't you? Well, let me tell you, choppin' wood's a darn sight better'n sloppin' hogs any day. But I'll be sure to give Pa yer message," he added with a smirk.

● ● ●

GOT AN APPLE pie coolin' on the windowsill. Be ready in a few minutes if you want a slice," Malene smiled, looking up from her sewing as Clint entered the kitchen.

"Better save it fer yer beau," Clint snarled, pulling off his battered cap and hanging it on the peg by the door before turning to his wife.

"What's that supposed to mean?" Malene exclaimed, putting down her sewing and looking quizzically at her husband. "Fer the love o' mud, what's gotten into you? It's gonna be a good harvest—you said so yerself. Ain't nobody took sick, an' now that mare's fixin' to foal . . . . Seems to me you should be kickin' up yer heels 'stead o' snarlin' like a mad dog. Somethin' happen in town?"

"Ran into Joe Phelps. You got a date fer the barn dance—if you want it," Clint answered, taking a glass from the cupboard beside the sink and bending over to take a bottle of water from the ice box—without looking at his wife.

"Thought I'd go with you—that is, if you ever get around to askin' me," Malene smiled again. Ignoring her husband's comment, she stood and walked over to run her fingers lovingly through his thick hair. She'd only hoped to make him a little jealous at that barn dance so long ago. She'd had no idea it would haunt him so.

"I've just about finished makin' the girls' dresses, an' I think I can get mine done in time," she added, returning to the kitchen table when she got no response. "How do you like this pink gingham fer Lori Beth?" she asked, shaking out the half-completed dress and holding it up for her husband to see.

"Ain't goin'," Clint responded sullenly.

"Who ain't goin'?" Malene asked calmly.

"Lori Beth. Told her so myself last week when she was pesterin' me so. An' after what I heard at the store this afternoon, she sure as shootin' ain't goin'," Clint asserted.

"What was that?" Malene sighed, sitting down again and wadding the dress into her lap. If Lori Beth couldn't go, then she couldn't either. An' she'd been lookin' forward so much to the dance. Weren't many chances to get out o' all the work fer an evenin'.

"Elliott Kingsley says all the guys in town been lookin' at Lori Beth when she walks by. Hinted that's why Willie nearly cut his hand off."

"That what's got you so upset?" Malene laughed. "Clint, every girl in Clint's Bend would give her right arm just to get one look as she walked down the street. Goodness knows, we all got just so much time before we're all stretched out o' shape and birthin' babies . . ."

"That's just why she ain't goin'. I ain't gonna see her end up cookin' an' cleanin' some fella's house before she's outa school, an' I told her so. We both know what goes on at them barn dances," Clint asserted, draining his glass and putting it into the sink.

"You can't hold the girls back forever. Leah Belle's fifteen now. When I was fifteen . . . ," Malene continued.

"I don't give a hang if Leah Belle goes to that dance. I'll have Jake take her. He can introduce her to some o' his buddies. Maybe one of 'em might even give her a whirl around the floor—as a favor to Jake—to keep her from being a wallflower," Clint added. "Speakin' o' Leah Belle, where is she? It's just about milkin' time."

"I'm right here, Pa," Leah Belle answered, pushing the screen door open with her shoulder and setting a large pitcher of milk down on the counter. "Your plain little wallflower done finished all her chores. Guess that's all I'm good fer around here," she added, tears springing to her eyes.

"Maybe yer ma needs some help in here then," Clint answered, failing to acknowledge his daughter further as he pushed past her out the screen door.

"Yer pa didn't mean nothin', Honey," Malene soothed, gathering her daughter in her arms. "An' you heard he's gonna let you go to the dance. Lori Beth's been askin' fer days, but you're the one he's gonna let go."

"He don't have to worry 'bout me 'cause no one's gonna ask me to dance nohow. I heard what he said," Leah Belle answered defiantly.

"Now that ain't so, an' I don't want to hear you talkin' like that," Malene countered, lifting her daughter's chin to look into her eyes and tenderly wiping away the two streams of tears making their way down her cheeks. "You just watch. When you put on that new dress I made you an' we fix yer hair . . . Well, you gonna be beatin' the boys off at that dance."

● ● ●

A FULL HARVEST moon hung over Elliott Kingsley's sprawling, red tobacco barn. The lilt of a banjo—alternating with the lively strains of a fiddle—wafted onto the cool night air. Elliott and Alice, his bride of thirty-five years, stood in the doorway to greet each new-comer and direct him to the refreshment table—laden with newly-pressed apple cider and overflowing platters of Alice's famous cookies and gingerbread.

Together, the two watched as wagonload after wagonload of young and old spilled out into the night and poured into both sides of the weathered barn—some young men dancing gaily through the dry, scattered leaves before they even reached the lighted interior. The aroma of dried tobacco still hung in the humid air of the empty barn, and small bits of dried tobacco leaves clung to the rough wood siding.

"Best way I know to end a harvest," Elliott said, his merry brown eyes twinkling. These dances had been an annual event in town since his granddaddy had started them—just after the War between the States. Granddaddy said folks were grumblin' too much 'bout what they'd lost when they all needed to be thankful fer what the good Lord had provided.

Seemed to Elliott not much had changed in over fifty years, so he an' his daddy before him had kept the dances going. He sup-posed he looked forward to them even more now than he had as a lad. Wasn't as much to look forward to now.

And Alice seemed to love them just as much—fussin' an' a cookin' fer a whole month before each one as she did, he thought, looking lovingly at his wife and wrapping his arm around her shoul-ders. "After thirty-five years, I've still got the prettiest gal in the county on my arm," he bragged—loudly enough for those around them to hear.

"Now, Elliott, I'm sure there are those who would argue with you there," Alice blushed, running a finger around the tightly-stretched waistband of the new calico dress she had made from last year's pattern—secretly admonishing herself for not fitting the pattern to this year's figure. But there just hadn't been time, she smiled to herself. It would do, at any rate, for this one evening, she decided as she pulled a gray curl in place across her forehead and smiled at Elliott—her gray eyes mirroring his love.

They had first met at one of his daddy's barn dances—longer ago than she cared to remember. Probably half the county could trace their beginnings to one of the Kingsley's "big doin's"—as Elliott called them.

"Stop fiddling with yer sash! You look just fine," Jake scolded as he helped Leah Belle from the wagon in the deserted field and looked around. It seemed he'd waited for hours while Ma fussed with Leah Belle's dress and then with fixin' her hair—with him watchin' the clock all the while. The dance was already in full swing. He could hear the fiddles. And if some other fella had found Carrie Sue, well . . .

But he'd promised Pa, and he'd have to stay with Leah Belle and be sure she had partners. "Come on," he responded irritably, taking hold of Leah Belle's hand and pulling her toward the brightly-lit barn. At least they could get inside where he could keep an eye on Carrie Sue.

"Remember," he warned his sister, "be polite. An' don't dance too close or too many times with the same fella. This is yer first barn dance. We don't want nobody to git the wrong idea. Pa don't want no gossip."

"Now you're soundin' just like Mamma!" Leah Belle retorted, angrily pulling her hand from his grasp. "If you ask me, I think Pa's more worried that his plain little gal ain't gonna git asked to dance at all. That's the kind o' gossip Pa's afraid of."

"Come on, Leah Belle. Fer God's sake, don't make a scene. If the fellas don't ask you to dance, then I'll go git some of my buddies . . . ," Jake began.

"Oh, thanks a heap," Leah Belle scoffed. "If I ain't purty enough to git a beau on my own account, then my big brother's gonna do it fer me. How much did Pa pay you to make you agree to that?"

"Leah Belle, I swear, if Mamma weren't home with Nate with a runny nose an' Pa didn't have to sit up half the night waitin' fer that mare to foal, I'd leave here right now an' not come back. But I can't leave you unattended. I promised Ma . . . . An' that's the truth of the matter," Jake answered, taking her hand and helping her from the wagon.

"Honestly," he continued as she made a face at him, "folks'd think you didn't want to come to the dance. Then there's Lori Beth home cryin' her eyes out 'cause Pa says she's too young to come," he added, spitting on the ground at his feet and grinding the globule into the dirt in disgust. "Sisters, I can't figger 'em out."

"Hey, Jake," Carrie Sue called, running toward them from the lighted interior of the barn. "I've been waitin' fer ya. We've been here fer hours. Willie an' I was the first ones here. How do you like my new dress?" she asked. Smiling, she twirled in front of Jake to let him get the full effect as the thin, blue fabric, which exactly matched her deep-set blue eyes, swirled about a pair of trim ankles. "Mamma an' I just finished it this afternoon."

Jake let out a low whistle and grinned.

"It's beautiful, Carrie Sue," Leah Belle offered quietly, enviously taking in the tall, slender young woman. Her white skin was flushed from the heat in the barn, and her long, straight, white-blond hair seemed to glow in the moonlight. It was clear Carrie Sue would have looked good in a flour sack from her mother's pantry.

"Yer folks come?" Carrie Sue asked then, looking into the darkness behind Jake and Leah Belle.

"Nope. Nate's sick with a cold. Lori Beth weren't in no mood to take care of him, so Ma stayed home. Pa's got a mare he's worried half to death over 'til she foals. Says he won't leave the barn 'til the little fella gets here. So me and Leah Belle just come by ourselves. Didn't want to miss it!" Jake grinned.

"Well, you darn near missed at least half of it," Willie laughed, walking up beside his sister and reaching around to clap Jake on the back. "We been here fer ages."

"Hey, who's this?" he asked as his eyes came to rest on Leah Belle standing just behind Jake. "Can't be little Leah Belle, now can it?" Willie continued, pulling her forward by the arm. Echoing Jake's low whistle at Carrie Sue's appearance, he looked over Leah Belle in her new pale-yellow dress, which only served to make her freckles more prominent on her pale skin and her eyes seem more faded. Her hair, which Malene had so carefully pinned on top of her head for the occasion, hung now in long, lifeless tendrils across her face and down her back—after the long wagon ride. It was hard to believe she and Lori Beth were even related—much less sisters.

Willie grimaced as he thought of the plan he had been hatching since his encounter with Clint. It had seemed so perfect. And he had been so anxious to get to the dance that he had pulled Carrie Sue out of the door in her new dress with their Mamma still following with a mouthful of pins.

Now, however, looking at Leah Belle, he wasn't sure he could go through with it. Maybe, if it was real dark, he could just pretend she was Lori Beth, he smiled to himself. After tonight, just let old Clint Causey try to hold his head up in town! If everything went according to his plan, he'd make sure the word got out by morning.

"Like some punch, Leah Belle?" Willie offered, linking the arm he held into his elbow. "Now, you just come with me, little lady." he added, smiling and winking at Jake over Leah Belle's head. "I'm sure Jake an' Carrie Sue can amuse themselves fer a while."

CHAPTER THREE

ANGEL BY MOONLIGHT

WILLIE, SHOULDN'T WE BE gittin' back inside?" Leah Belle asked half-heartedly as she leaned back in the crook of Willie's elbow against the back side of the old, red barn, where the beat of the music caused the wooden boards to vibrate ever so slightly. It was almost as soothing as being afloat on the Roanoke River in Pa's old rowboat—only twice as nice with the warmth of Willie beside her.

"Just look up at that old moon, Leah Belle," Willie answered, ignoring her question and turning to point and gaze at the full, orange Carolina moon hovering just above the distant line of pine trees. "Now, you know, God must've put that old moon up there fer a reason. Wouldn't seem right to waste it by goin' back inside this old barn with only the empty rafters to look up at, now would it?" he asked.

"Ain't cold, are you?" Willie continued after a moment, tightening his arm about her shoulders and looking into her eyes in the scant moonlight.

"Warm as toast," Leah Belle whispered back in a husky voice, shaking her head and snuggling closer to him—her head on his shoulder. "Wallflower," Pa had said. Well, guess after tonight he'd have to eat his words. Willie had danced every dance with her. Then, he'd spent the last half hour with her—just walkin' in the moonlight.

"Never knowed a gal with such soft skin," Willie continued, running the fingers of his free hand gently over her face. "Is the rest o' you this soft?"

"I . . . I don't know . . . ," Leah Belle hesitated, feeling her body go limp as an electric charge seemed to run through it. She raised her eyes to look at Willie. He was handsome enough whenever she passed him at the lumber mill—with those muscles of his bulgin' an' his white-blond hair hangin' kind o' sexy-like over his blue eyes. But tonight she knew he was the most beautiful thing she'd ever seen—dressed in a starched shirt an' tie with his hair all slicked back an' smelling o' soap and fresh laundry. She couldn't believe this was really happening to her—plain little Leah Belle Causey.

Oh, wouldn't she have a thing or two to tell Lori Beth when she got home, too! She'd seen the way Lori Beth looked at Willie every time they was in town and passed his house. It wouldn't hurt to make her at least a little jealous. She hoped her sister would still be awake. She knew she'd want to hear all about the dance.

"Seeing you in that pale yeller dress all decked out in moonlight—well, it kinda makes you glow . . . . You know, like an angel, almost. Yeah, that's it," Willie whispered, looking into Leah Belle's eyes, "an angel.

"Boy, I sure must've done something to please the Lord fer him to be sending me my very own angel tonight," Willie continued, rolling his eyes upward as he leaned closer to Leah Belle.

"Hey, ever heard that kissin' an angel under a Harvest Moon'll bring you good luck the rest o' yer life?" he added a moment later, his eyes searching hers.

"You made that up," Leah Belle giggled—not daring to move as she returned his gaze.

"You wouldn't keep a fella from havin' good luck the whole rest o' his life, would ya?" Willie pleaded, looking so deeply into her eyes that Leah Belle thought she'd melt on the spot.

The only thing she could hear was her heart beating so loudly it drowned out the sound of the music inside. The only things she could see were Willie's blue eyes staring into hers. And the only things she could feel were Willie's arms around her, his hot breath on her face, and his warm lips pressing hers and—oh, God—, his tongue forcing her lips to part as he laid her gently back onto the soft hay.

"Pa don't want no gossip." Jake's words rang in her ears.

"Willie," she tried, as soon as she could breathe, "maybe we should just . . ."

"What's the matter, Darlin'? Ain't you havin' a good time?" Willie asked, kissing her neck and beginning to work his way down to the neckline of her dress.

"But Pa's worried that . . . ," Leah Belle continued, attempting to sit up.

"Yer pa's worried that some fella's gonna take a shine to you an' take you away so you won't be around to do all them chores every day," Willie finished for her as he slid down beside her, propping himself up on one elbow and looking into her eyes.

"Maybe he's right. 'Spect I was darned lucky I was the first fella who laid eyes on you tonight. But don't you worry none. We don't have to tell yer pa how we feel right away, do we?" he asked, slowly unbuttoning the front of Leah Belle's dress and running his hand inside. He smiled as he felt her body quiver.

"How we feel?" This couldn't be happening to her. And Pa thought she'd be sitting in one of them chairs alongside the wall all night. 'Course she couldn't tell right away. She knew how Pa felt about the Phelpses. But he just didn't know Willie. He'd feel different when he did, Leah Belle decided, wrapping her arms around Willie's neck.

● ● ●

LEAH BELLE! LEAH Belle, are you out here?" Jake called, pulling Carrie Sue by the hand as the two made their way cautiously into the looming shadows beside the old barn. The fiddle and banjo had long since been packed up. The only sound now was a whisper of voices carried on the slight breeze from the parking area in front of the barn. The full moon peeking in and out of the clouds provided the only light for hitching up horses and turning wagons for the trip back to town or to neighboring farms.

"She can't have gone too far," Carrie Sue reasoned, carefully holding up the hem of her new dress with her free hand as she picked her way through the fallen leaves and scattered hay. "It's too far fer her to walk home. An' I think she would've let you know if she was takin' a ride with someone else."

"Leah Belle mostly keeps to herself. She ain't the sort to take up with nobody," Jake responded, shaking his head as they rounded the corner and approached the sloping pile of hay just behind the barn.

"Now, if it was Lori Beth . . . ," he continued, stopping in mid sentence as he tripped over something and lurched forward—pulling Carrie Sue with him into the pile of hay.

"Hey," Willie yelled angrily, sitting up, his blue eyes luminous in the filtered moonlight. "Can't you two find yer own pile of hay?"

"Hi ya, Willie," Carrie Sue laughed. "Sorry to disturb ya. We didn't mean nothing. We're just lookin' fer Leah Belle. Party's over—'case you been too busy to notice," she smiled, cutting her eyes toward the female figure just sitting up beside Willie.

No wonder she hadn't seen him in the past hour! Seemed every gal in the county was willing to throw herself at her brother. She didn't know why. She didn't think he was nearly as good looking as Jake Causey. Who was it this time?

"Leah Belle!" Jake screamed, as the moon came out from behind a cloud bank—illuminating the torn and rumpled yellow dress, the hay clinging to Leah Belle's hair, and her wide eyes and flushed face.

"Git outa that hay this instant!" Jake called, reaching across Willie and grabbing his sister's arm—twisting it painfully as he pulled her to her feet. "What in Hell was you two doin' in there?" he asked accusingly, looking first at Willie, and then watching as Leah Belle self-consciously pulled her skirt down and tried to button the front of her dress.

"Same thing you two been doin', I 'spect," Willie grinned—his white hair and teeth glowing in the faint moonlight. "Me an' little Leah Belle's had us quite an evenin', ain't we, Honey?" he questioned, grabbing Leah Belle's other hand and falling to one knee in the dirt in front of her. "Pleasure's been all mine, Ma'am!" he added—planting a mock kiss on the back of her hand.

"Stay away from her, Will Phelps!" Jake spluttered, pulling the simpering Leah Belle away from Willie and pushing her behind him. "She's only fifteen, fer God's sake! It's her first dance, an' I promised Pa . . ."

"Didn't seem to bother you none when you left her with me an' took off with my sister," Willie added triumphantly.

"If you think you can do what you just did an' git away with it, you got another think comin'," Jake yelled. He'd promised Pa to look after her, and now look what had happened. His guilt fueling his anger, Jake lunged at Willie, catching him by the throat.

"No . . . ," Leah Belle screamed, grabbing Jake's hands and pulling them away from Willie's neck. "Don't go blamin' Willie. It . . . it weren't all his fault," she added in a whisper, her pale eyes downcast. "Please, Jake, let it be. Let's just go home. Can we?"

"I'll take you home, all right—an' be darned glad of it. It's where you should've stayed in the first place," Jake yelled as Leah Belle burst into tears—while still refusing to let go of her brother's hands.

"Jake, please, let it be," she sobbed. It had been such a perfect evening. She'd never dreamed . . . But now . . . with Jake carryin' on like this, Willie would probably never want to see her again—like as not.

"This ain't over, yet, Willie. So don't think it is," Jake muttered angrily, backing off at last.

"Willie! How could you?" Carrie Sue began, pulling the shaking Leah Belle into her own arms and feeling the hot tears on her shoulder. "Sometimes I just don't know you at all!"

"Leah Belle, git to the wagon an' wait fer me there," Jake ordered.

"Don't worry, I ain't gonna mess up his pretty face," he added when his sister hesitated. "Carrie Sue, go with her, would ya?" he asked as Carrie Sue nodded and turned Leah Belle toward the parking area.

"Evenin', Darlin'," Willie called after Leah Belle, performing a mock bow and pretending to sweep an imaginary hat off his head as she turned to look back.

"Now, you gonna tell me what you was thinkin'?" Jake asked as soon as the girls were out of earshot.

"Just thinkin' how mad your pa's gonna be when he finds out one o' his little gals spent the evening in the hay with one of them 'trashy' Phelps boys!" Willie laughed.

"You tellin' me you planned this whole thing . . . to embarrass Pa?" Jake asked, incredulous. "Didn't you never give a think to Leah Belle's feelin's when she finds out?"

"So, it's all right fer you to go sneakin' off behind the wood-pile with my sister every chance you git. But it's not all right fer me to have my fun with yer sister. Is that it, Jake Causey?" Willie retorted, spitting on the ground in front of Jake.

"Think she's too good fer me, don't you—just like yer pa? Well, let me tell you, ain't a fella in this whole county would've looked at yer sister twice before tonight. An' when word gits out about what happened just now, ain't a fella 'round here what'd even be caught talkin' to her. An' you can tell that to that high-an'-mighty pa o' yers, too!

"Now, 'pears to me the party's over, an' the air 'round here is just a little too chilly fer me," he added, striding toward the parking area. "Come on, Carrie Sue. Ma'll be worried."

"I . . . I'm so sorry, Jake . . . ," Carrie Sue called over her shoulder as Willie led her away—her eyes locked pityingly on the silhouetted pair beside the Causey wagon.

"Leah Belle, what in God's name was you thinkin' by takin' on so with Willie?" Jake whispered as Willie and Carrie Sue disappeared around the side of the barn and he helped his sister onto the wagon seat.

"I was thinkin' how wrong Pa was an' how good it felt to have some fella interested in me—until you had to go and spoil it all," Leah Belle added angrily. "Now, Willie'll probably never want to see me again."

"After what he done tonight, he sure as Hell better never try to see you again," Jake retorted, jumping up on the driver's seat and picking up the reins. "An' when Pa finds out . . ."

"You ain't gonna tell, are you, Jake?" Leah Belle gasped, her eyes luminous as she turned to her brother.

"Don't know what I'm gonna do yet," Jake answered honestly, guiding the horse slowly onto the dirt road.

"I don't see you worryin' none 'bout what Pa Phelps is gonna do when he finds out about you an' Carrie Sue," Leah Belle responded sullenly.

"Ain't nobody gonna find out 'bout us," Jake answered.

"An' ain't nobody gonna find out 'bout Willie an' me neither—lessen you tell," Leah Belle countered.

"Leah Belle, let's drop it fer now. Things'll look a lot different to both o' us in the morning," he continued, refusing to look at his sister—his eyes riveted instead on the vast rows of silver corn stalks glowing in the filtered moonlight. Things were going to look a lot worse in the morning, he was afraid. But he couldn't tell Leah Belle that. Just let her have this one evening.

Damn that Willie! Oh, he had no doubt he would spread his conquest all over town to embarrass Pa—as he had threatened. Carrie Sue'd told him about Willie's run-in with Pa just last week and how angry her brother had been. But to use poor Leah Belle to get his revenge . . . well, that was unforgivable, Jake thought to himself, the fist on his free hand drawn up in anger. He shouldn't have listened to Leah Belle. Not many girls in town would take up with a guy whose nose was plastered all over his face.

What was done was done, though. He'd let Willie get away with it, and now they would all have to live with the consequences. The last thing he wanted to do was to tell on Leah Belle. A girl should be able to count on her brother, fer God's sake, he added to himself, slamming his fist down on the seat beside him. But he couldn't let Pa find out from some outsider in town.

Oh, why had he ever agreed to take Leah Belle to that stupid barn dance? And why hadn't he stayed with her—as he had promised Pa? He guessed he bore at least a part of the blame for what had happened, and now it would be up to him to try to straighten things out—if that was possible.

CHAPTER FOUR

WEDDING BELLS

I'LL KILL HIM!" CLINT Causey yelled, his narrowed blue eyes flashing as he jumped up from the kitchen table. He grabbed his worn Navy-blue and white plaid jacket from the wooden peg beside the door, slammed his battered, brown felt hat over his wiry, brown hair, and lifted his shotgun from the wall above the brick fireplace—all in one fluid motion.

"Jake, are you sure 'bout all o' this?" Malene asked, rising from the table and looking at her son.

"I didn't want to have to tell," Jake nodded, turning to his mother and shaking at the anger on his father's normally-placid countenance. He'd expected Pa to be angry when he told him about Leah Belle and Willie, but he'd never in his life heard Pa this angry.

"You done what you had to," Malene responded. "Now yer pa an' I need to talk this out alone," she added, gesturing toward the dining room door with her head as she walked toward her husband.

With one last glance at his father, Jake quickly rose and crossed the room. He wouldn't want to be in Will's shoes right now, he decided as he quietly pulled the kitchen door closed behind him.

"Clint Causey," Malene said as soon as Jake was out of ear-shot, "put that gun down an' let's talk before you make a fool o' yerself rushin' over to the Phelpses.

"Now, I ain't no happier about this than you are. I thought Leah Belle had more sense. But she ain't the first gal to be sweet talked into somethin' she didn't intend. An' you wouldn't be the first pa to rush off half crazed an' do somethin' you didn't intend neither," she continued, stepping smoothly between Clint and the back door. "But we gotta think this through. You know, rushin' over there's just what Willie wants."

"I knowed them Phelps kids'd bring trouble some day—comin' outa the same barrel as they did. I should've finished things eigh-teen years ago. Now look what's happened! Ain't but one thing to do now, an' I ain't gonna let you talk me out of it. So, git outa my way, woman!" Clint continued, holding the shotgun across his chest and staring Malene down as he tried to reach the door.

"You ain't goin' nowhere 'til you hear me out," Malene re-sponded calmly as she folded her arms across her chest and re-fused to move away from the door—holding her husband's gaze with her own.

"You ain't gonna say nothin' I ain't heard before. An' it ain't gonna make no difference," he persisted angrily. "Seems you're always takin' Joe's side. Maybe I should've let you marry him after all. That what you wanted?"

"It's just reason I want, 'stead o' anger," Malene answered calmly. "Seems you got little of it whenever you hear his name."

"I've heard it one too many times already today. Ain't no reason left fer what Willie done. Now, git outa my way!" he added as he shoved her gently with the side of the gun.

"Clint, I ain't takin' nobody's side," Malene answered quietly, gently pushing the gun away. "But it seems to me the damage has already been done, an' there's not much we can do about that.

"Now, you gotta think about how Leah Belle's gonna feel if you go runnin' off at the mouth an' makin' a scene in town. So far she don't know Willie was usin' her to get back at you. You gotta leave her a little happiness—an' dignity."

"You askin' me to forget all this ever happened?" Clint asked incredulously.

"I'm just askin' you to look at the facts. You taken a good look at Leah Belle lately?" Malene questioned in a whisper. "We gotta be honest. She ain't no Lori Beth. Ain't a fella this side o' the Roanoke River gonna take a second look—once they gits the first. She ain't never gonna git a fella on her own. And that Willie Phelps certainly is a handsome devil. Most gals 'round here'd give their eye teeth if he'd just give 'em one look.

"So what if Willie thought he was playin' one on you. I says we play him one right back," Malene continued. "'Stead of killin' the fella, why not go to Joe, tell it like it were, an' set the weddin' date. Despite yer differences, he don't want a scandal in town any more than you do. I know how you feel about Joe. But everything that happened with the three of us was a long time ago. An' I chose you, didn't I?"

"Not 'til after that damned guy got his hands all over you on that hay ride," Clint exploded. "Knowin' them kids o' his would be at Elliott's, I never should've let Leah Belle go. Should've figured it'd run in the family. But," he considered, lowering the gun a bit and looking thoughtfully at his wife, "just maybe you got a good point. We sure ain't gonna marry Leah Belle off no other way . . . ."

• • •

LEAH BELLE, HONEY, yer pa an' I need to talk to you. Can we come in?" Malene called through the bedroom door a few hours later.

"I'll be down in a while," Leah Belle answered, wiping her eyes. Oh, Jake just couldn't wait to tell their parents everything, could he? And after she'd thought he'd understood. She wasn't sure just what he'd said, but she'd heard her father's bellow— something about killing Willie—just before Jake came running up the stairs to his room.

Well, if Pa was threatening to kill Willie, there was no tellin' what he'd do to her, she sobbed. It had started out as such a perfect evening. Then, Jake had had to go and spoil it all . . . .

"I'm not sure she's ready . . . ," Malene said, noting the catch in her daughter's voice.

"Hell, I wasn't ready fer all she throwed at me neither," Clint yelled, turning the door handle and rushing into the room to find Leah Belle lying prone across her bed—her face buried in her pillow.

"Clint," Malene called, entering the room behind her husband and closing the door. "It ain't right fer Lori Beth an' Nate to be hearin' all this."

"Then you talk to her, woman!" Clint exploded. "Little snip throws herself at that good-fer-nothin' kid o' Joe Phelps at the dance in front o' the whole town—makin' us all laughing stocks, an' now she's not ready . . ."

"Pa, it wasn't like that," Leah Belle screamed, raising her face from the pillow and turning red-rimmed eyes to her father. "You an' Jake are both tryin' to make it all sound so dirty. But it wasn't like that at all. I know you can't believe I could get a fella on my own, but Willie came to me. He got me some punch an' asked me to dance. Wasn't nothin' dirty about it at all—'cept in Jake's an' yer minds."

"Leah Belle, yer pa's been over to the Phelpses," Malene added softly.

"Oh, Pa, no! You didn't . . . ," Leah Belle wailed. She'd heard what he said earlier, but she'd never believed . . .

"Just hush a minute, Leah Belle, an' hear yer pa out," Malene continued, sitting on the side of the bed and nodding to Clint.

"Saw Willie an' both his folks," Clint answered. "We had a long talk, an' we all agreed on a weddin' date in three weeks. Been to see Reverend Saunders, too, an' he's set the banns."

"A what?" Leah Belle gasped.

"Weddin', Honey. It's gonna be you an' Willie . . . ," Malene interrupted, attempting a smile.

"I can't believe . . . I mean . . . We was only together last night. How do I know Willie even wants . . . ," Leah Belle asked, looking from one parent to the other.

"Willie's willin' fer the weddin' to take place—said so himself, didn't he, Clint?" Malene interrupted, her eyes pleading with her husband.

"He damned well better be if he hopes to see his next birthday," Clint grumbled. "An' that goes fer you, too, young woman—draggin' the Causey name through the mud without a thought of what you was doin'.

"Well, you wanted that Phelps kid bad enough to let him get you in the hay, an' now you're gonna get what you asked fer," he added, grabbing the door handle and storming from the room—his footsteps echoing in the stairwell.

"Sweetheart, don't mind yer pa. It's gonna work out just fine. Don't you see? You an' Willie gettin' married—well, maybe the good Lord planned it all this way so that yer pa an' Willie's pa can bury their hatchets fer once," Malene said, rising and patting her daughter on the back. "An' just think o' how jealous all the other gals in town are gonna be when they hear the news!

"Now, when you feel more like it, we can go to town an' shop fer some material fer yer weddin' dress. We got a lot to do in the next three weeks."

• • •

I WON'T GO! I won't. You can't make me!" Lori Beth sobbed into her pillow, beating her fists against her bed.

"'Pears to me you ain't got no choice in the matter," Malene answered calmly as she leaned over to lay the new, pale-green dress she had just completed for Lori Beth on the bed beside her. "Weddin's gonna take place anyway—whether you're there or not," she continued.

"Seems to me all you got left right now is yer pride. You sure ain't gonna have Willie—not if yer pa's got anything to do with it. An' I don't see why you'd want him after what he done to you," she added with a sigh—sitting beside her younger daughter on the bed and rubbing her heaving back.

"Lori Beth, Honey, you got years ahead o' you. You can have any fella you want when the time comes," she added in a soothing voice. "You've seen 'em. Why, they're jammin' Main Street every time you walk by."

"Willie's the only fella I ever wanted. An' now Leah Belle's taken him. I hate her! I hate her! She did this on purpose to get back at me. An' you an' Papa helped her!" Lori Beth sobbed— her head still buried in the pink cotton spread.

"Now, you don't really believe that, Lori Beth," Malene answered quietly. "You an' Willie been meetin' in secret. Nobody else knew. You told me that yerself. Neither yer pa an' I nor Leah Belle had no idea how you felt about Willie. She's yer sister. She wouldn't hurt you on purpose.

"It's Willie who's to blame fer leadin' her on so. You know him. Why any girl'd be proud as punch to have him even look her way. An' Leah Belle'd never had that before. She just got carried away by Willie's attention. You gotta see that. I can't let you go blamin' yer sister," Malene sighed.

"I can, an' I will—'til the day I die!" Lori Beth vowed, raising her tear-stained face to look at her mother. "I never want to see her again as long as I live," she hissed through clenched teeth.

"Well, she's gonna be movin' to that big, old, ramshackle house o' the Phelpses down by the lumber yard soon as the weddin's over," Malene sighed. "So you don't have to see her after to-day—if you don't want to.

"But, Honey, half the town's gonna be watchin' as we go by today. Yer pa's got his pride—an' so do you. Much as we all hate the thought, we all gotta be there together today—holdin' our heads up like yer sister done just won the biggest prize in the county. Now, come on an' git dressed. Yer pa's not gonna wait fer any o' us. An' I gotta hustle Nate along, too."

● ● ●

THE OLD, GRAY horse kicked up a cloud of gray dust and dried gold and brown leaves as he slowly pulled the heavy wagon up the slight incline toward the small, white frame church. It was a beautiful, crisp fall day under a cloudless blue sky. The beauty of the day, however, was lost on the driver, who looked only at the road ahead of him as he turned the wagon from the main road into the parking area.

Carelessly flipping the reins over the hitching post in the gravel lot, Willie took a quick look around, jumped from the wagon, ran a hand over his hair, and made his way toward the side door of the church.

Hidden beneath the dried, brown leaves still clinging to the spreading oak tree, Lori Beth watched him approach. Looking around for any means of escape and seeing none, she remembered her mother's words, squared her shoulders, and waited. He was handsome in his new dark-blue suit with his long, blond hair all slicked down, she had to admit—with a pang she could feel clear down to her toes.

Looking surprised as he finally raised his eyes from the ground and noticed Lori Beth eyeing him, Willie shook his head—as if to clear it of a bad dream. "Afternoon, Lori Beth," he offered sadly.

"Afternoon, yerself!" Lori Beth answered back, tossing her head and looking through the low-hanging branches toward the front of the church, where several wagons were now drawing to a stop.

"Lori Beth," Willie began slowly, looking around to be sure no one else was within earshot, "I been meanin' to talk to you—only . . . I didn't know how to begin . . . ."

"You could begin by tellin' me what you was doin' at that barn dance. Here you was, declaring yer love fer me by the river that afternoon an' then pullin' my sister into the hay soon as the moon rose!" Lori Beth whispered indignantly.

"It was supposed to be a joke. You gotta believe me. You know how yer pa feels about all us Phelpses, don't you? Well, I just thought I'd show him a thing or two—take his little girl in the hay an' then brag about it in town—you know.

"You gotta admit, he's had it comin'," Willie offered, his arms opened wide, begging her understanding.

"An' you never stopped once to think of all the folks you'd be hurtin'? Did you ever think about yer mamma—an' Carrie Sue? An' did you ever think about how embarrassed Leah Belle would be with you spreadin' yer conquest all over town?" Lori Beth asked.

"Jeeze, Lori Beth, you know yer sister. Ain't no guy ever gonna look at her the way they do at you. I thought she'd be kinda thrilled at the attention," Willie added, confused.

"Did you ever think o' my feelings?" she continued.

"Heck, it was a joke! I thought you'd laugh at it as much as me—considering how much you an' Leah Belle always fight an' all . . . ," Willie went on, his face dropping. He couldn't bear that green-eyed stare another minute.

"Well, Willie Phelps, I 'spect there's a lot o' folks laughing out there. But seems to me the joke's on you now. An' this time it's fer good. Ain't no gettin' outa what's gonna go on inside there in a few minutes," Lori Beth added triumphantly, as she jerked her chin toward the church building where the old, out-of-tune piano had just struck up.

"See you in church!" she added, turning on her heels and striding off.

CHAPTER FIVE

PEACE IN THE FAMILY

MALENE, SEEN LORI BETH?" Clint called excitedly. The door banged shut behind him with a blast of cold air as he walked to the glowing brick fireplace on the far wall of the kitchen. Removing his heavy work gloves, he rubbed his rough, reddened hands together for a moment before turning to his wife.

"Ain't seen her since she come home from school," Malene answered, looking up for a moment from the sink—where she was peeling potatoes. "But you know where she is . . . ," she continued, blowing a stray wisp of hair from her eyes.

"Still in her room?" Clint asked, sliding into the nearest chair at the kitchen table. The excitement in his voice faded as he noticed his wife's face.

"An' still cryin' her eyes out," Malene nodded, drying her hands and walking over to the table—where she took a seat opposite her husband. "I swear, Clint, I'd never've thought she'd carry on this long! She screams any time any one of us speaks Leah Belle's name. An' she don't want to talk to none of us.

"She blames Nate fer bein' sick so's I couldn't go to the dance. She blames Jake fer takin' Leah Belle. An' she thinks you an' me pushed Leah Belle into Willie's arms to spite her. I can't talk no sense into her head. Lord knows I've tried," Malene concluded, shaking her head sadly.

"Maybe what I've got to tell her will put some life back in them big green eyes," Clint smiled mysteriously, pulling a piece of paper from his pocket. "I've just come from town."

"Sell the calf?" Malene asked, brightening. "We sure could use some extra money with Christmas comin' on."

"Got what I asked fer it, too," Clint nodded.

"How much you git?" Malene questioned, watching as her husband unfolded the paper in his hands.

"Got this receipt . . . ," Clint began, handing the paper to her across the table.

Grabbing the paper from Clint's hands, Malene looked intently at it before letting out a shriek. "Clint Causey! This ain't no bank note. What's the meanin' o' this? You tellin' me you traded our calf fer a—fer a—pack o' pictures?" she cried, her eyes burning.

"Now, just listen afore you judge," Clint added soberly, reaching across the table to take the paper from his wife's trembling hand. "You know how Lori Beth's always twirlin' in front o' her mirror an' lookin' at herself?" he asked, waiting for his wife's nod.

Receiving only a stony glare from her, however, he continued. "Now, you know she does it. Seems she knows what a looker she is already—almost as purty as her mamma—near as I can tell," he continued, grinning broadly at Malene in hopes of softening her resolve.

"If you're hopin' to soft-pedal me . . . ," Malene added—looking at him at last.

"Well, truth is, after I sold that calf, I was just a walkin' past the General Store thinkin' what I was gonna buy my beautiful wife for Christmas, when I seen this poster," Clint explained. "It said a man what takes photographs was gonna be in town next week to take pictures o' any folk what signed up.

"So's I got to thinkin'—what did my beautiful wife want fer Christmas? Seems to me ain't nothin' she wants more than peace in this family again, I told myself. An' what would bring some peace? Why, to see little Lori Beth smile again.

"What would make her smile? Why, a chance to look as beautiful as her mamma—an' to git a keepsake o' it to carry with her always," Clint concluded triumphantly.

"So you spent all our Christmas money fer some pictures o' Lori Beth?" Malene asked incredulously, shaking her head slowly as she looked at her husband. "I think you've been touched in the head!"

"Now, just give it a chance, Malene. I listened to you 'bout Leah Belle an' Willie. Maybe it were right . . . or maybe it were wrong. But there ain't another thing I can do about it now.

"'Pears to me, though, we got another problem that maybe I can fix—an' that's Lori Beth. I swear, it's worth all the money I could git fer my whole herd just to see that little gal smile again an' to have you happy," Clint sighed.

"Well, the money's been spent now, an' I don't suppose you could git it back if you wanted," Malene sighed resignedly. "So why not go on upstairs, tell Lori Beth 'bout the pictures, an' see how it works.

"Just don't complain to me when you don't git no Christmas presents," she added, rising from the table and heading back to the sink.

● ● ●

HEY, LORI BETH! I seen yer picture in town in the window of the General Store," Willie called, stopping with one foot on the log he was cutting and putting down his ax. He pushed up the sleeves of his plaid flannel shirt, and watched as Nate and Lori Beth—a pile of books secured by a strap slung over her shoulder—walked by on their way home from school.

"Sure does brighten up the town—if you ask me. You always was a looker!" he grinned.

"Lori Beth, Willie's talkin' to you," Nate said, punching his sister on the arm and motioning toward Willie with his chin.

"Ain't got nothin' to say to him," Lori Beth added softly, kicking at a leftover pile of snow on the side of the road. Pulling her gray wool cape closer about her and looking straight ahead with her nose in the air, she continued to walk past the lumber yard without pausing—expertly skirting the many puddles in the rutted dirt road.

"Nate, yer sister said to tell yer folks she's doin' fine. Will ya do that?" Willie tried again, pushing his hat off his forehead and squinting into the bright January sunshine toward the pair.

"They knows she's all right," Nate answered coldly. He paused to pick up a frozen chunk of brown snow from the ground beneath a large oak. Throwing it aimlessly back at the trunk, he watched as the small, brown crystals slid slowly to the ground.

"She's gittin' big already!" Willie added proudly, pulling his hat back down and picking up his ax once more. "Gonna have me a son by summer. Pa says he hopes he's a big 'un so's he can take over some o' this here work. Got more than enough fer us Phelpses."

"That's good, Willie. We gotta go now," Nate answered, hurrying to catch up with Lori Beth, who was several paces ahead— her eyes never leaving the path.

"Hey, Lori Beth, you ain't never congratulated me on being a pa!" Willie called at last, tired of playing the game.

"'Pears to me folks don't go around congratulatin' other folks fer gittin' somethin' they ain't never wanted in the first place," Lori Beth called back loudly over her shoulder.

The five lumber hands, who had been working beside Willie, had stopped to watch the exchange. At Lori Beth's words, they burst into peals of laughter as Willie turned quickly and worked at pulling a log from the bottom of the pile beside him—the red creeping up his face.

CHAPTER SIX

CLOSER TO HEAVEN

DARN THAT LEAH BELLE," Lori Beth fumed. She kicked a rock ahead of her and watched as it disappeared into a clump of new pale-green grass beside the muddy path to the river. "First, she went an' stole Willie away. Then, she moved off to the Phelpses an' left all her chores behind. What with feedin' the chickens, gittin' the eggs, milking the cows, gittin' the water from the well, helpin' Ma in the kitchen, an' doin' the laundry—there just ain't enough hours in the day.

"At least I still have school every day fer the next month. An' I don't have to do no work there," she smiled. "Old Miz Gordon don't care none about them kids that's gonna be finishing their schoolin' in a few weeks. So if I happen to just let my eyes wander . . .

"Now, Billie Johnson ain't too hard to look at," she smiled to herself. "Matter of fact, Bubba Thomas ain't bad either. Fact is, they both look pretty good down at the swimmin' hole—now that the weather's warmed up. Maybe after I finish my swim, I can just wait around . . .

"After all, Mamma ain't home today, so won't nobody be lookin' fer me. An' no tellin' how long Mamma'll be over to Miz Stallings. Can't never set no clock when young 'uns are gettin' born. "Soon, I 'spect she'll be over to the Phelpses helpin' out old Leah Belle, too," she sighed, her face falling. "It's just not fair! Leah Belle's got it all—a new home, Willie, an' now a new baby comin'!

"But I'm not gonna think o' Leah Belle today. It's much too pretty to think downin' thoughts," she decided, as she looked upward through the gray-green haze of new growth, which hung over the towering oak trees.

The morning's brief shower was long since past. The new pale-green leaves were just bursting forth, and the robins were singing. The sun was still high, so it was too early for the lumber mill hands to take their dip in the river. "That means I can have the whole swimmin' hole to myself," Lori Beth smiled, flipping the large towel she had slung over her shoulder at a bumble bee. It was a glorious day.

The swiftly-flowing, gold-tinted river—swollen by the recent spring rains—sparkled in the afternoon sun as it eddied and flowed around the large, gray trunk of the fallen oak, which leaned out across the water and formed a perfect bathing pool this side of the current. Spying the swimmin' hole at last, Lori Beth began to run.

As she reached the bank, she threw her towel and a bar of lye soap onto the upturned roots of the old, gnarled tree. Then, with one fluid motion, she pulled her thin, calico dress over her head and hung it over a low-hanging branch—out of the way of the water. Her shoes, stockings, and thin chemise followed, until Lori Beth was, at last, poised above the water hole peering down at the reflection of her own young body.

"Let Willie have skinny, old Leah Belle," she scoffed as she smiled at her reflection. "I ain't so bad. Bet there's plenty o' boys what'd want what I got to offer," she added to herself. Looking at her slim hips and high, proud breasts, she felt rather vindicated before sliding slowly off the high, muddy bank into the dark water.

This must be close to what old Reverend Saunders meant when he spoke o' Heaven, Lori Beth decided as she lay on her back and felt the cold water slide over her body. An' there weren't no one around to tell her to git back to work or to git on home, neither. She'd left Nate in town to visit with Bobby Joe Dempsey. An' Papa and Jake had just been fixin' to go into town to git their broke harness fixed an' to pick up Mamma when she left Miz Stallings's house.

She wished she could come down here fer a swim every day. But by the time she usually finished her chores, the boys from the lumber yard were already over here splashing around and havin' fun and tellin' tales 'bout all the gals in town. Judgin' by the sun, though, today she'd have at least an hour or so before the whistle blew and the boys got free. In the meantime . . .

"Hey there, Lori Beth! Look at you—struttin' your stuff for every guy in town to see. Ain't you got no shame?" came a voice from behind her. Lori Beth, hearing the voice, suddenly swung her feet downward and tried to hide in the brackish water.

"Won't do you no good to hide. I can outwait you. An' I got yer clothes," the voice taunted.

Looking behind her at last, Lori Beth spied Willie. His tan breeches were rolled up to his knees, and his shirt and shoes were already on the riverbank. He was balancing on one bare foot on the upturned roots of the old oak as he reached out to pull Lori Beth's clothing from the branch.

"You put those back right now, Willie Phelps!" Lori Beth screamed in frustration.

"Come on outa there an' make me!" Willie teased, grinning as he dangled the clothes just over her head.

"What're you doin' out here?" Lori Beth demanded. "I ain't heard the whistle yet." Hadn't he already done enough to humiliate her?

"Just enjoyin' the view," Willie laughed, raising a pale blond eyebrow and smiling lewdly. "If I'd knowed the afternoons was this beautiful out here, I'd a been takin' off work this early every day. Bet the rest o' the guys gonna bug their eyes out when they sees what the current's done washed up in the old swimmin' hole!"

"Willie, leave my clothes be and git outa here so's I can git dressed," Lori Beth ordered.

"I would, Darlin'. But I ain't got what I come fer yet. An' I ain't leavin' 'til I gits it," Willie teased.

"Ain't nothin' I'd ever give you, Willlie Phelps," Lori Beth screamed.

"I come down to yer house to git some o' that liniment yer mamma rubs on gal's bellies when they's stretched all outa shape—like yer sister's is," Willie continued, ignoring Lori Beth's outburst. "But there weren't no one home.

"Then, when I come out here to find someone, somehow that didn't seem like what I wanted at all. Think maybe a little kiss—like them you used to give out—might git me to leave. Wanta come up here an' give it a try?" Willie continued.

"You're disgusting!" Lori Beth called back. The muck on the bottom of the river where she was kneeling was thick and slimy. She longed to climb out of the water, but she sure as shootin' wasn't goin' to do it with Willie watching her every move. And he didn't seem disposed to move until she did something. Maybe, if she could get him to come in, too, she could slip by him, grab her towel, and . . .

"Why don't you come after what you want?" Lori Beth called defiantly.

"Thought you'd never ask me!" Willie added, grinning. Then, pausing long enough to throw Lori Beth's clothes over a limb high above his head—and well above hers—he jumped into the water beside her.

Taking the moment to effect her escape, Lori Beth rushed through the water toward the tree—and her towel. "Not so fast, Darlin'," Willie called, diving expertly toward her, catching her around her knees, and holding her captive. Moving his arms up her body, he suddenly surfaced, shaking the water from his long hair before taking an appraising look at the young woman before him.

"Well, I'll be. Will you look what I just caught in the old swimming hole!" he announced, holding her firmly around the waist.

"You let me go, Willie Phelps," Lori Beth screamed, pushing at Willie's chest and kicking at him with her feet, "or I'll call my papa an' . . ."

"Yer pa's in town," Willie laughed, grasping both of Lori Beth's wrists with one hand and holding them out of the way. "I seen him an' Jake over to the General Store afore I come out here. 'Fraid they ain't gonna be much help.

"Now, are you gonna give me what I want?" he asked, his face menacingly close and puckered for a kiss—as Lori Beth turned her head to avoid his advance.

"I can wait," he continued angrily. "Think maybe I'll just keep you right here until that whistle blows an' all them guys you Causeys stick up yer noses at git down here fer a look-see," he added, tightening his grip on her wrists.

"Willie, let me go!" Lori Beth ordered, her voice rising hysterically as she continued to kick at him and pull away. "Ain't you done enough to me an' my family already?"

"From where I'm standin', little lady, you an' yer family owe me one," Willie answered calmly, without lessening his hold. "Seems poor little Leah Belle got herself in the 'family way.' An' good old Willie was kind enough to rescue her so's her pappy can go on ridin' through town with his nose in the air like nothin' ever happened."

"Willie, that ain't fair," Lori Beth answered defiantly. "You was the only boy Leah Belle was ever with, an' you know it. You planned that whole evenin' to embarrass Papa. You told me so yerself—standin' right there in front o' the church on yer weddin' day."

"But I done the right thing by all o' you, now didn't I?" Willie asked. "Seems you owe me somethin' fer saving that Causey pride o' yers," Willie continued, holding Lori Beth at arm's length—his eyes roaming lewdly over her body.

"I don't owe you a darned thing. You cooked yer own goose, an' now you gotta live with it!" Lori Beth concluded triumphantly, ceasing her struggle. All right, let him look. She had nothing to hide. Let him see what he'd been so willing to throw away, she decided.

"Not fer long, I ain't," Willie smiled, shaking his head. "That's what I come to tell you."

"What'd you come to tell me?" Lori Beth demanded, her eyes not leaving Willie's face. He could be so exasperating.

"That you can still have me if you want me," Willie answered, his face breaking into a wide grin. "I done what was right by Leah Belle. An' I'll stick by her 'til the young 'un comes—give it a name an' all that. My pa'll take him in. He needs another hand or two at the mill. Then, when old Leah Belle gits back on her feet . . . Well, we can do it kind o' quiet like, so's the whole town don't find out I left her right away.

"I got an uncle works in the mill over in Elizabeth City. He's a foreman. But, hey, I can cut wood with the best of 'em. Yer sister can tell folks I went over there to make a little more money fer the boy. Then you an' I can just disappear together," Willie answered—smiling as he pulled her tightly to his chest. "What d' ya say, Darlin', do I git my kiss now?"

"Willie Phelps! Of all the low-down, selfish tricks," Lori Beth hissed, her breath coming in gasps. "Here you are—plannin' to leave Leah Belle with no husband an' a young 'un to raise— an' you think I'm gonna just fall into yer arms an' let you take me away to . . . ," Lori Beth stopped as Willie's mouth found hers— the force of his kiss grinding her lips against her teeth as he bent her backwards.

"Let me be, Willie!" Lori Beth pleaded as soon as she could speak—pushing against Willie's chest to free herself.

"You know you wanted that," Willie added, looking into her eyes. "You been missin' it as much as me. Don't tell me you ain't. Now, here we are—all alone out here. What's the harm? Ain't nobody gonna find out if you don't tell."

"It just ain't right," Lori Beth countered, shaking her head— the tears rolling down her cheeks.

"What ain't right?" Willie questioned, his eyes studying hers. "Yer sister done took yer beau. Yer folks pushed her into my arms—yer pa totin' that old shotgun o' his an' makin' me marry her to save his pride. Now, you're standin' here tellin' me what ain't right?

"Seems to me what you an' I done been through—that's what ain't right," Willie continued, his eyes holding Lori Beth's for a long moment—his arms still holding her tightly.

"But we . . . ," she began, her eyes pleading.

"Won't never let on 'bout how we feel. You can go on ignorin' or insultin' me every day on yer way home from school if you want to, an' I won't never say a word. Then, I'll make up some excuse an' meet you down here every afternoon—just like we used to do. Ain't nobody gonna know the difference," he smiled. "Won't hurt Leah Belle or yer pa—or anybody," he added, pulling her to him once again.

Lori Beth knew she should push away, but something Willie said made sense somehow. She and Willie really were the wounded parties. Leah Belle had taken him away from her. Her mamma and papa had only been thinkin' o' themselves when they made him marry Leah Belle. They knew they couldn't get her married off any other way. Willie'd had to marry a gal he didn't want, and now he'd have to raise that young 'un . . . .

All those days and nights she'd cried herself to sleep . . . An' Papa thinkin' he could wash all the hurt away with those dumb old pictures of her.

Who cared about some old photographs, anyway? It was Willie she wanted. Always had been, she decided at last, as she wrapped her bare arms around Willie's neck and allowed him to carry her to the clearing—under the gnarled, old oak—where he laid her gently in the dappled shade.

CHAPTER SEVEN

THE SINS OF THE FATHER

MIGHT'VE KNOWN LEAH BELLE'D pick the hottest day o' the year to have that baby!" Nate fumed as he carefully felt his way down the attic steps carrying his end of the old, scarred cradle.

"Can't believe old Willie's gonna be a pa!" Jake chuckled, looking up at his brother as he backed down the steps ahead of Nate, supporting the other end.

"An' Leah Belle's gonna be a mamma. Suits her, though. She always was bossy enough," Nate laughed.

"You fellas stop jawin' an' hurry up with that cradle. Mind you don't drop it!" Malene called from the kitchen. "Yer pa's got the wagon hitched already, an' we gotta git goin'. Little Leah Belle's gonna need all the help she can git to git that young 'un into this world.

"Can't say when yer pa an' I'll be back. Baby's gonna come when it feels like it an' not a mite sooner. So don't expect us 'til you see us. I left some o' yesterday's chicken fer you—if you git hungry," Malene continued as she followed Nate and Jake and the cradle out of the door and down the side steps to where Clint stood waiting patiently beside the wagon.

"Where's Lori Beth?" Jake asked, looking across the parched yard back toward the house after the cradle had finally been loaded. "Why can't she fix us supper?"

"Where've you been all day?" Nate questioned disgustedly as he wiped his perspiring forehead and looked up at his brother. "Lori Beth's been cryin' since Willie come to fetch Mamma. Says she ain't never comin' out o' her room again."

"Malene, is that true?" Clint turned from the back of the wagon where he was securing the cradle, his concerned blue eyes searching his wife's face. "Maybe we'd better not go just yet. 'Pears to me little Lori Beth needs her mamma . . . ."

"So does my other girl—a lot more than Lori Beth does right now," Malene interrupted. "Lord, Clint, she's been carryin' on for nigh on to nine months now. I've about had it with her. What she needs is a good paddlin' down to the wood shed—like you give the boys.

"I'm just hopin' once this young 'un gits here she'll stop moonin' over Willie Phelps an' find herself another beau. Then, maybe we can finally git some peace around here—an' git some work out o' her," Malene concluded as she took her husband's offered hand and climbed onto the wagon seat.

"That damned Willie Phelps!" Clint added angrily as he climbed onto the driver's seat beside her. "Both them babies was too young to have beaus yet—much less a weddin'—an' now a kid. Wouldn't none o' this happened if he'd been lookin' at girls his own age. An' look what it's done to this family!"

"Oh, I suspect if it wasn't Willie, it would have been some other boy in town," Malene sighed, adjusting her white gloves and reaching up to secure her small-brimmed, straw hat before the long ride.

"We can't protect them forever, Clint. Remember, I had Jake when I wasn't any older than Leah Belle. You didn't seem to think I was too young," Malene continued, a slight smile creasing her face.

"It's not the same, an' you know it. We'd been seein' each other fer over two years," Clint answered—not meeting her eyes. "Well, we've lost Leah Belle. But I won't let it happen to Lori Beth," Clint continued as he picked up the reins and clucked to the tired, old horse. "I'll see that she never again . . .

"Look in on Lori Beth, will you, Jake?" he called, turning back to his son. "See that she's all right fer me. An', Nate, you'll do the milkin' today, understand? No need to bother yer sister with her feelin' so poorly," he added as he turned the wagon in the drive.

"Yes, Sir," Nate answered without question—as Jake put his arm around his younger brother. The two watched until the wagon approached the main road, turned left, and was soon lost in a cloud of dust.

"'Spect Leah Belle was right after all," Nate observed, breaking the silence as he turned at last to Jake. "Don't seem nothin' Lori Beth does is ever wrong—accordin' to Pa. Now, if that was me . . ."

"Guess that's the way things is with papas an' girls," Jake shrugged.

"An' like they is with you an' Ma?" Nate questioned, his deep-blue eyes searching his brother's hazel ones. "Guess that leaves me out—just like it done Leah Belle. No wonder she gone off an'. . ."

"Nate Causey! Don't hand me that. I seen all the favors you git—just because you're the baby," Jake interrupted, ruffling Nate's tousled hair and smiling at him. "Don't you talk to me none 'bout bein' left out!

"Tell you what," he added after a moment. "It's mighty hot today. An' with Pa gone, we ain't got nothin' to do 'til we bring the cows in. Why not just grab that chicken Ma left in the kitchen an' take us down to the river to do some fishin' fer the afternoon?"

"But, Lori Beth . . . ," Nate said.

"Can just go stew in her own juice. I'm tired o' listenin' to her weepin' an' wailin'. Ain't nothin' that special 'bout Willie Phelps. Even Carrie Sue says she don't know why all the gals in town go so crazy over him—an' she's his sister," Jake broke in, closing the subject.

"Ain't gonna be no gals runnin' after him when he's pushin' a baby carriage 'round the lumber yard," Nate added, smiling at his own observation. "You git the chicken. I'll git the fishin' poles. Race ya to the point!" he called over his shoulder as he began to run toward the barn.

● ● ●

LORI BETH, ARE you okay? Pa asked me to look in on you," Jake offered, knocking lightly at the door of Lori Beth's room.

"Go away, Jake. I don't want to see no one," Lori Beth called from behind the closed door.

"Ma left some chicken in the kitchen—if you're hungry," Jake offered.

"I ain't hungry, an' I don't want company," she grumbled.

"Well, suit yourself. I just wanted to tell you Nate an' I are goin' out fishin', in case you need anything afore we go," Jake called through the door.

"I don't need a darned thing 'cept fer all o' you to leave me alone," Lori Beth bellowed—so loudly the door vibrated.

"Hey, I can take a hint!" Jake yelled back. "Ain't nobody gonna bother you fer the rest o' the day—least o' all me!" he added, exasperated, as he stormed down the stairs.

He was still fuming several minutes later when he entered the kitchen. Walking to the pantry, he reached onto the top shelf and took out the tattered, old, wicker picnic basket. How long had it been since the family had used it? Come to think of it, he couldn't remember how long it had been since they'd had a meal together without some kinda fightin' or Lori Beth running off to her room. Well, he still had Nate. An' the two of them could still enjoy the day, he decided. Placing a large, red-checked napkin in the bottom of the basket, he piled in two of the three pieces of chicken, four pieces of fresh bread, and some of last night's corn fritters before slamming the top down, securing the leather straps, and racing out of the screen door after Nate.

● ● ●

HEARING THE SCREEN door bang shut and feeling the sudden silence in the old house, Lori Beth rose from the bed at last and walked to her wash basin. She'd thought they'd never leave. It'd been harder and harder to see Willie lately—now that school was over an' she didn't have a reason to be goin' in an' outa town.

She'd had to make up any excuse she could to go into town—or to run after a lost cow—every afternoon so's she could meet Willie at the river. An' today she suspected they'd have to make it real short—since he'd need to be back home fer the baby's birth. She'd watched her Mamma at birthin's too many times not to know that the papa was not allowed around 'til after the birth. But he sure better be there when that first scream came.

She remembered once when old Wally Hanson had been drunk behind the wood shed. The whole town had been out searchin' fer him to see his new young 'un. When they finally found him, he was just a bawlin' that thirteen was an unlucky number, an' that meant he'd have to go one more!

Oh, she was angry at all the fuss folks had been makin' 'bout Leah Belle an' the baby. But, she had to admit, she was glad to see this day, she decided, drying her face and picking up her brush. Willie'd said he'd stay with Leah Belle only until the baby was born, an' it seemed that time had come.

Maybe today he'd tell her his plans about them runnin' away together. She already had her case packed an' hidden under her bed. She'd done that this mornin' when she'd heard Willie down-stairs. She knew she couldn't risk seeing him in front o' her parents without one o' them givin' away how they felt.

Reaching into her chest, she pulled out the new dress Mamma had made. She knew Willie'd like it since it was green an' matched her eyes. He was always tellin' her to wear that color. She smiled as she slipped the dress over her head and tied the sash behind her back, twirling in front of the mirror to get the full effect.

Yes, he was gonna like it all right—'specially since it had all them little buttons right down the front . . . Maybe she'd wear it again when they went travelin' to Elizabeth City. She'd want Willie to be proud o' her when they met his relatives.

Carefully watching her reflection in the mirror, she lifted a wide, green ribbon from the dresser and loosely tied it around her hair. Willie liked her hair loose, but she didn't want it to get tangled before she got to the river. Then, biting her lips and pinching her cheeks to add color, she took one last look in the mirror. Smiling at what she saw, she turned and slowly opened the door of her room.

It was quiet in the house as she slowly crept down the hall. Jake and Nate seemed to have left already. But she watched care-fully from the landing before she descended the dark stairs—just in case they were still there. She didn't want anyone following her today.

● ● ●

WILLIE WOULD CALL it a "scorcher," Lori Beth observed as she left the cool darkness of the house and squinted at the cloudless sky above the sunny chicken yard. Guess July was supposed to be that way, though.

Maybe, after she'd seen Willie, she'd go back to the swimmin' hole one last time to get cool. She wasn't dumb enough to think Willie could leave town today. There'd be too many folks around the house fer a while wantin' to see Leah Belle an' the new baby an' offer their congratulations. But maybe they could leave to-morrow—or the next day. He'd promised "soon."

The shade under the spreading oaks was pleasant as she walked briskly down the familiar dirt path to the dark river—lying lazily today in the filtered sunlight. Lori Beth smiled up at a jay hollerin' from a branch just above her head. Guess she'd sounded just about as angry when Jake had come to call. But she hadn't wanted to miss seein' Willie, so she'd had to git rid o' Jake. Seemed she'd done a good job, too, since he an' Nate were nowhere around. She hadn't even needed to invent an excuse.

"Hey, Lori Beth!" Willie called, stepping out from behind the large, sprawling oak—a smile plastered on his face. "Did ya hear I'm about to be a pa! What d'ya think? Don't that just beat all?"

"I'm glad it'll all be over soon," Lori Beth smiled, twirling around slowly and feeling the soft fabric swirl around her legs as she attempted to catch Willie's eye. "How do you like my new dress, Willie?"

"Gonna name him William Phelps, Junior," Willie continued, his eyes staring at a branch over Lori Beth's head. "But me an' Leah Belle thought we'd best call him 'Billy' so's folks don't git confused. Pa says he's gonna put him to work at the mill—soon's he's big enough to swing an ax!"

"Don't seem to me there'll be much trouble 'bout you two gettin' mixed up if you an' I are over in Elizabeth City," Lori Beth added. "Already got my bag packed," she continued proudly.

"What'd you go an' do a damned thing like that fer?" Willie questioned, snapping back to reality and turning angrily to her. "I ain't ready to go yet."

"You said after the baby was born . . . ," Lori Beth added, her eyes searching Willie's.

"I said 'after' the birth—not right away!" Willie admonished. "What kinda pa would I be if I run off the minute my own son was born? Little fella gotta have his pa aroun' fer the Christenin'—

'specially if he's gonna have my name. Damn, Lori Beth, I ain't never had any creature named after me afore," he said earnestly.

"Then, just when do you plan on us leavin' town, Willie?" Lori Beth asked, confused. "I mean . . . I gotta know. I swear, I don't know how much longer I can stay in that house with all that talk about Leah Belle an' the new baby . . . ," Lori Beth sighed.

"I'll let you know, Lori Beth. I gotta write my uncle first—see if he needs a hand an' all that. Might be he's got all the help he needs right now," Willie shrugged.

"But, Willie, you said it was all set," Lori Beth gasped, her mouth agape.

"Well . . . , it just about is . . . ," Willie hedged. "But . . . Hey, Lori Beth, it's gittin' late," he added, looking up at the sun. "I gotta git goin'. Yer ma said it weren't gonna be long. Carrie Sue might be out lookin' fer me just about now, an' I promised Leah Belle . . . "

"Well, fine, Willie Phelps! Just you go on back home an' hold that squawlin' baby o' yers. Give him yer name, change his stinkin' diaper, an' put him to work in yer pappy's lumber yard. Then see if I care!" Lori Beth exploded, wiping furiously with the back of her hand at the tears flowing steadily down her face.

"But Lori Beth . . . ," Willie answered, confused. "I didn't say it'd be forever. It's just like—I gotta be around here fer a little while—'til all the excitement dies down an' all, you know. An' it wouldn't be fair to leave Leah Belle just yet.

"In the meantime, we can keep right on meetin' here—just like always. Ain't nobody found out yet, has they?" he asked, reaching out for her hand.

"Ain't nobody like to find out anything neither—if they sees you down here alone from now on!" Lori Beth yelled back, pulling her hand away and running back down the path—her streaming tears making dark stains on the new, green dress.

CHAPTER EIGHT

A PLUCKED CHICKEN

HEY, PA, DID WILLIE get that strappin' boy he was lookin' fer?" Jake called—running out of the barn as he heard the wagon approach later that afternoon.

"Scrawniest little gal I ever seen!" Clint called out, shaking his head as he threw the reins to his son and jumped from the wagon.

"Now, Clint. All babies are scrawny when they're born," Malene admonished, taking the hand her husband offered and climbing down as well.

"Not like that one, they ain't!" Clint added. "Why, you fellas ain't gonna believe . . ."

"How scrawny is she, Pa?" Nate interrupted, throwing the fork back into the haystack beside the barn and running over for the news, a wide grin spreading over his freckled face. Pa could really tell a story when he wanted to. And Nate sensed there was going to be one now.

"Don't you fellas go eggin' him on none," Malene ordered from the steps—while a small smile tugged at the corners of her mouth. "I'll call you all when supper's ready," she added, unpinning her hat as she pulled open the screen door and disappeared inside.

"Come on, Pa, an' tell us how old Willie took the news—him tellin' everybody 'bout how big an' strong his son was gonna be an' how he was gonna take over at the lumber yard . . . ," Jake laughed. "I can just see his face when Ma told him it was a girl!"

"That what it was? Looked more like a plucked chicken, if you ask me," Clint offered, his grin covering his face and his blue eyes shining.

"You mean like this, Pa?" Nate called, his grin mirroring Clint's as he bent his knees, tucked his hands under his armpits, and strutted around the dusty chicken yard—flapping his makeshift wings and cackling.

Peering out the kitchen window, Malene smiled at her son's antics and the peals of laughter that erupted. It was good to hear laughter in the house again—even if it was at the expense of her son-in-law and her first grandbaby. An' Clint had been right—that little gal surely was scrawny. After one look at the baby, Willie had disappeared behind the wood shed, an' nobody had seen him again. Served him right. But she did feel sorry fer Leah Belle.

If the baby'd been a boy, maybe things might've worked out fer Leah Belle an' Willie, she decided, crossing the kitchen and walking through the living room. As it was . . . , but she mustn't think too far down the road. Baby gals—no matter what they looked like—had a way o' wrappin' themselves around their pappy's heartstrings. She glanced at the portrait of Lori Beth on the mantle and remembered the grin that had lit Clint's face on the day he an' Lori Beth had brought that package o' pictures home from the General Store.

Maybe little Annabelle would do just that with Willie. They'd just have to wait an' see, she sighed as she picked her way up the darkened stairs. At least it had been an easy birth an' Leah Belle had come through it fine. A mamma couldn't ask fer more than that fer her daughter.

Right now, she had another daughter to worry about, she thought, as she paused in front of Lori Beth's closed door. Much as she'd never admit it, she knew how hard Leah Belle's wedding had been on Lori Beth. And now that Leah Belle had given Willie a child . . . Well, she could understand Lori Beth's heartbreak. It wasn't going to be easy, but she'd have to make her face the facts— the sooner the better.

"Lori Beth, it's Mamma," Malene called, knocking softly. "Can I come in an' set a spell?"

"I don't want to see no one!" Lori Beth sobbed from the other side of the door.

"Lorinda Elizabeth Causey! This is yer mamma. I'm askin' to come in an' see you. An' I ain't takin' 'no' fer an answer," Malene answered back angrily, pushing the door inward.

As the door swung shut behind her, Malene stopped, expecting to see Lori Beth lying prostrate on the bed weeping her eyes out. Instead, she found her in the darkened room, dressed in her new dress, and sitting in the middle of her bed. The battered old chamber pot was clutched between her bent knees, her hair was loosened and matted around her face, and her head was bent over the pot.

"Lori Beth, Jake didn't tell me you was sick!" Malene cried, sitting down on the edge of the bed and beginning to rub Lori Beth's back.

"He didn't know it," Lori Beth added defiantly. "Ain't nobody would've cared nohow, seein' how all o' you been so caught up in Leah Belle's birthin'."

"Now, you know that ain't so," Malene admonished. "We only done what any family would've done in our same place. Leah Belle needed her mamma around. An' when yer time comes, God willing, I'll be there fer you, too. But it don't mean she's any more important than you are, Sweetheart. Lord knows I can't be two places at once.

"You've just been taking things too hard lately. An' now look at you—you've done made yourself sick with all yer carryin' on," Malene observed, rising, walking to the wash basin, and wetting the cloth hanging on the side of it—while never taking her eyes off her daughter.

Lori Beth had been so proud of that new dress . . . She wouldn't have just . . . There was a lot more here than met the eye, Malene told herself. But now was not the time. "How long you been sick up here?" she asked gently.

"I dunno—since sometime this afternoon. I guess it was something I ate," Lori Beth sobbed—her red-rimmed eyes turning to Malene as she took the cloth her mother offered her and wiped her mouth. "I'm feelin' better now."

"Well, maybe you'll feel better hearin' it's all over down to the Phelpses," Malene offered, sitting down on the side of the bed. "Leah Belle came through just fine. Had her a little girl. Named her 'Annabelle'—after Willie's ma. Made Anna Phelps right proud. I can tell you that."

"A girl?" Lori Beth questioned, her eyes searching her mother's face.

"A little scrawny, yer pappy says. But, then, most newborn babies look that way," Malene continued, rising.

"There'll be time enough fer you to see fer yourself later. Right now, I think you need yer rest. You just lie back now, Honey, an' try to git some sleep," Malene continued, taking the cloth and removing the chamber pot. "I'll bring yer supper up later," she added, pulling the door closed quietly behind her.

"Lori Beth all right?" Clint asked, concerned, as he appeared at the top of the stairs.

"I think she's gonna be just fine," Malene smiled. "She's done cried it all out by now."

● ● ●

A GIRL—AND a scrawny one, too! Might've expected that outa old Leah Belle, Lori Beth mused, a smile playing over her lips. An' Willie puttin' on such airs about his son an' namesake. Gonna be named after him an' take over the lumber business, was he? Now, she, scrawny, little Annabelle Phelps, was gonna be the namesake o' that poor, tired grandma o' hers an' work in the kitchen at the dilapidated, old house aside the lumber yard—feedin' all them strappin' hands afore they went out to chop wood!

Just let Willie take one look at what Leah Belle done give him. He'd change his mind right fast, now—maybe not even wait 'til the Christenin' to leave town. After all, little Annabelle would have her proud, new grandma there to be named after.

An' now—one day—she could be the one to give him his son— William Phelps, Junior. They could still call him "Billy" if Willie wanted. An' he could work in his great uncle's lumber mill over in Elizabeth City while Lori Beth tended the house his papa would build her. Seemed God hadn't forgotten her after all.

She'd look fer Willie tomorrow down by the river, an' they'd make their plans . . . , she decided as, exhausted, she drifted off to sleep.

● ● ●

No, MAMMA, No! It's not . . . It can't be!" Lori Beth shrieked— tears streaming down her face as she looked up at the stern face of her mother, who stood with her hands on her hips beside the bed. "It's just somethin' I ate. I told you that."

"Lori Beth Causey, you know as well as I that you've eaten the same things the rest of us has fer the past week—an' none o' the rest o' us is sick. An' it 'pears to me you ain't gittin' no better.

Now, I want you to tell me if there's any cause fer me thinkin' what I'm thinkin'," Malene ordered—her eyes never leaving her daughter's face.

"No, Mamma. I told you. You don't understand. It just can't be!" Lori Beth sobbed.

"It can't be, or you don't want it to be? There's a difference, Lori Beth. I need you to be honest with me if I'm gonna help you," Malene persisted.

"You can't help me. Nobody can," Lori Beth sobbed harder, burying her face in her pillow.

"That's just what Leah Belle thought," Malene answered, softening as she sat down on the bed and put her hand lovingly on Lori Beth's back—rubbing absently up and down. "But look at her now. She's got a fine husband. They're happy. An' they got a new young 'un, an'. . . ," Malene crooned.

"No, she don't. An' no they ain't. Papa says the baby is as scrawny as a plucked chicken. An' Willie wanted a boy, too," Lori Beth snapped defiantly—her eyes flashing.

"Guess I shouldn't have brought Leah Belle up," Malene sighed. "I'm just tryin' to tell you that nothin's hopeless. Yer pa an' I can take care o' things fer you—just like we did for Leah Belle. Maybe right now you think it ain't what you want. But things have a way o' workin' themselves out—if you just give 'em a chance.

"Now, who was it? Billie Johnson, Bubba Thomas, or maybe it was . . ."

"No, Mamma! I told you, 'No.' Can't you just leave me alone? I've just been eatin' all them blackberries growin' down by the cow pasture. Should've knowed they wouldn't set well . . . ," Lori Beth continued, turning over, beating at the pillow a moment, and then lying back with her eyes closed.

"All right, Lori Beth. I'm not gonna push you. An' you can deny it all you want fer now. But sooner or later we're both gonna have to face some facts. The sooner the better, I say.

"Just remember—when you get ready to talk, I'll be here. But I sure hope it's before all the rest o' the town is already talkin'," Malene added, shaking her head as she rose. Looking down at the distraught figure on the bed one last time, she slipped into the hall and pulled the door closed behind her.

CHAPTER NINE

A NAMESAKE

LARGE, GREEN BOTTLE FLIES swarmed above the dented, metal trash can by the mill door, while in the dirt beneath it three noisy, black starlings picked over a crust of dried bread that had fallen from the can. The town had been up for hours—taking advantage of the slightly cooler morning for chores and duties. Now, as the unrelenting sun hung straight overhead, everyone who could had long since taken up residence inside.

Biding his time, Nate Causey looked up and down the deserted street. Leaning back against the dusty window of the mill office, he sucked lazily on a peppermint stick—while sneaking sideways glances toward the Phelpses' rambling, old house with the peeling paint on the far edge of the lumber yard. He's always thought it strange that it didn't have no yard—just dirt and piles of boards out front.

'Course he didn't know much about such things, but he reckoned Pa was right when he'd said that—'stead o' sellin' it all—they'd all do better to put some o' that lumber to work fixin' up their own place. But maybe that was what they was doin' with all them long boards holdin' up the porch roof an' the shorter ones stickin' out from under the front steps.

Didn't really matter much to him, he shrugged. He just wanted to get things over with so he'd have time to stop in town before lunch. Bobby Joe had promised to trade him that aggie he'd been wantin'. He wished Willie would hurry.

That note Lori Beth had asked him to deliver must be mighty important if she'd been willing to part with her whole week's allowance to get him to deliver it. He'd been plannin' to go to Bobby Joe's today anyway, he thought. He could've brought it fer her on his way, an' she wouldn't have had to pay a dime. But he'd never tell her that.

He was always looking fer a reason to go into town lately. It weren't no fun at all around home anymore. Jake an' Pa seemed to take off every mornin' to check the fences or tend the crops. So Nate was left at home with Mamma an' Lori Beth.

Mamma seemed cross all the time now. An' Lori Beth was always eatin' them berries an' makin' herself sick. Then Mamma would make him do all Lori Beth's chores. Come to think o' it— maybe Lori Beth did owe him all her allowance. After all, he'd been doin' all her work fer nigh on to a month now!

The screen door on the side of the Phelpses' house opened ever so slightly, then banged shut again. Nate straightened up and turned to watch. Lori Beth'd said to give the note to Willie— alone. That might be hard if all the hands came out together after their dinner.

Chewing the last of the peppermint stick and licking his fingers, Nate reached his hand tentatively into the deep pocket in his denim overalls. Yep, the note was still there, he smiled as he withdrew the folded paper. Wonder what was so all-fired important that Lori Beth'd had to write about it? He could find out if he read the note. But he'd promised Lori Beth.

Oh, he'd learned to take care of himself around his older siblings, but Nate was still honest. If he'd promised not to look, then he'd never think of it.

The door opened again, and Nate—still leaning aimlessly against the building—strained to see who would come out. He was in luck. It was Willie, an' he was alone—but probably not fer long, Nate decided as he heard the din of voices from inside the screen door.

"Hi ya, Willie," Nate called cheerfully, pushing himself away from the wall and strolling across the lumber yard. "How's little Annabelle?"

"Strongest little gal you ever seen," Willie answered, shading his eyes with his hand as he looked into the sun in the direction of Nate's voice—a smile breaking across his face. "She can already grab my finger an' pull up," he added as Nate approached.

"That's great!" Nate answered, wondering why that was something to get so excited about. But, then, he'd been wondering about a lot of grown-up things lately.

"Wanta come see her?" Willie asked. "Purtiest little gal in town! Mamma says she's a Phelps all right—with all that blond hair an' all. Gonna give the boys a fit in a few years.

"I got a few more minutes o' lunch time, an' Leah Belle'd be pleased as punch to see you," he continued, starting back toward the house.

"Can't stay today, Willie. I gotta git back home," Nate answered, shaking his head. "I just come to give you somethin'," he added—holding the paper out in front of him.

"Fer Leah Belle?" Willie asked, reaching out for the paper.

"Don't think so," Nate commented thoughtfully, shaking his head. "Got yer name on it," he continued, looking down to make sure it still said "Willie."

"Let me see," Willie answered, reaching out to take the paper.

"Lori Beth said to tell you to read it alone—so's nobody else sees you. That's why I done waited 'til you was alone," Nate added proudly.

"Thanks, Nate. You done a right good job," Willie smiled, reaching into his pocket and tossing a shiny dime to the little boy.

"Thanks, Willie," Nate called, grinning as he slipped the dime into his pocket. "You tell Leah Belle an' Annabelle I said 'Hi,'" he added as he skipped off down the street. Hadn't been a bad morning at that.

"Wonder what Lori Beth wants now?" Willie sighed as he walked behind the shed, leaned against the rough, unfinished wood, and slowly unfolded the paper Nate had handed him. He'd already told her he couldn't go to Elizabeth City right now. It wouldn't be fair to leave little Annabelle just yet.

After that, Lori Beth had run off. Said she never wanted to see him again. But he'd known she didn't mean it, Willie grinned to himself. Even if she hadn't come down to the river the last few weeks, he'd known she couldn't stay away fer long. That little gal was too hot.   Oh, he'd give her a hard time. But he'd still agree to keep on seein' her, he smiled. He knew a good thing when he seen it. If he played his cards right . . .

Yep, that was what she wanted. "Meet me at the river," was all the note said. There was no name or nothin'. But Nate'd said it was from her. Well, if he got his work done, he could take off early today an' slip down to the river without nobody missin' him. It'd be just like old times again, he smiled—whistling as he picked up the saw he'd left lyin' on a nearby stump and chose a fresh log from the woodpile.

● ● ●

WHAT DONE TOOK you so long?" Lori Beth yelled accusingly, as Willie appeared around the wood pile in a new plaid shirt with his hair all slicked down and a big grin on his face.

"Missed me, Darlin'?" Willie smirked.

"Oh, Willie, if you wasn't such a cussed fool!" Lori Beth snapped angrily. "I told you I never wanted to see you again, an' I meant it. Only . . ."

"Only you couldn't stay away fer long," Willie boasted, stopping to take an appraising look at the pathetic figure in the faded, blue calico dress. With her swollen face and red, puffy eyelids, she bore little resemblance to the girl he was accustomed to meeting. He'd heard from Carrie Sue how Jake said she'd been carryin' on, but he hadn't believed it 'til now.

"An', by the looks of you, you've been doin' a powerful lot o' cryin'," he continued. "You done lost weight, too, Lori Beth. I never knowed you'd take on this way over me."

"Don't go givin' yerself any airs!" Lori Beth sneered. "It ain't on account o' you. But, then . . . , maybe it is," she said hesitantly.

"You been puttin' yourself through all kinds o' misery fer no reason, Darlin'," Willie smiled, reaching out to pull her into his arms, but receiving no response. "You know, I come down here every day fer a week after you left the last time. But you never showed. When little Nate brought that note, I was glad to see you'd finally come to yer senses."

"Willie . . . ," Lori Beth began, "I need to know if you've written yer uncle yet."

"Well, it's kind o' busy around the yard right now," he hedged. "An' with Leah Belle an' the baby both needin' me when I git home . . . ," he added, shaking his head. With all the women giving orders in his house right now, he sure didn't need one more female trying to run his life.

"You really don't plan to write him at all, do you?" Lori Beth retorted, biting her lip to hold back the tears.

"I told you I'll do it—just as soon as I git the chance. Ain't gonna make no difference when we go. We can just go on meetin' right here—like we always done. We got our whole lives out there," Willie added. Darn the woman. Why'd she want to go an' mess up a good thing. She oughta know he couldn't just up an' leave . . . .

"You're wrong, Willie. It's gotta be now," Lori Beth interrupted his thoughts, her eyes filling with tears. "You gotta promise me you'll write that letter today an' then tell me when we can go."

"I know you love me, but I wish you wouldn't take on so," Willie sighed, exasperated. "Pa's got an awful lot o' work needs doing before the weather changes. An' Leah Belle—she needs me, too . . ."

"Old Leah Belle don't need you half as much as I do," Lori Beth sobbed. "She's already got a name fer her baby!"

"What're you tryin' to tell me, Lori Beth?" Willie pulled back suddenly, holding Lori Beth at arm's length and looking into her green eyes—swimming with tears.

"I'm tryin' to tell you that I'm gonna have that son you was so all-fired anxious to have," Lori Beth snapped back. "I done it fer you. I knowed how much you wanted him," she added, her voice breaking. "But, now, I . . . I don't know what to do. You gotta tell me what to do."

"You done gone an' got yourself in trouble, an' now you ask me what to do about it?" Willie asked incredulously, dropping her arms and backing away. "You want me to leave my wife an' new baby an' take off with you to give yer baby a name?

"How'd I even know it were mine, Lori Beth?" he continued. "I've seen you struttin' through town with every eye just a watchin' you. An' I've seen you down by the swimmin' hole just a waitin' fer them hands to show up. Every red-blooded man around these parts knows what you got to offer . . . ."

"I was just waitin' fer you, Willie. I got no interest in them other fellas," Lori Beth screamed. She couldn't believe what she was hearing. Didn't he know how she felt?

"I got a wife already—an' a baby. Ain't I got enough trouble?" Willie retorted. "I sure don't need another sniveling Causey woman or another young 'un in my life right now.

"An' if you think yer pa can fix this one, you got another think comin'. He knowed he'd never find a husband fer Leah Belle, so I got stuck. She ain't the looker you are, I admit. But maybe yer pa done me a favor at that, 'cause, at least, I know she ain't foolin' around behind the wood pile with every other fella in town . . . ," he concluded.

"That's unfair. You know you're the only fella I've ever been with," Lori Beth sobbed.

"I got only yer word on that," Willie shrugged. "'Sides, you know you can have any fella you want in town. Most of 'em would be right proud to hang you on their arm come the next Harvest Dance.

"Why don't you just pick out some fella you want an' send your pa to his pappy with his shotgun—like he done to me?" he asked.

"I don't want another fella. You were mine before Leah Belle took you away. You done stayed with her until the baby was born, an' I let you. But, now, I need you, an' . . . ," Lori Beth choked on her words.

"You let me?" Willie laughed. "Seems you didn't have no choice in the matter, if you ask me. An' you still ain't got no choice.

"You think yer pa's gonna ask me to leave one o' his gals to go to another? Not on yer life! Not with the pride old Clint Causey's got, he ain't. An' if you don't believe me, try him an' see. Go on. Go tell yer sweet pappy you done gone an' got yerself in trouble, an'—like as not—he'll turn that old shotgun on you an' run you outa town," Willie called over his shoulder as he turned and disappeared behind the woodpile, taking the path back to the mill.

"But, Willie, I love you. You said we'd go away together. You promised . . . ," Lori Beth screamed, running after him. "You can't just leave me here. We gotta talk," she sobbed as he continued walking—refusing to turn around or acknowledge her further.

A leaden weight pressed against her chest. Her temples throbbed; her eyes burned; and her legs turned to jelly. "Willie, wait . . . ," she gasped one last time, watching through her tears as his wavering image stepped at last into the clearing behind the lumber mill—without ever turning back. Falling on her knees, then, she let the tears flow in earnest.

She'd planned it all to be so different. She'd imagined Willie's happiness when she told him her news. An' she'd imagined the new life they'd have in Elizabeth City. She wouldn't even have cared if he'd still stayed married to Leah Belle. She'd have taken Willie any way she could have him. Wouldn't nobody in Elizabeth City ask to see the license, nohow. But stayin' here in town—well, she didn't have no choice. As Mamma'd said, wouldn't be long before folks would begin to talk.

An' Papa'd be so disappointed in her. She wasn't blind enough not to realize she'd always been his favorite—what with him spendin' all his money for the calf on them pictures of her he was so proud of. Then with him vowin' not to let her end up like Leah Belle . . . Well, it would kill Papa, like as not.

Oh, she had no doubt Papa'd do the right thing by her. He'd find her another fella. Willie was right there. All she'd have to do is point her finger at any boy in town, an' the poor fella'd have no defense. Papa'd see to that.

But she didn't want no other fella. She just wanted Willie. Willie was the only one she'd ever wanted.

Maybe she could just go away somewhere an' have this baby—someplace where no one would know her. She could say her husband was dead, an' people would feel sorry fer her . . . .

But she didn't have any place to go, an' she didn't have any money, either. She'd never bothered to save any o' her allowance, an' she'd given her last dime to Nate this morning to deliver her note to Willie. It wasn't fair! It just wasn't fair, she sobbed, her chest heaving.

The world swam before her eyes in sunlit greens and shimmering blues as the towering oaks and swollen river swirled around her—and finally became one.

CHAPTER TEN

AIN'T WE GOT ENOUGH TROUBLE?

Seen Lori Beth this afternoon?" Malene turned, her eyes showing her concern as Jake banged through the screen door and planted a fleeting kiss on his mother's lined cheek.

"Ain't she in her room?" Jake asked, grabbing a warm corn muffin from the platter Malene had just placed on the table, stuffing it into his mouth, and talking through the mouthful. "Seems she's been there every time I seen her fer the past two or three weeks."

Malene shook her head. "I was outside in the garden pickin' peas—just after dinner—when she brushed past me. Said she was goin' fer a walk, but her eyes was all red—like she'd been cryin' again. I asked her did she want company, but she said she needed to be alone. Said it'd make her feel better to git out a bit," Malene answered.

"I didn't pay her no nevermind, 'cause I agreed with her there," she continued. "But she's been gone fer nigh on to three hours now. I wouldn't say this to yer pa an' all, but I'm worried about her, Son. She ain't been herself at all lately. She won't even talk to me. Now, she's gone an' disappeared."

"Bet she's gone off to town," Nate observed, nonchalantly stepping into the kitchen. He let the screen door slam behind him and leaned against it while he sucked a lemon stick.

"Nate Causey, where'd you git money fer them candy sticks?" Malene called accusingly, as she turned around and spied him. "I thought you done spent all yer allowance last week on that bag o' marbles you was so proud of. You ain't done somethin' dishonest, has you? 'Cause if yer pa finds out . . ."

"No, Ma'am," Nate replied. "Lori Beth done give me her allowance. You can ask her if you want to."

"Why would she go an' do a thing like that?" Jake broke in. "Lori Beth ain't never willingly parted with a dime—near as I can remember."

"Can't say," Nate shrugged, as he continued licking his candy.

"Can't say, or won't say, Nate Causey?" Malene questioned, examining her younger son's eyes. "Yer sister's been missin' fer nigh on to three hours now. You walk in here sayin' she's given you all her allowance, an' then you say she's probably gone to town . . . . Tell me, young man, why would she go into town if she ain't got no money?" Malene concluded.

"Maybe to see Leah Belle," Nate shrugged again. "I don't know."

"I swear you ain't got the sense God gived one of them cows out there," Malene answered, exasperated. "You know she ain't spoken to her sister since the weddin'. Why do you think she'd go over to the Phelpses' house now?"

"I thought that might be what the note was about," Nate hedged.

"Note, what note?" Jake asked, grabbing his brother by the shoulders, turning Nate to face him, and bending down to the boy's height—his face menacingly close to Nate's. "Yer ma's worried sick over Lori Beth, an' you're standin' here talkin' riddles," he accused. "If you know somethin', you'd better say it—an' right now."

"I just took a note from Lori Beth to Willie. That's all. I thought maybe she was askin' him to work things out with Leah Belle," Nate answered, wriggling out of Jake's grasp and refusing to look at him, while popping the candy stick back in his mouth. "I don't know no more."

"Willie!" Malene called, catching Jake's eye. "Jake, I may need yer help," she continued, drying her hands. Removing her apron, she laid it over the back of a chair, took a quick look at the stove, and headed for the door.

"Jake and I'll be out fer a little while, Nate. But not a word o' this to yer pa. You hear yer mamma?" she threatened, turning to the frightened little boy.

"I hear you, Mamma. Don't worry. I don't want no part o' what's goin' on with Lori Beth," he called over his shoulder as he ran for the stairs—relieved to be free.

● ● ●

Know where you're goin'?" Malene called, carefully picking her way behind Jake as they crossed the sparse, dry grass and baked dirt of the cow pasture—while avoiding the numerous cow patties dotting the landscape.

"Over here," Jake nodded at last, grabbing Malene's hand and helping her over the split-rail fence at the edge of the pasture before leading her onto the shade-dappled dirt path beneath the leafy canopy. "Down by the river," he added, pulling his mother behind him.

"Jake, if she's gone to meet Willie and he ain't come, an' she's down to the river . . . You ain't thinkin' she's gone an' done somethin'. . . ," Malene stopped—her free hand flying to cover her mouth.

"Now, Mamma, you always tell us not to go borrowin' trouble," Jake added, his grin reassuring his mother. "Ain't no gal loves life more than Lori Beth. She ain't gonna go an' do somethin' foolish. If Willie didn't come to meet her, she's probably down here drownin' in tears—more 'n likely. An' if he is with her, he ain't gonna be no more good to her—or to Leah Belle—when I git my hands on him."

"Where d'ya think she'd be?" Malene called, stepping over a moss-encrusted log and looking down the path ahead of her.

"Down behind the big wood pile," Jake added confidently, then shrugged as he noticed his mother's eyebrow raise. "It's a favorite meetin' place fer all the kids," he added, running ahead.

"Look," he called a moment later, pointing at a shoe on the path ahead of them. "It's Lori Beth's, ain't it? Like I said . . ."

"She's over there," Malene gasped, running up beside him and pointing to a figure lying prone under the big oak tree at the edge of the river. "Oh, my God, Jake, she's . . ."

"Done cried herself out, Mamma," Jake laughed as he walked over to Lori Beth, prodded her outstretched arm with the toe of his shoe, and watched her flinch involuntarily. "Ain't nothin' wrong with her. I told you," he scoffed, shaking his head.

"Then Willie didn't . . . ," Malene whispered.

"Good thing fer him he didn't show. Must've known what Pa or I'd do if we catched him over here," Jake whispered back as he leaned over Lori Beth, grabbed her arms, and pulled her to a sitting position.

"Mamma, Jake, what're you two doin' here?" Lori Beth demanded angrily, blinking her eyes and turning from one to the other. "I told you I wanted to be alone, Mamma," she added. Her red-rimmed eyes and mottled face attested to her bout with tears as she looked at each of them.

"Been up to me, I'd a let you rot out here," Jake retorted angrily. "But you been gone over three hours now. You had yer mamma worried sick, Lori Beth,—disappearing like that with no word," he concluded, glaring at his sister. Sisters! he decided—he'd just about had it with both of 'em.

"I told you I was goin' out, Mamma,—right there in the garden 'fore I left," Lori Beth replied in her own defense, getting to her feet and brushing the grass and dirt from her skirt. "I just lost track o' the time, that's all."

"That's the first word from either you or Nate today that I can believe," Malene smiled wryly. "Now, come on. It's late. Let's git you home afore your pa gits in. We can talk later."

• • •

ALL RIGHT, LORI Beth, I've put up with enough o' yer foolishness this past month. It's time you an' I had our little chat," Malene called, wiping her hands on her apron before partially closing the door of Lori Beth's bedroom. Then, sitting on the bed beside her daughter, she waited.

"I don't want to talk, Mamma," Lori Beth answered at last—her swollen eyes pleading with her mother. Meeting only Malene's unblinking gaze, she turned her face to the faded, flowered wallpaper—wiping furiously at the tears which continued to flow down her face.

"Then I suppose it's up to me to do all the talkin'," Malene sighed.

"What d'ya mean?" Lori Beth asked, turning back to examine her mother's face.

"I mean that it's time we brung the facts out into the open—so we can deal with 'em," Malene continued. "I'm afraid it ain't gonna be pleasant—from where I'm sittin'. But it's gotta be done. Now, here's what I know. You can fill in anything you want as I go on. Then we've got some decisions to make," she added, holding Lori Beth with her eyes.

"Now, you an' I both know you're in the 'family way,' Lori Beth," Malene spoke softly, putting her arm around her daughter's shoulders. "An' it ain't gonna be long before the rest o' the town knows it, too."

At Malene's words, Lori Beth burst into tears again—unable to meet her mother's glance. "What am I gonna do, Mamma?" she sobbed, burying her face on her mother's shoulder.

"This mornin', I would've sent yer pa over to Billie's or Bubba's house to set the date an' git you two hitched so this young'un would have a father," Malene began.

"You can still do that," Lori Beth brightened, nodding as she finally met her mother's gaze.

"An' trap some innocent young man, Lori Beth? I should say not. Yer pa an' I done taught you better'n that," Malene reprimanded strongly. "We Causeys don't have much money. But we do have honesty. You've got yerself in a pretty pickle right now. There's no mistakin' that. But I'll not let you drag some innocent young man down to help you hold yer own head up."

"But, Mamma, I could say . . . ," Lori Beth argued.

"You could say the father was any boy in town—if you wanted to. An' yer pa would believe you, too, like as not. You might even find a fella willin' to go along with you. I've seen how they look at you. But that ain't what you're gonna do," Malene asserted.

● ● ●

MALENE, THAT TOMATO plant o' yers is outdoin' itself. I brung you in all I could carry, an' there's still . . . ," Clint stopped. Looking around the empty kitchen, he laid five bright-red tomatoes on the table before going back to open the screen door once more and stick his head out.

"Nate, where's your mamma?" he asked, smiling at the sweat-carved tracks that made their way down the red, freckled face as Nate turned from his game of marbles.

"Ain't she in the kitchen?" Nate asked, sticking his tongue out as he took careful aim. "They all come in just a while ago."

"They? Who's 'they'?" Clint questioned, confused.

"Mamma, Lori Beth, an' Jake. Lori Beth was cryin' fit to kill. Mamma had her arm around her. I don't know where they'd been or what happened. I ain't sayin' no more," he added, turning quickly back to his marbles.

"Must be mighty important fer Malene to leave the supper fixin's," Clint muttered under his breath as he retraced his steps into the kitchen. Taking a muffin from the platter, he stuffed it into his mouth before making his way through the dining room door.

Climbing the stairs, Clint heard voices as he approached the second floor. Lori Beth's door was open. They must be in there, he decided as he brushed the crumbs from his mouth with the back of his hand and walked slowly down the hall.

Poor little gal. She'd sure been puttin' herself through all kinds o' misery lately. Wonder what the problem was this time.

● ● ●

THEN, WHAT AM I gonna do, Mamma?" Lori Beth asked, turning her tear-stained face to her mother.

"Don't appear to me there're too many choices left right now," Malene answered, sadly shaking her head. "Being as how he's already fixed things once in this family, don't seem to be much yer pa can do this time."

Hearing his name as he approached, Clint paused outside the door to listen.

"What do you mean?" Lori Beth sobbed.

"Well, since yer pa's already forced Willie into marryin' Leah Belle, don't seem to be a thing he can do to make him own up to bein' the father o' yer baby, too," Malene sighed.

"Malene! What's the meanin' o' this?" Clint spurted, bursting into the room, his eyes ablaze.

"Papa!" Lori Beth called in alarm—turning at the sound of her father's voice.

"Just tell me if what I just heard is true, Lori Beth," Clint demanded.

"Clint, it don't concern you," Malene added, rising, walking toward her husband, and putting her hand on his arm.

Pulling away from his wife's touch, Clint walked to the bed and took Lori Beth's chin in his hand. "I asked you a question, young lady. An' I'm still waitin' fer an answer," he continued.

Bursting into fresh tears, Lori Beth hung her head—refusing to meet her father's eyes.

"I guess that's all the answer I need," Clint bellowed—stepping back from the bed and glaring in disbelief at his daughter. "My God! You do all you can to make a decent living an' raise yer family right—an' this is the thanks you get. Wasn't enough yer sister had to drag the Causey name through the mud . . . . An' believe me, they're still talkin' in town—despite her weddin'. Ain't none o' us gonna be able to hold our heads up when this gits out!"

"Clint, please. Rantin' an' ravin' ain't gonna solve a thing. Lori Beth's upset enough right now. If you'll just let me handle this . . . ," Malene interrupted.

"The same way you handled both our daughters?" Clint blurted out, turning on his wife. "Well, I'm sick an' tired o' that 'reason' you always want to talk. Ain't done nothin' but bring us more trouble.

"We both know there ain't but one way to handle what Willie Phelps has done to this family. Should've done it a year ago. An' I'm gonna see it's done right this time," he yelled, storming into the hall and slamming the door behind him.

The thudding on the stairs vibrated throughout the second floor of the house. The only other sounds were Lori Beth's loud screaming and Malene's soft sobs as she followed her husband down the stairs and through the dining room door in time to see him lift his shotgun from the rack over the kitchen fireplace.

"Clint, no!" she yelled at last—rushing around the table. "That ain't the way to handle this. Ain't we got enough trouble without you gittin' yerself in trouble with the law?"

"I'm warnin' you, Malene. Stay outa this," Clint called, waving the gun barrel at his wife. "This is man's work. We done tried it yer way once. Now, I'll handle it my way. You just look after the young 'uns," he bellowed.

Holding the gun between him and his wife, he reached behind him, removed his battered old felt hat from the peg, and jammed it on his head. Then, still clutching the shotgun, he pushed the screen door open with his shoulder and thundered down the back steps.

CHAPTER ELEVEN

LET THE LAW HANDLE IT

W HERE'S P A OFF TO in such a hurry?" Nate asked, turning to his mother as she rushed onto the back porch a moment later.

"Quick, Nate," she hissed, motioning him to her, while ignoring his question.

"What's goin' on, Mamma?" he asked, confused, as he left his marble game and hurried to her side, alarmed by the tone of her voice.

"I have a very important errand fer you to run," Malene began, tenderly grasping her son's thin shoulders and looking at him through tear-filled eyes.

"As important as Pa's?" Nate inquired, his eyes aglow.

"More important," Malene nodded. "An' it's something only you can do."

"Tell me, Mamma!" he cried eagerly.

"Now, listen carefully, Son," she began, as they both stopped to watch Clint pass in the wagon—his shotgun poised on the seat beside him.

"Bye, Pa," Nate called cheerfully, waving and then turning a questioning look at Malene as Clint, ignoring him, continued to stare forward—his jaw set firmly.

"Don't mind Pa," Malene whispered quietly as the wagon bounced down the driveway. "He's just headin' into town to do somethin' he thinks is right."

"But it ain't right?" Nate asked, confused.

"I . . . I don't really know, Son," Malene answered honestly. "But what I'm askin' you to do is right."

"What is it, Mamma?" Nate called eagerly, his hands in his pockets and an expectant look on his face.

"Listen carefully, Nate," Malene said, turning him to her and searching his eyes. "I want you to go down to the lumber yard right now—as fast as you can run. Can you do that?" she asked, waiting for his nod. "Take the short cut down by the river, where you won't be seen . . . ."

"But, Mamma, you said I wasn't old enough . . . ," he interrupted.

"You are now," she smiled wanly. "This is a man's job, Son. Are you up to it?"

"Yes, Ma'am," Nate answered proudly.

"Then, I want you to go straight to the lumber yard. If Willie's there, tell him to git outa town right now an' don't come back until night time. Tell him I said to," Malene cautioned, looking into Nate's blue eyes—so like his father's. Poor Clint! She supposed a father had no other choice—but she did.

"What if he's not there, Mamma?" Nate asked.

"Then, run to the house an' find Leah Belle. Tell her to git to Willie fast an' git him outa town," Malene continued.

"Yes, Ma'am," Nate answered.

"An', Son," Malene cautioned, "don't let yer pa see you."

"Am I helpin' Pa to do right?" Nate questioned.

"I hope so, Son. I hope so," Malene sighed. "Now, hurry, Nate, please," she added, watching the youngster run off.

● ● ●

WILLIE, NATE JUST come to the house. Said Mamma sent him to tell you to git outa town right now an' don't come back 'til dark!" Leah Belle called breathlessly as she ran barefooted across the lumber yard toward her husband.

"Did he say why?" Willie asked, laying his saw across the nearby pile of logs and wiping his sweating hands off on his overalls before turning to his wife. "I mean, she'd better have a pretty good reason. Pa's expectin' me to cut all this wood today so's we can git it down river . . ."

"All's I know is Nate said Pa just tore outa the barn in his old wagon totin' his shotgun an' Mamma asked him to come find us," Leah Belle answered, shaking.

"Oh, my God," Willie whistled. "Did he say how long ago yer pa left?"

"Couldn't be long. Nate was blabbin' 'bout how proud he was that Mamma let him come by himself down by the river soon as Pa left."

"I'll have to tell Pa I'm goin'," Willie answered, striding quickly across the lumber yard toward the shed.

Willie, what's goin' on?" Leah Belle asked, running behind him. "I don't understand . . ."

"Guess you'll find out when yer pa gets here," Willie called over his shoulder. "Truth is, I was haulin' some logs down to the river this afternoon when I saw Lori Beth—sittin' there under the old oak tree an' cryin' fit to kill."

"Did you find out what was wrong?" Leah Belle questioned.

"Sat right down there an' asked her," Willie nodded. "But you ain't gonna want to hear it . . . ," he paused, studying his wife's face.

"Come on, Willie! Is all this why Mamma's askin' you to git outa town? Lori Beth's always cryin' 'bout somethin', but Mamma don't overreact, so . . . ," Leah Belle added, waiting.

"Well, 'pears she's gotten herself in trouble with some guy in town," Willie continued, shaking his head.

"Oh, Willie, no!" Leah Belle wailed.

"Might've known it would happen sooner or later with her runnin' after all Pa's hands an' all," Willie shrugged. "Anyway, you won't believe it . . . . Then maybe again you will—knowin' yer sister an' all."

"Believe what?" Leah Belle asked, still stunned at what she had heard.

"Well, you know how she was always runnin' after me?" Willie added, pausing until Leah Belle nodded. "Truth is, she asked me to take her away somewhere so's she wouldn't have to face people here. Can you believe it—her askin' me to leave you an' little Annabelle an' take her away?" Willie asked.

"What'd you say?" Leah Belle asked suspiciously. She hadn't been deaf all those weeks before her wedding when Lori Beth had been in the next room bawling that Leah Belle had stolen Willie from her.

"'Course I told her she'd have to solve her own problem and git yer pa to take his shotgun to whoever was responsible," Willie concluded with a shrug.

"Then, why's Pa comin' here?" Leah Belle asked. "Willie, you ain't . . ."

"Leah Belle, you know better'n that," Willie answered, bending down to kiss his wife. "Got me all I want—what with you an' little Annabelle. I ain't got time fer nobody else. An' you seen me every day out here workin' or takin' Pa's logs to the river.

"Lori Beth, though, she was awful angry." Willie continued, shaking his head. "Said if I wouldn't take her away, she'd tell yer pa the kid was mine an' have him come after me."

"Oh, my God! So that's why he's comin' an' Mamma said fer you to git," Leah Belle gasped. "Willie, I seen Pa when he's angry. He don't stop to ask questions. An' you know he believes everything Lori Beth says . . . . You gotta get outa here right now," she continued, grabbing his arm and pushing him toward the shed door. "Tell yer pa you're gonna take the logs down river, an' hurry!"

"First, I gotta know who you believe," Willie said, putting his arm around Leah Belle. "If you're gonna believe yer sister, then I might as well wait around fer yer pa an' let him see if that old shotgun really works . . . ."

"Willie, good Lord, 'course I believe you," Leah Belle answered, her eyes wide. "Now hurry an' git. Little Annabelle an' I need you. An' don't worry. I'll handle Pa when he gets here," she concluded, turning and running toward the back door of the house.

● ● ●

THE OLD, WOODEN wagon rumbled across the gravel beside the sprawling lumber yard—its wheels spitting out piles of sawdust and wood shavings as it drew to a halt beside the weathered front steps of the boxy, two-story house, which stood on the back of the property.

Black shutters—having long ago succumbed to dry-rot and lost most of their slats—hung from rusted hinges like gap-toothed hags. Strips of yellow paint lay on the small, bare wood porch and curled from the faded siding—the dark, aged wood beneath providing a striking contrast to the piles of new wood laying across saw horses littering the yard. Any trees that had dared to grow on the property had met Joe's saw long before most folks in town could remember—their rotting stumps standing sentinel about the yard decorated with empty bottles or a forgotten ax or rusted saw.

As Clint carefully lifted his shotgun from the wagon seat and jumped to the ground, he felt a guilty pang at what he and Malene had forced on Leah Belle. Baby or no baby, no kid of his deserved to live like this—or to be mixed up with Willie Phelps, he added to himself, clenching the barrel of his gun tighter as he took the steps two at a time.

Looked like it was up to him to set things right once and fer all—even if it was a little after the fact. He'd bring Leah Belle an' Annabelle home. Malene would be glad o' the help once again. An' they would deal with Lori Beth when the time came. Lord knows, nobody could blame a pa whose daughters had both been violated.

Anna Phelps, hearing footsteps on the porch, put down her duster, wiped the perspiration from her face with the sleeve of her dress, blew a limp strand of dishwater-blond hair from her eyes, and looked down, dismayed, at her bony figure in its faded house dress. They didn't usually have callers when the men were at work. "Carrie Sue, you expectin' company?" she called upstairs.

"No, Ma'am," Carrie Sue called as she started out of her bedroom door to see who their visitor might be—almost running into Leah Belle, who had burst from the room she and Willie shared across the hall.

"It's okay, Ma Phelps. My pa's come to see me," Leah Belle called loudly, retying the simple housedress she wore as she bolted down the stairs.

"Land sakes, Leah Belle. First yer brother an' now yer pa," Anna answered sharply. "Next time you're expectin' company, you let me know. The house is a mess, an' I must look a fright," she added, turning to the cloudy hall mirror and pulling her damp hair off her neck.

She wished she'd taken time to wash her hair—or at least put on a little paint, she decided, running her little finger across a sparse eyebrow and biting her lips to add color. Fer all their airs, those Causeys was no better'n a band o' gypsies—just comin' an' a goin' whenever they pleased—never mind askin' leave or announcin' a caller.

"It's all right," Leah Belle explained. "He'll only be a minute, an' he won't be comin' in."

"Better ask him in anyway. Don't want yer mamma thinkin' us Phelpses ain't hospitable," Anna called to Leah Belle's back as her daughter-in-law hurried out the front door.

If she'd a knowed Clint was comin', she would've spent the mornin' bakin' them brownies he used to love so. Well, there was some apple pie left from dinner. She could serve that, Anna decided as she hurried up the stairs. At least she could change her dress an' brush her hair. It wasn't every day Clint Causey came to call. An' he was still the best-lookin' man in town.

• • •

PA, WHAT'RE YOU doin' in town in the middle o' the afternoon?" Leah Belle called as she threw open the door and met her father on the porch. Her eyes widened at seeing the gun by his side, but her voice remained steady. "Did you come to see Little Annabelle?"

"Lookin' fer that no-good husband o' yers," Clint shouted, looking around. "They told me he weren't at the lumber yard. If he's in the house, you better tell him to git out here. We got a big score to settle, an' I don't think he'll be wantin' to settle it in front o' the women folk."

"Willie, ain't here right now, Pa," Leah Belle hedged, looking hurriedly around the lumber yard. "He's down to the river with a load o' logs. Don't expect him back before nightfall—maybe even tomorrow. But I can give him a message . . . ."

"You tell him fer me that he done messed with my family one too many times," Clint bellowed. "You tell him I'm goin' to town to swear out a warrant, but I'll be back to finish what I should've done months ago," he continued, climbing back onto the wagon seat and angrily standing the gun on end beside his leg. "He can't hide from me forever. When I catch up with him . . . ,"

"Yes, Sir. I'll be sure to tell him," Leah Belle nodded. Despite the many months away from home and her new life at the Phelpses, Clint's bark still sent shivers through her as she hurried back up the front steps and stood nervously by the door to watch her father depart.

"Clint not comin' in?" Anna called from the vestibule as she came down the stairs in a new dress with her hair freshly combed.

"No, Ma'am. He had things to do in town," Leah Belle answered as she ran up the stairs past her mother-in-law and entered her own bedroom once more.

● ● ●

THE HEAT ROSE in waves off the pavement as Clint drove down dusty Main Street. The town was totally deserted, he noticed. Guess folks had all finished their business early fer the day. They was probably all stretched out on their front porches fannin' themselves an' drinkin' lemonade. Least, that's where he'd like to be right now.

Damn those Phelpses. Lord knows he was too old for all this foolishness. He should've settled his score with Joe Phelps years ago—when he'd had enough strength to fight things out like a man. Weren't really a fair fight totin' a gun—even if he never intended to use it, he thought, glancing down at the shotgun at his feet. Willie'd be as good locked up as dead—maybe more so since dead folks somehow always seemed to end up heroes . . . . Maybe Malene was right. He'd voted fer old Sheriff Bentson. Why not let him do his job?

Only ten minutes to spare, Clint noticed as he pulled the wagon to a stop across from the red-brick courthouse with its fluted, white marble columns and glanced above the front door at the town clock reading 4:20. They were pretty punctual about closin' at 4:30. But ten minutes should be enough time to fill out the warrant, he decided. That way, the sheriff could deliver it tomorrow. Maybe he'd even hang around down the road a bit in the mornin' an' wait to see 'em leadin' that good-fer-nuthin' Willie Phelps off to jail—like he should've had 'em do last fall—'stead of makin' him a son-in-law.

Maybe it was just as well Willie hadn't been around, he thought as he paused to tie up his horse in front of the General Store. He'd been so angry he just might've used that gun. Maybe things would be better this way.

"Let the law handle it," Malene always said. But she didn't understand it wasn't that easy—especially when the family's pride was at stake. An', then, there was poor little Lori Beth. It hurt too much to think of what she'd be goin' through the rest o' her life. No one could blame a pa . . . .

Still, he'd been pretty hard on Malene back there. He'd have to work harder at controlling that Causey temper, he decided, shaking his head. But he'd make it up to her. Maybe he'd bring her some flowers if Elliott was still open when he came out. An' she'd be proud o' him fer doin' the right thing this time. He smiled to himself as he crossed the street and hurried up the wide, white marble steps.

A sudden, loud backfire reverberated along the deserted street. With no auto in sight, Clint turned—puzzled at the noise—just as a searing pain ripped through his back. He lunged backwards and then pitched forward as his legs and arms reacted to the shock. His clouded eyes briefly noticed the crowd suddenly pouring from the open doors of the courthouse—before everything went black.

"It's Clint Causey," an elderly, white-haired man with a long, white beard—stained yellow from years of tobacco spitting—called from the doorway of the General Store. Crossing the street, he looked up at the crowd of bystanders now gathered on the courthouse steps above him.

"Is he . . . ," a well-dressed, dark-haired woman with a market basket over her arm called—looking out from the store's doorway before sliding to the ground in a faint.

"Near as I can tell," the elderly man nodded, looking down at the still figure at his feet. Then, locking his fingers around his stained, red suspenders, he sidestepped the bright-red river of blood cascading over the white marble steps and pooling into the dark street below and hurried back across the street.

"Somebody better go git Malene," a middle-aged man with long, graying sideburns called from the door of the Savings and Loan— next door to the General Store—as he paused to glance briefly at the carnage before him. He shook his head before hurrying on.

"And the doc," a distinguished, silver-haired man in a business suit called from the courthouse door. "C'mon, let's close up here," he added, motioning to the bystanders as he glanced upward at the town clock.

"Anybody see who did it?" a young man with dark, curly hair and bright-blue eyes asked as he rounded the corner of the court-house—a briefcase tucked under one arm. He paused to look, horrified. Things like this didn't happen in Raleigh.

"Weren't nobody out here," the elderly man with the tobacco-stained beard shrugged at him. Taking one last look, he shook his head and reentered the General Store. "Durn this Prohibition," he called. "Elliott, yer sarsaparilla ain't nearly strong enough fer what I just seen. Who d' ya know with a little business on the side?" His voice carried through the doorway and hung on the still, hot air.

CHAPTER TWELVE

A TIME TO MOURN

SOMEONE'S COMIN', MAMMA," NATE called breathlessly as he ran
around the corner of the porch and pushed open the screen door to
the kitchen.

"Is it yer pa?" Malene asked, laying a large spoon on the side
of the cast-iron stove and covering the pot she had been stirring
before crossing the kitchen to the door. "'Bout time he got back.
Supper's been ready fer ages."

"Don't think it's Pa," Nate answered, shaking his head. "It
ain't a wagon," he called, leading his mother around the side porch
to the front steps and pointing down the lane. A cloud of gray
dust enveloped the boxy, black Model T Ford slowly approaching
the Causey home—its motor belching black smoke as it bounced
over the rutted drive.

"Good Lord, Nate! It's Sheriff Bentson," Malene called, grabbing Nate's arm and squeezing it subconsciously. "You don't
suppose yer pa has gone an'. . . Nate Causey, you did find Leah
Belle an' warn her like I asked, didn't you?" she asked worriedly.

"Yes, Ma'am. Like I told you, I gived her the message. She said to tell you she'd tell Willie to git," Nate nodded emphatically. "Do you think Pa did that thing you was worried about?"

"I don't know, Son," Malene answered. "But there's got to be some reason yer pa ain't home yet an' the sheriff's comin' up the road. He ain't never been out here before. Hurry, Nate. Go find Jake fer me. I may need him."

"He's in the barn, Mamma. I'll git him," Nate called, hurrying off.

"Who's that comin', Mamma?" Lori Beth asked, opening the front door and stepping out onto the front porch beside her mother. "That car's sure kickin' up enough dust," she added, waving her hand in front of her face.

"It's the sheriff, Lori Beth. Lord only knows what . . . ," Malene called softly, turning in time to see her daughter's eyes open wide with fright.

"Oh, Mamma, no! Do you think Papa really shot Willie?" Lori Beth cried, her voice coming out in a screech.

"Hush, Lori Beth. Don't say such things," Malene cautioned, "'specially not in front o' the sheriff. We don't know what's goin' on. Best to just act like we don't know nuthin'. We'll invite him in all friendly like, an' wait to hear what he's got to say.

"Why don't you go on back in the house fer me an' git out that cherry pie I fixed fer supper. . . ."

"Mamma, I can't just pretend I don't know nuthin' when—at this very moment—Willie might be . . . ," Lori Beth blurted out, her eyes spilling over with tears.

"If you can't control yerself, then you git on up to yer room, Lorinda Causey. An' don't you come down 'til the sheriff's gone. You hear me?" Malene ordered sternly. Grabbing Lori Beth's shaking shoulders firmly, she turned her around and pushed her to the door.

"If yer pa's gotten hisself in trouble, I won't have you makin' it any worse fer him by lettin' on why he went to town today. Now, git on upstairs. An', fer God's sake, stop yer bawlin'!"

"If you an' Papa had just left me alone, Willie an' I would've worked out all our problems," Lori Beth screamed hysterically. "Now, look what yer meddling's gone an' done," she added, giving her mother a withering glance before turning and running through the door.

Malene could feel the porch beneath her feet vibrate from the thunder of Lori Beth's anger as she raced up the stairs to her room once more. Sighing, she turned expectantly toward the sheriff as he approached.

"Afternoon, Sheriff Bentson," she managed to smile as the shiny, black roadster came to a halt at the base of the steps, the door opened, and the sheriff stepped onto the running board.

The presence of Mack Bentson, a tall, burly, middle-aged man with red hair flecked with white, usually threw a scare over even the most righteous of citizens. Today, however, he looked anything but threatening as he blinked into the late afternoon sun streaming across the front lawn and tried to focus on the lone figure of Malene Causey.

Although he didn't know the family well, he had always admired the woman. She and Clint were decent folks and had never caused him a moment's problem in town. It was times like this he hated this job.

"Afternoon, Malene," he responded as he climbed the three steps to stand beside her on the porch.

"Got some cherry pie inside," Malene began nervously, wadding her apron with her trembling hands. "That is, if you got time fer a visit."

"This ain't really a social call . . . ," Mack answered hesitantly, juggling his ring of keys from hand to hand as he spoke. But maybe what he had to say would be easier inside, he thought.

"Afternoon, Sheriff," Jake called, approaching around the corner of the house with Nate at his heels. "Is there something we can help you with?"

"Afternoon, Jake. Your mother was just offering me some pie. Maybe if we all go inside . . . ," he tried.

"It'll only take a minute," Malene sighed, relieved, as she led the way around the porch to the kitchen door and pushed it open— hurrying to the old ice box in the corner.

The last thing he wanted right now was a piece of pie, Mack thought as he followed Malene into the kitchen. But at least it would give him time to decide how to tell her. God, it never got easier, did it?

"Malene, I don't need the pie, but I do need to talk to you," Mack began, pulling out a chair at the table, seating himself, and concentrating on straightening the fringe on the tablecloth in front of him while Malene waited—the open ice box door still in her hand. "Perhaps, though, it'd be best if young Nate were to leave the room . . . ," he added after a moment.

"Pa ain't done it!" Nate shrieked out suddenly. "I done warned Leah Belle to git Willie outa town so Pa wouldn't do wrong."

"Hush, Nate!" Malene shouted, slamming the door, grasping Nate by the shoulders, and propelling him across the room. "Jake, take him to his room, will you? I'm sorry, Sheriff. I don't know what's come over him."

"Jake, I'll need to talk to you, as well. Will you come back down as soon as you've seen to your brother?" Mack asked— receiving a curt nod as Jake left the room, pushing the protesting Nate ahead of him.

"Malene," Mack began again, looking at her for the first time since coming into the kitchen. "Did you know Clint was goin' to town this afternoon?"

"I seen him when he left," Malene nodded.

"Does he always take his shotgun with him when he goes into town?" Mack continued, his eyes shifting to the vase of flowers in the center of the table.

"He was gonna git it fixed," Malene answered quickly, her jaw set firmly. "Said the catch didn't work. He was afraid it might go off when he didn't mean it to . . ."

"What's the trouble, Sheriff?" Jake asked, pushing back through the swinging door—his jaw set as firmly as his mother's.

Such strong people . . . But they would need to be, Mack sighed. "Take a seat Malene, Jake. What I've got to tell you ain't pleasant . . . ," he began.

"Sheriff Bentson! Willie Phelps? I mean, is he . . . ," Lori Beth screamed, pushing open the kitchen door and running into the room hysterically—tears streaming from her eyes.

"Lori Beth, git back to yer room!" Malene called sternly, rising, grabbing her daughter by the shoulders, and turning her around quickly. "You shouldn't be up. She's feelin' poorly, Sheriff," she added in explanation. "I'll just take her back upstairs . . . ."

"All you care about is Papa!" Lori Beth screamed. "Well, somebody's got to care about Willie, too," she added as her voice trailed off up the stairs.

"You gotta excuse my sister," Jake apologized when Lori Beth's protests were no longer audible. "You know how emotional young girls can git . . . ."

"Jake, do you have any idea why your pa went to town today?" Mack asked.

"No, Sir," Jake answered, shaking his head. "I didn't even know he'd left until it come time to bring the cows in. Pa don't usually leave the farm during the day," Jake observed honestly.

At least one member of the family was telling the truth, Mack observed, meeting Jake's candid eyes.

"Lori Beth's been feelin' poorly fer a spell," Malene explained as she reentered the room and took the seat across the table. "I'm sorry, Sheriff. Now, what was it you needed to know?"

"I guess I need to know if Clint had planned to meet anyone in town today," Mack asked, looking from Malene to Jake.

"Not that I know of," Jake answered, shaking his head. "I told you I didn't even know Pa was gone."

"And you, Malene?" Mack continued, turning to her.

"I told you already he was goin' to git his gun fixed . . . ," Malene said softly, pulling the vase of flowers toward her and removing a dead blossom—while refusing to look at the sheriff.

"His gun? But, Ma . . . ," Jake protested.

"He checked it out this afternoon—after you'd gone to fix the fences," Malene spoke up quickly, turning to her son. "Came in here a fussin' an'—'scuse me, Sheriff,—a cussin'. Said the catch was broke. He wanted to take it into town today so's he could git it back sooner."

"You're sure he wasn't meetin' anyone?" Mack asked, watching as each shook his head. "Then, either of you got any reason to suspect anyone might have had a grudge against Clint?" Mack went on.

"Everyone loves Pa," Jake asserted. "Just ask around town. Folks'll tell you. Ain't got an enemy in the world."

"Why are you askin', Sheriff?" Malene questioned—a cold feeling starting in her stomach and creeping up her chest as she watched the sheriff clasp and unclasp his hands on the table in front of him.

"Malene, Jake, I got something I gotta tell you. I swear, it never gits easier," Mack answered, his eyes riveted on the table-cloth once again.

"Well, it ain't gonna git any easier by waiting," Malene spoke slowly. "Just tell it like it is. Clint ain't home yet, an' you ain't here on a social call. You tryin' to tell us he's in jail?"

"No, Malene, he ain't in jail . . . ," Mack hedged.

"Well, that's a relief," Malene sighed. "Then, where in heck is he?"

"Over to Doc Mason's. Malene, Jake, Clint was shot this afternoon—in the back—with a revolver. He was just goin' up the courthouse steps when . . . ," Mack began, shaking his head.

"How bad is he hurt? Jake, hurry an' git the old wagon hitched up. I gotta git to him," Malene called, jumping from the chair and reaching for her hat on the hook by the door—without waiting for an answer.

"I'll take you both, Malene, in my car. But there's no need to hurry," Mack hesitated. "He didn't suffer none—if that's any comfort to you," he concluded.

"You mean he's . . . ," Malene gasped, reaching out to steady herself on the chair back—the blood draining from her face as she suddenly grasped the situation.

"Pa's dead?" Jake screeched, his eyes darting from Mack to Malene. "Who done it? Who'd want to shoot him? Pa ain't never wronged no one!"

"That's what I want to find out," Mack answered sadly.

"Didn't nobody see who done it?" Malene asked, incredulous.

"It was late. The street was deserted, and the folks in the courthouse were just closin' up. I questioned everyone who was nearby, but nobody seems to have seen a thing," Mack announced. "Either of you got any idea why he would've been goin' to the courthouse?"

"I . . . I don't know," Malene whispered, tears filling her eyes. "I thought he was . . . , but it don't matter none now."

"Malene, you said you saw Clint leave today. Was he angry?" Mack persisted.

"I . . . Yes, yes, he was, but not angry enough to git hisself killed!" Malene sobbed, the tears rolling down her cheeks and onto the bodice of her housedress.

"Was Willie Phelps involved?" Mack asked, waiting while Malene and Jake exchanged glances. "It's no secret there's always been bad blood between the Phelpses and Clint.

"I could ask Lori Beth," he answered slowly when neither would speak. "She seemed mighty worried about that young man as soon as she saw me."

"It was a personal matter," Malene confided, her chin set.

"Nothing remains 'personal' in a murder investigation," Mack announced, standing. "I don't want to intrude on your grief any more than necessary, but I've got to warn you. I'm gonna have to pick up Willie Phelps for questioning and see if he owns a revolver. Then, I'll need to talk to each of you again as well.

"Somebody pulled that trigger, Malene, and I intend to find out who it was. You may not want things out in the open, but I'm gonna find me a motive and a suspect—with or without your help. Nobody gets away with murder in Clint's Bend if I have anything to do with it.

"Now, why don't you just run upstairs and tell the children you're going to town for a while. There'll be time enough later to tell them what's happened," Mack concluded.

● ● ●

LORD, LEAH BELLE, here comes more o' yer family," Anna Phelps announced, dropping the faded drapes back across the living room window. Hearing no response, she walked into the vestibule and called up the stairs, "Leah Belle, d'you hear me? Yer ma and Jake is out front fixin' to come callin'. I swear, I ain't never seen the likes . . ."

"Sorry, Ma Phelps. I was just checkin' on little Annabelle," Leah Belle called, running down the stairs as Carrie Sue entered from the kitchen.

"She okay?" Anna asked.

"Fast asleep," Leah Belle nodded.

"Want me to wake her? Yer ma might be wantin' to see her," Carrie Sue offered.

"Let's let her sleep fer now," Leah Belle answered, hurrying to the door as she saw Malene on the porch through the narrow vestibule window.

"Mamma, what brings you out . . .?" Leah Belle asked, stopping mid-sentence as she noticed her mother's face and stepping back to let her enter.

"Howdy, Miz Causey," Carrie Sue called, smiling. "Mamma, I'll just go keep Jake company," she called, running out the open door.

"Good t' see ya, Malene," Anna offered as Malene entered. "Been a while. Seems we're seein' the whole Causey family today. Ain't no one here but the gals an' me. An' we just finished supper. We weren't expectin' no one. But I do got some cookies bakin' in the oven if you can set a spell," she added apologetically.

"This ain't a social call, Anna, but thank you," Malene began, removing her gloves and unpinning her hat. "Truth is, I gotta talk to Leah Belle, an' I'd like to do it alone."

"Suits me. Lord know I got enough to do around here anyway," Anna shrugged, backing off as she, too, noticed Malene's face. "You can use the parlor, Leah Belle. I'll be in the kitchen cleanin' up the supper fixin's if you need me."

"Thank you. If you'd just listen fer Annabelle . . . Come on in, Mamma. You look awful. Has something happened?" Leah Belle asked, leading her mother to the sofa.

"Leah Belle, Honey, you gotta brace yerself fer some bad news," Malene announced, reaching for her daughter's hand as she took a nearby chair.

"Why, what's happened? I saw Pa just a little bit ago. Said he was goin' to town . . . . ," Leah Belle said.

"Guess that's where he was headin' all right," Malene answered, shaking her head. "Least, accordin' to the sheriff, that's where they found him."

"Found him? Mamma, I don't understand what you're tryin' to tell me. You mean the sheriff picked Pa up?" Leah Belle asked.

"With the help o' several other people, I suspect," Malene continued. "Leah Belle, Honey, yer pa was shot an' killed this afternoon on the courthouse steps. I'm sorry. I don't know no better way to say it," she concluded as the tears rolled down her cheeks and she buried her head in her hands.

"But who'd want to shoot Pa?" Leah Belle persisted.

"That's what the sheriff an' the rest o' us want to know. But there's more you gotta hear," her mother said, raising her head and drying her eyes on her sleeve.

"What else could there be?" Leah Belle asked.

"I know you saw Nate this afternoon, too," her mother answered.

"He comed to tell me to git Willie out o' town fer a spell," Leah Belle nodded.

"Did Willie go?" Malene asked, her eyes fixed on her daughter. "I need the truth, Leah Belle."

"Yes, Ma'am, he done took the logs down river fer his pa. He won't be back 'til tomorrow."

"An' you're sure he's out o' town?" Malene continued.

"Mamma, what's this all about?" Leah Belle demanded. "You're sittin' here tellin' me Pa's dead, an' then you're askin' me where Willie is. When did you ever care where he was or what he was doin'?"

"I might as well come right out an' tell you," Malene sighed. "The reason yer pa was over here today an' I sent Nate to see you first is that Lori Beth's expectin' a baby, an' she says Willie is the father."

"Mamma, that's a lie!" Leah Belle interrupted angrily. "Let her go find another fella to blame this on. You've seen her—struttin' all over town. Wonder this hasn't happened before now. Lori Beth's been tryin' to take Willie away from me since we planned our weddin'. She'd do anything to hurt me, an' you know it.

"Well, I ain't gonna believe a word o' it, an' I won't let her break up my marriage. I'm sorry Pa's dead, but you ain't gonna pin his murder on Willie. I won't let you," she added defiantly.

"I wanted to keep the whole story from you, but it don't seem there's a way, now that the sheriff's involved," Malene added.

"The sheriff? You mean you told the sheriff that story—without askin' me or givin' Willie a chance to defend hisself?" Leah Belle asked, incredulous.

"Didn't need to say much. Seems everybody in town knows how Willie an' yer pa felt about each other. Would've come out one way or another," Malene shrugged.

"So you an' Lori Beth had to spread yer vicious lies on top o' it all. Now, the sheriff's gonna arrest Willie fer somethin' he ain't done!" Leah Belle cried, her voice rising hysterically.

"The sheriff's gonna arrest Willie?" Anna screamed, dropping the plateful of cookies she was carrying into the room. "Why in God's name they gonna arrest my boy? He ain't done nothin'."

"That's what I been tryin' to tell Mamma," Leah Belle wailed. "But she's gone an' spread Lori Beth's lies to everyone."

"Malene, is this true?" Anna asked, turning to Malene.

"Anna, I got a lot o' things I gotta do right now. An' it don't look like Leah Belle wants to hear any more o' what I got to say. So I'm just gonna have Jake drive me on home, an' Leah Belle can give you her version o' the story," Malene answered, rising.

Turning to her daughter, she continued. "Leah Belle, I gotta go home now an' tell Lori Beth an' Nate. Then, I gotta deal with Reverend Saunders. Funeral's day after tomorrow. It'd mean a

lot to all o' us if you'd come an' sit with the family," she concluded as she walked to the door.

"Funeral? What funeral? Who died? Leah Belle, what is yer
ma talkin' about?" Malene could still hear Anna Phelps's shrill
voice as she pulled the door closed and picked her way slowly
down the wobbly front steps.

● ● ●

THE AFTERNOON SUN reflected off the tin roof of the small, white
church outside of town and painted a rainbow across the wood
floor inside the open doors as it streamed through the stained-glass
windows. Slowly winding its way out of the double doors, the
little procession climbed past the weathered oak and on up the
dusty dirt path to the top of the hill—overlooking the muddy
Roanoke River as it meandered around the small cemetery.

A plain, wooden casket covered with a bouquet of bright daisies rested on the shoulders of Jake, Doc Mason, Mack Bentson,
and an elderly man with a white beard—stained with tobacco juice.
("After all, I seen him fall," he had offered at the doctor's office
where he'd been keeping vigil until Malene arrived.)

Reverend Saunders, Malene, Lori Beth, and Nate followed
closely behind as the casket was laid on the parched, yellow grass
of the Causey plot. No other occupants of the town were visible at
the church or on the streets. The word "Murder" had locked
every door as surely as a quarantine notice.

Willie had already been picked up for questioning. It was common knowledge that Willie owned a revolver, yet a search of the
Phelpses' home had not turned up the weapon. Nonetheless, Sheriff Bentson was determined to solve the murder, and he needed a
suspect.

Leah Belle had refused to attend the funeral. "My pa was just
as guilty as Mamma in believin' Lori Beth's story. He ain't never
cared one mite about me, so why should I care about what hap-

pened to him?" she told Carrie Sue when the young woman had offered to babysit for Annabelle.

As the casket was laid beside the gaping hole and the bearers stepped back to join the mourners, a tall, slender young woman— her white-blond hair caught in a net beneath a wide-brimmed straw hat—slipped from behind a tree. Slowly, Carrie Sue made her way to Jake's side—where she wordlessly slipped her hand into his, tears cascading down her face.

CHAPTER THIRTEEN

THE STATE VERSUS WILLIE PHELPS

WEAK RAYS OF WINTER sun slid across the roof of the county library and came to rest on the white marble steps of the old courthouse—now alive with activity. Nobody could remember ever having had a murder trial in town before, and nobody wanted to miss a chance to be a part of the history-making process. It would be something to tell a grandchild about someday. And—with the harvest already in—it would provide the liveliest winter entertainment the town of Clint's Bend had ever known.

A scattering of automobiles and a myriad of wagons flanked Main Street. The occupants called greetings to one another, while elbowing fellow townspeople out of the way as they hurried to reach the tall, green double doors at the top of the stairs where bystanders were being admitted to the courtroom one at a time.

A worn wooden wagon drew slowly to the dusty curb in front of the General Store—angling into the only space available in the crowded square. From nearby wagons, the street, and the court-house steps, all action stopped as people turned as one to watch the occupants of the old wagon alight.

Looking to neither left nor right, Jake alighted first. His only concern was his mother in her stark, black mourning dress and black straw hat. Fixing her attention on pulling on her new white gloves while waiting for her son to circle the wagon, Malene ignored the staring faces on all sides.

As Jake took her hand and helped her to the ground, Nate leaped to the street on the other side of the wagon, rounded it, and took his mother's hand from Jake. Standing tall and straight in his newly-made suit, Nate guided his mother expertly across the street and through the throng of bystanders. Malene looked down only once—at a rust-colored stain on the old marble steps—before lifting her chin and fixing her eyes imperiously on the double doors so far above her.

All eyes turned back to the wagon where Jake was now helping Lori Beth to alight. Her condition, although covered in part by a dark-green wool cape, was still quite apparent as she neared her term.

Leaning heavily on Jake's arm, her eyes downcast, Lori Beth tried to ignore the stares and repeated whispers, which surrounded the pair as they followed Nate and Malene's path up the steps. Jake, too, looked down at the rust-colored stain before fixing his eyes on his mother and brother, who were just entering the courthouse.

Once inside, the family was ushered into a small anteroom beside the courtroom where the trial would take place. Although they were still fully visible, they were, at least, removed from the crush of the crowd. Malene breathed a sigh as she took a seat on the high-backed, wooden bench and motioned for Lori Beth to sit beside her.

"You'd think we was a circus come to town," Lori Beth whispered under her breath. "I declare, Mamma, every soul in town was out there in the street, an' all o' them was starin' at me as if I was stark naked."

"I'm so sorry, Lori Beth. I would've spared you all this if I could've," Malene offered, reaching over to cover Lori Beth's small, cold hand with her own warm, calloused one.

"Why are they gonna make me testify when I don't know nothin'?" Lori Beth asked, her eyes searching her mother's. "I don't think I can do it—with all them people in that courtroom starin' an' judgin' me. I just wanta go away somewhere where nobody knows me . . . ."

"Perhaps after the trial—an' the birth . . . ," Malene answered.

"Lori Beth," called a whispered voice. Looking up, Lori Beth's stomach flipped as she caught sight of Willie—flanked by two marshals. He was dressed in a dark-blue suit with his flaxen hair slicked down. His eyes were riveted on Lori Beth's midsection. Turning at last, he said something to one of the marshals, who shook his head. The other marshal, however, after hearing the exchange, put his hand on the arm of his fellow marshal, and the two backed discreetly away.

"Miz Causey, Lori Beth . . . ," Willie began, hesitantly, "I can't tell you how sorry I am . . . ."

"You might've thought of that before you pulled the trigger, Will Phelps!" Jake called loudly enough for those passing in the hallway beyond to hear.

"Jake, for Lord's sake, let's not make this more of a spectacle than it already is," Malene hissed. "Half the town's watchin'. Let's just let Willie have his say," she pleaded.

"It's just that, Miz Causey . . . ," Willie continued, wringing' his hands in front of him, "they got the wrong man. I ain't done it. I swear to you. I mean . . . I ain't even seen Clint Causey at all that day . . . ."

"See, it's like I told you, Mamma. I told Leah Belle to tell Willie to git—like you said to," Nate nodded beside Malene.

"Hush, son," Malene scolded, turning to Nate. "It ain't proper to be discussin' any o' this before the trial. An' I suspect you'd better be savin' yer explanations fer the judge as well, Willie. But do give my best to Leah Belle. Tell her we understand why she ain't been to see us," she concluded, turning her head from Willie in dismissal.

"Lori Beth," Willie began plaintively, watching from the corner of his eye as the marshals began to move toward him once more. "I just wish to Heaven things could've been different. If only . . ."

"You made yer own trouble, Willie . . . , an' I made mine," Lori Beth answered hesitantly, holding Willie with a candid glance for a single moment before subconsciously laying her hands on her midsection and dropping her eyes to her lap.

"All the wishin' in the world ain't gonna make things no different. Guess I've learned that from all that's happened," she whispered as the marshals approached Willie once more and led him into the courtroom.

● ● ●

THE PROSECUTION CALLS Miss Lorinda Causey," Don Lockridge, a tall, young man with dark, curly hair and piercing blue eyes called loudly as he approached the bench.

"Will Lorinda Causey please take the stand?" The thin, balding man in the long, black robe looked over the courtroom from behind his high, wooden desk—his dark eyes under heavy, gray brows seeking and then lighting on Lori Beth.

"Do I really have to go up there, Mamma?" Lori Beth whispered nervously, holding onto Malene's hand—her eyes wide with fear.

"The judge is callin' fer you, so you ain't got no choice," Malene nodded. "Just tell the truth, Lori Beth. That's what yer pa would've wanted. No amount o' wishin' gonna bring him back, but you can still make him proud o' you," Malene whispered back, attempting a wan smile as she squeezed her daughter's hand and helped her to rise from the hard, wooden bench.

Lord, it was hard enough facing life without Clint, Malene noted sadly as she watched Lori Beth's unsteady gait down the row and into the aisle. But the hardest thing of all had been seeing the toll his death, her pregnancy, and her guilt had taken on Lori Beth. Gone was the confident, cheerful, young girl. In her place was a tense, fearful stranger, who had not smiled since Malene and Jake had taken her and Nate into the living room of their home so many months ago to deliver their devastating news.

Then, there was Leah Belle, the poor, innocent young woman on whom so much had been thrust. The demands on her had been too many, too soon, Malene shuddered. She had not even been allowed to speak to Leah Belle during the trial—so smothered was she by Phelpses. She stole a glance at her other daughter, seated on the opposite side of the courtroom—her eyes never leaving Willie's back as he sat at the table in the front of the room watching Lori Beth approach.

Maybe she had been wrong, Malene sighed. Maybe she had been meddling in God's affairs by insisting Clint force Willie into marrying Leah Belle. Saving the family pride surely could not have been worth Clint's death and what the rest of the family was going through now. And—despite their efforts—in a cruel twist of fate, the family was now to endure what they had sought so hard to avoid.

If they had let things pass, at least she would still have had Clint by her side—Clint, the one person she knew who always seemed to make things right. Oh, he had always had a quick temper. She'd seen that from the time they first started courtin'. But his outbursts had occurred only when his pride was hurt. And his pride had never been for himself—only for those he loved.

Despite Clint's anger, he would have taken whatever befell them all and made the most of it. And he would have loved little Annabelle with all his heart and given her a place in his home—no matter her parentage. Of that she was certain.

Then there was Lori Beth—his pride and joy—so full of life with her radiant gold hair and vibrant gold-green eyes. What would Clint have thought to see her as dejected and humiliated as she was today—her hair straight and limp from her pregnancy, her body so misshapen, and her red-rimmed eyes never leaving the floor as she slowly made her way toward the bench and onto the witness stand.

Perhaps the Lord had known what he was doing after all in taking Clint, Malene sighed. She knew he could never have endured the pain in those sad eyes.

"Raise your right hand, Miss Causey," Judge Edwards said, as Lori Beth stood behind the podium. "Now, do you swear to tell the truth, the whole truth, and nothing but the truth, so help you, God?" he questioned, his piercing gray eyes catching Lori Beth's as she nodded.

"You must answer 'I do' aloud," Miss Causey, he ordered irritably. A soft murmur ran like a current around the courtroom as all eyes turned to stare at Lori Beth.

Looking only briefly at the sea of faces, Lori Beth cast her eyes at the table in front of her and whispered, "I do." She turned her eyes pleadingly to the judge.

"Your witness, Mr. Lockridge," the judge began. "You may be seated, Miss Causey," he added as an afterthought.

"Miss Causey," Don Lockridge began, attempting a smile at the clearly distraught young woman, "I'll try to make this as brief as possible. Can you tell the court how long you have known the defendant, Willie Phelps?"

"He lives just down the way—on the road to town. So, I guess I've known Willie all my life . . . ," Lori Beth answered slowly, looking involuntarily at the nearby table, where Willie's eyes were fixed on her.

"In that time, were you aware of any animosity between your two families?" Don continued.

"Objection, your Honor," the portly, white-haired defense attorney, William Green, called. "The Prosecution is leading the witness."

"Sustained, Mr. Green," the judge answered. "The Prosecution will please rephrase the question."

"Miss Causey, did you ever hear Willie Phelps threaten your father?" Don Lockridge asked.

"I . . . I don't know what you mean . . . ," Lori Beth hedged, while avoiding Willie's eyes.

"I must remind the witness that she is under oath . . . ," the judge commented quietly, leaning over the bench to look at Lori Beth.

"He . . . he didn't like my papa none, if that's what you mean. Everybody in town knew that. He was always tryin' to play tricks on Papa . . . . But that don't mean he wanted him dead," Lori Beth burst out, tears coming to her eyes.

"Just answer the questions, Miss Causey," Judge Edwards reminded her.

With a quick glance at the judge, Don Lockridge continued, "On the day on which your father was shot when Sheriff Bentson came to your house, did you have reason to suspect that he and Willie might have had an altercation?"

"I knew Papa was goin' to see Willie, if that's what you mean," Lori Beth nodded.

"Did Willie know that?" the prosecutor asked.

"I'm not really sure . . . . Yes, I guess he must have known Papa would be comin'," Lori Beth concluded at last, her eyes pleading with the attorney to end the questioning.

Noticing her distress, Don Lockridge nodded imperceptibly. "Thank you, Miss Causey," he smiled gently. "I have no further questions, Your Honor," he added, stepping back from the witness stand.

"Your witness, Mr. Green," the judge continued.

Rising and walking to the witness stand, William Green paused a moment to look out at the courtroom. Spreading his tweed suit coat wide and locking a thumb under each suspender as it crossed his ample midsection, he began, "Miss Causey, one can see you are clearly 'in the family way.' I think that is how they put it delicately," he smiled.

He rocked on his heels and stretched his suspenders while he directed his gaze at each of the jurors inside their dark, wooden enclosure. "Can you tell us the name of the father of your child, since I see from my manifest that you are still a 'Miss,'" he added, reading from a sheet of legal paper in his hand.

"Do I have to answer that?" Lori Beth asked, turning to the judge—her eyes filled with tears.

"Mr. Green, I must object to this line of questioning," the judge replied.

"Let me rephrase my question," Mr. Green began again, turning toward the jury with an oily smile. "Is the father of your child in the courtroom, Miss Causey?"

"I object, Your Honor," Don Lockridge called, looking from Lori Beth's distraught face to Judge Edwards's immobile profile.

"Mr. Green, unless you can prove that this line of questioning is totally relevant to the case . . . ," the judge responded, leaning across the bench and holding the portly Mr. Green with his eyes.

"I think you'll find it very relevant, Your Honor," William Green answered—turning for a brief moment to Willie, who looked only at the table in front of him, refusing to meet his attorney's eyes.

"Very well. You may continue," the judge sighed, settling back in his chair.

"I repeat, Miss Causey. Will you tell the jury if the father of your child is in this room?" Mr. Green asked again, as Lori Beth reluctantly nodded.

"You will need to answer the question for the record, Miss Causey," the judge interjected.

"I said, 'Yes,'" Lori Beth whispered, her eyes downcast.

"Is it true that the father of your child is also your sister Leah Belle's husband—as well as the defendant in this trial—Willie Phelps?" Mr. Green added, triumphantly, as all eyes turned to Lori Beth.

There was not a sound in the courtroom as Lori Beth looked pleadingly across the room at her mother. Malene nodded imperceptibly. "Just tell the truth" rang in Lori Beth's ears as she nodded at last.

"You must answer 'yes' or 'no' to the Defense's questions," Judge Edwards responded, exasperated.

"Yes," Lori Beth cried out at last, wiping her eyes with her sleeve.

Noticing her tears, William Green dramatically pulled a crisp, white handkerchief from his pocket, shook it open, and handed it to Lori Beth before continuing.

"And, Miss Causey, is it true that you had met with the defendant on the day your father was shot?" Mr. Green asked.

"At the river," Lori Beth answered softly—as a buzz ran around the courtroom.

"Order in the Court," Judge Edwards called, bringing his gavel down soundly in front of him.

"Is it true that you arranged this meeting to ask Mr. Phelps to leave your sister and their child to run away with you?" William Green triumphed—looking out over the courtroom.

"Objection, Your Honor. The Defense is leading the witness," Don Lockridge said, jumping to his feet. Every once in a while, he began to question his great desire to go into the legal profession.

He had seen the young woman's father gunned down on the steps of the courthouse and had witnessed the shunning of her family. Now, he was not going to stand by and watch that oily William Green continue to embarrass her in front of the whole town. Miss Lorinda Causey deserved a chance to preserve some of her dignity—which he knew had been sorely stripped away over the past several months.

"Sustained, Mr. Lockridge. The Defense will please rephrase his question," the judge ordered.

"Miss Causey, let's get right to the point. When Willie Phelps refused to leave his wife and daughter for you, how did you feel?" Mr. Green continued.

"I was hurt," Lori Beth answered. "He'd promised to . . ."

"Hurt enough to implicate him in your father's murder when Sheriff Bentson came to your home?" William Green interrupted, pausing as another buzz ran around the courtroom.

"Objection!" Don Lockridge called loudly, jumping to his feet again and slamming both hands on the table in front of him for emphasis.

"Sustained, Mr. Lockridge," the judge acknowledged. "Mr. Green, I must warn you . . . ," he cautioned angrily as his gavel resounded throughout the courtroom.

"I'll withdraw the question, Your Honor. I have no further questions," William Green concluded, leaning back on his heels, pulling his suit coat together, straightening, and catching Willie's eyes with a slight smile.

"You may step down, then, Miss Causey," the judge added, turning to Lori Beth. Sighing in relief, Lori Beth stepped down from the platform. Looking only at the floor ahead of her, she made her way slowly back down the aisle and across the row. Malene grabbed and pressed her hand and offered a wan smile as she slid into her seat. What more could—or would—William Green subject her daughter to?

"Will you call your next witness, Mr. Lockridge?" Judge Edwards requested—with a glance at the large clock on the back wall of the courtroom. He'd only had time for a piece of toast for breakfast—and it was quickly approaching noon . . . .

"At this time, I'd like to call Mrs. Leah Belle Phelps to the stand," Don Lockridge announced, looking across the courtroom. At the mention of her name, Leah Belle rose from her side of the courtroom. She wrapped her long, thin hair behind her ears and stopped a moment as Anna Phelps squeezed her hand in passing. Then, walking directly to the front of the room, she paused before the table where Willie sat. Their eyes locked wordlessly for a moment before Leah Belle followed the judge's direction and took the witness stand, smoothing the skirt of her yellow, flowered dress before turning to the judge.

"Place your left hand on the Bible and raise your right hand, Mrs. Phelps. Now, do you promise to tell the truth, the whole truth, and nothing but the truth, so help you, God?" the judge repeated his former question to Leah Belle.

"I do," Leah Belle answered in a clear voice with her hand raised and her head held high—her eyes never leaving Willie as she seated herself.

"Mrs. Phelps, can you please tell the court the events that transpired on the day your father, Clint Causey, was killed?" Don Lockridge requested.

"Willie, my husband, had just gone back to work after havin' his dinner, when my younger brother, Nathaniel, come runnin' up to the house," Leah Belle began.

"Was your brother in the habit of comin' to visit you unannounced?" Don Lockridge continued.

"No. He'd never come by himself before. That's what surprised me," Leah Belle added.

"Did he have a reason for his visit?"

"He said Mamma had sent him," Leah Belle nodded. "He said I should find Willie an' tell him to git outa town fer the rest o' the day."

"Did he say why?" Don Lockridge prodded, his eyes holding Leah Belle's.

"He said Mamma said to do it an' that he was helpin' Pa do right, if I remember correctly," Leah Belle concluded. She cut her eyes to Malene, who sat stone faced, watching her older daughter, while still clutching Lori Beth's hand.

"Did you warn your husband?" the prosecutor asked.

"I went over to the lumber yard right away an' told him what Mamma had said," Leah Belle nodded. "His daddy heard me an' sent Willie off with a load of lumber that they was takin' down to the river," she added, sneaking a look at Joe Phelps, who nodded his head.

"Did you actually see your husband leave the lumber yard and go to the river?" Don Lockridge persisted.

"No . . . I mean, I have a little baby, Annabelle. She was back to the house. I had to git back to her. I couldn't stay . . . ," Leah Belle answered, flustered.

"Then," the attorney went on, "you have only your father-in-law's and husband's word that Willie actually left that day. Is that correct?"

"But I knowed they was takin' the logs down river," Leah Belle added, looking helplessly at Willie. "An' he didn't git back fer supper . . . ."

"Thank you, Mrs. Phelps. I have no further questions, Your Honor," Don Lockridge answered, smiling as he stepped away from the bench.

"Your witness, Mr. Green," the judge announced, sneaking a look at the clock on the back wall.

"No questions, Your Honor," William Green stood, addressing the bench. There was nothing Mrs. Leah Belle Phelps could say that would help his case at the moment.

"Thank you, Mrs. Phelps. That will be all," Judge Edwards announced with an audible sigh. "The Court will now adjourn for lunch. We'll reconvene in one hour."

"All rise," the bailiff ordered.

Stacking his papers, Don Lockridge shook his head. There would be no lunch for him. With Miss Causey's testimony, he had succeeded in showing probable cause. And he'd poked a small hole in Willie Phelps's alibi. But he had a long way to go. And they still hadn't found the murder weapon.

CHAPTER FOURTEEN

ANOTHER GOODBYE

THIS ALL THE MAIL we got, Son?" Malene asked, taking the single envelope from Jake's hand as he exited the small, red-brick post office.

"All Mr. Parker gave me," Jake shrugged as he took his mother's arm and helped her to their wagon a short distance down the street.

"Got a local postmark," Malene mused, turning the letter over in her hand. "Seems we've seen every person in town at the courthouse. Wonder who'd need to be writin' us?" she added as she climbed onto the wagon seat and slipped a fingernail under the envelope flap.

"Who's it from, Mamma?" Jake called as he climbed onto the driver's seat and turned to look at his mother—her face now ashen.

"Where are Lori Beth an' Nate?" Malene called in a frightened voice a moment later. She looked hurriedly back toward the courthouse doors—now spilling out the trial's attendees for the day. "Go find 'em, Jake, an' hurry!" she cried, her hand on her heart and her eyes wild with fear.

"I seen Mr. Lockridge stop Lori Beth on her way out. Nate's with her. They're all right," Jake offered.

"Don't argue with me, Jake Causey. Just do as I ask. Go find 'em an' git 'em back to the wagon this minute," Malene ordered before collapsing onto the seat and burying her face in her hands.

"I'll go right now, Mamma," Jake answered, alarmed by his mother's actions. "You just wait here," he called over his shoulder. He dodged a wagon just pulling out behind him before running back across the street and up the steps of the courthouse.

Her face buried in her hands, Malene, nonetheless, was fully aware of Jake's actions. As soon as his back was turned, she slipped her right hand out of the fold of her black cloak and read the horrifying words once again—carefully this time. Each letter had been cut individually from old mail order catalogs and haphazardly glued onto the piece of paper. "Lori Beth and the baby will die," the note said. There was no further message, and there was no signature.

The meaning was clear enough, but who had sent the note? Who hated Lori Beth enough to want to kill her—and an innocent baby? "God, please help me," Malene pleaded. "Haven't we suffered enough?" she whispered, rolling her eyes upward as she refolded the note and slipped it back into her pocket. She had to do something. But who could she trust? There was no one in town . . .

"I found 'em, Mamma!" Jake called, waving from the steps of the courthouse. Don Lockridge walked beside him, holding Lori Beth's arm and helping her down the long flight of steps. Nate, weaving his way impatiently through the crowd, skirted past Jake and took advantage of an opening in the crowd to jump down two steps at a time and appear first at the wagon.

Of course, Malene sighed, watching her daughter approach— Don Lockridge. He had no ties in the town, and he was the prosecutor. She could trust him. He'd know what to do.

"Mrs. Causey," Don Lockridge called as soon as he and Lori Beth were within earshot—his blue eyes showing his concern, "are you all right? Jake said you seemed ill. We can call Dr. Mason for you . . . ."

"That ain't necessary," Malene answered, her head held high as several bystanders stopped to observe the proceedings. "But I need to speak to you—if I could," she added.

"You've had an exhausting day," Don Lockridge smiled as he approached. "And they're closing up inside," he added, looking back toward the large, green doors—now empty of people. "I could follow you out to the farm if you'd like. My car's just over there—in front of the library," he said, pointing a few yards down the street. "And perhaps my seats would be more comfortable for Lorinda than the wagon seat. Would you mind if I brought her with me?"

"That's a wonderful idea," Malene said, brightening. Lori Beth would be far safer in Don Lockridge's auto than in the open wagon. "But close the windows fer her, will you?" she added, looking around the street. It was impossible to guess from which area the danger might come. "This cold air ain't good fer the baby."

"Of course," Don added. "Over here, Lorinda," he said softly, continuing to guide her by the arm.

"Can I come, too?" Nate called, running behind Lori Beth as Don led her away. "I ain't never ridden in a real automobile."

"Then, we'll have to take a drive—soon," Don smiled at the little boy. "Maybe next Sunday—if that would be all right with your mamma. But I think three would be too crowded for right now."

"Come on, Nate. Mamma will need yer help while I'm puttin' the horse away," Jake called, grabbing the little boy around the waist and swinging him up into the wagon.

● ● ●

MAMMA, WHAT'RE YOU lookin' at?" Nate asked as the little procession slowly made its way back down Main Street. "You afraid Mr. Lockridge's car ain't gonna make it?"

"She's just worried about Lori Beth, ain't you, Mamma?" Jake explained. "It must've been hard on her answerin' all them questions today with everybody starin' an' a knowin' what went on with her an' Willie. But she done a good job, didn't she?" he smiled.

"Is Willie gonna go to jail?" Nate questioned, his blue eyes shining. "I ain't never knowed no one who went to jail before."

"Hush, Nate," Malene answered distractedly. "That's fer the jury to decide. It ain't none o' our business."

"But Willie said he ain't killed Pa," the little boy continued. "Don't you believe him?"

"I don't know what to believe anymore," Malene answered sadly—as Jake turned the horse north onto the river road. Looking back, she sighed at seeing the shiny, black automobile following closely behind—a cloud of dust hiding the small town of Clint's Bend in its wake.

● ● ●

LORI BETH, YOU gotta be worn out," Malene offered as the two entered the house together. "Why don't you go right up to yer room an' lie down. I can bring you a plate o' food later," she added, removing the pins from her small, black hat and pulling her gloves off.

"That's what I've wanted to do all day," Lori Beth sighed. She hung her new cloak on the wall peg and smoothed her dark-green dress over her extended midsection. "Mamma, do you think I'm gonna have to go back on that stand?" she questioned.

"No, Lori Beth. You told 'em all you knew. Now, it's time to think about you an' the baby. Yer pa'd want that," Malene tried to smile as she grasped her daughter's hand. She had made a decision. She'd lost one daughter today. After Leah Belle's testimony, it was clear her loyalties were now wholly with the Phelpses. Now—one way or another— she was going to lose another daughter. But it was better to lose her this way. . . .

Taking a deep breath, she began again, "Do you remember this mornin' when you said you'd just like to go away somewhere where nobody'd know you?"

"It's so embarrassin', Mamma—with everybody in town knowin' an' pointin' at me," Lori Beth whispered, her eyes filling with tears.

"I know how hard it's been fer you, Honey," Malene nodded. She lifted Lori Beth's chin to look into her eyes. "An' I've been thinkin' that maybe you're right. Maybe you should go away—at least until the trial's over. What d' ya think o' goin' to Grandma Blaine's in Roanoke Rapids an' havin' the baby there? We don't have to tell anyone here where you are. You can tell everyone there yer husband's away fer a spell, but he'll be comin' fer you after the baby's born."

"Oh, Mamma, could I?" Lori Beth asked, brightening. "I'd give anything to walk down the street again without everyone starin' at me. But I'll miss you. I'd so counted on you being there. I mean, I know nothin' about birthin'. Would you come—fer the birth, I mean?" she asked, her eyes filling with tears.

"You'll be in good hands with Grandma Blaine," Malene added confidently, remembering her mother, from whom she'd learned her own midwife skills. "But I'll be there if I can, Lori Beth," Malene nodded. "You can count on that.

"Now, you git on upstairs right now an' git some rest. After yer supper, I'll come help you pack. Tomorrow's Saturday. There's no court session, so we won't be needin' the wagon. Jake can have it ready an' take you over to Grandma's right after breakfast." She tried to smile as she pulled her daughter to her in one last embrace—smelling the fragrance of Lori Beth's hair and locking it into her memory.

As she watched Lori Beth plod tediously up the stairs for the last time—one hand in the small of her back and the other slowly pulling herself up the banister—Malene's eyes fell on the smiling Lori Beth still residing on the mantle where Clint had so lovingly placed the portrait only a year ago. How could she have been so angry at Clint for spending their Christmas money? Reaching out, she cradled the smiling image against her breast as if it were the baby—no, the two babies—her own and Lori Beth's—she was about to lose.

"Mamma?" Jake called, the screen door banging behind him as Malene replaced the photograph and hastily wiped her eyes. There was business to take care of. Maybe, mercifully, it would help her to get through all that she must, she decided, as she pushed open the swinging door and entered the kitchen.

"You needed to talk to me, Mrs. Causey?" Don Lockridge asked uncertainly as he waited beside the kitchen door.

"Come in, Mr. Lockridge, and take a seat," Malene answered politely, waving him to a chair at the kitchen table before turning to Jake. "Jake, where's Nate?"

"He's playing marbles again. I told him it was too cold . . . ," Jake began. "I'll get him if you want him."

"Let him play, Jake," Malene answered, shaking her head. "He's had too much sufferin' in his young life already. An' he mustn't hear what I'm gonna tell you two," she continued, sliding out a chair for herself as she pulled the crumpled note from her pocket and placed it in the middle of the table.

"Mamma, where did you get this?" Jake whispered loudly, his eyes widening in fear as he looked from the note in front of him to his mother.

"It was the letter you brought me in today's mail," Malene answered.

"Then, you have no idea who sent it?" Don asked as he pulled the note toward him—rereading it.

"None at all," Malene admitted, shaking her head.

"But who'd want to hurt Lori Beth?" Jake whispered again, taking a look toward the dining room door.

"Seems to me she's the one who's been hurt the most in all of this," Don added, shaking his head. "I felt so bad for her on the stand today. I know how much it took out of her. I would have avoided it if I could have . . . And now this," he continued sadly, pushing the paper back across the table.

"Does Lori Beth know?" Jake asked.

"I couldn't tell her," Malene whispered, shaking her head. "She's been through so much."

"Mrs. Causey, It's clear that Lorinda's not safe here. I think it's imperative that we get her out of town as soon as possible—since we don't know who the enemy is at the moment," Don added, thoughtfully.

"Think it's Willie?" Jake asked.

"He could have mailed a letter from jail, but I'm not sure he'd risk it—not with the trial going on and all," Don answered. "And a restraining order on him on suspicion wouldn't make much difference, since he's already being held . . ."

"With your permission, I'll take this note in to the sheriff, though," he added, picking up the note and putting it into his pocket. "But I don't want to raise false hopes. Unless someone physically threatens Lorinda, we may never know who wrote the note."

"I've already made a decision," Malene nodded. "She'll be goin' to my mother's home in Roanoke Rapids tomorrow mornin'. Jake," she added, turning to him, "I'll have to ask you to drive her. Nobody else must know—not even Nate. He means well enough, but he just might not understand the importance o' all this. You'll need to leave before dawn . . . ."

"Mrs. Causey, if I might make a suggestion," Don interrupted.

"Of course, Mr. Lockridge," Malene answered, turning back to him.

"It's just that . . . You see, it's possible that whoever sent that note may be watching your home. Lorinda's whereabouts must be kept secret—from everyone in town," Don added.

"I have an idea, if you'll allow me," he continued. "As you know, I've just recently been assigned here. My home is in Raleigh. I'm going to be going home this weekend to attend my cousin's wedding. When I leave tomorrow morning, no one will think anything of it. Roanoke Rapids is on my way. I could take Lorinda . . . ."

"Would you?" Malene interrupted, brightening. "We would be so grateful."

"Whoever wrote this note may be watching your home from the road," Don continued. "But I could meet you . . . say at the church by the river. Jake, could you take the wagon across the pasture and meet me there?"

"I don't see why not," Jake answered. "Pa an' I've taken the wagon across the field lots of times. An' the ground's dry . . . ."

"Be there before dawn," Don interrupted, rising and walking to the door. "I'll be waiting," he added, as he pulled the door open and disappeared through it—a blast of cold air enveloping the forlorn pair at the table.

● ● ●

LORI BETH, IF you really want to keep yer new home secret, you can't write us," Malene cautioned. She laid one last folded dress in the old wicker case and slammed the lid before meeting her daughter's eyes. "Someone at the post office could let yer address slip, an' . . ."

"But, Mamma, how will we keep in touch?" Lori Beth asked, her eyes filling with tears.

"Don Lockridge has agreed to deliver mail from us an' bring us any word from you," Malene nodded. "It's important, Lori

Beth. You need this time away from everyone an' everything here," she added, waving her arm to include the whole room, while taking one last look at Lori Beth in her bedroom. "An' you'll be back soon," she continued, turning her head to avoid meeting her daughter's eyes.

Unless Don Lockridge or Sheriff Bentson somehow discovered who had written the note, she knew Lori Beth could never come home again. Even if Willie were convicted of Clint's murder and sent to prison, they could not be sure he was the author. And they couldn't risk any visits whatsoever. They must rely on Don Lockridge for everything.

"Mamma," Jake called, knocking lightly at the door, "it's time. We've gotta git goin'."

"I'm ready," Lori Beth called cheerfully, swinging the door open. She had always loved Grandma Blaine, and it would be so good to get away from all this—for a little while, at least.

"This it?" Jake asked, surprised, as he lifted the single wicker case from the bed.

"It's all I need. I'll be back in two months," Lori Beth smiled. As she headed to the door, Jake and Malene met one another's glance for only a moment.

"Give my best to Grandma," Malene added, trying to smile.

"I love you, Mamma," Lori Beth said, grabbing her mother in a final embrace.

"I'll always love you," Malene added, the tears coursing down her cheeks, as Jake gently took Lori Beth's hand and led her from the room.

Malene listened as the footsteps died away down the stairs. Then, picking up Lori Beth's favorite rag doll from the chair under the window, she hugged it to her. Leaning over the sill, she watched in the pre-dawn darkness as the small lantern bobbed slowly around the side of the house and disappeared into the night.

Slowly, she replaced the doll, drew the curtains back over the window, and paused to straighten the spread. Then, taking one final look around the room, she leaned across the night table to turn off the light. Stepping into the hall at last, Malene paused to look at the closed door to Leah Belle's room across the hall. Then, wiping her eyes with the back of her hand, she reached behind her and gently pulled yet another door closed.

CHAPTER FIFTEEN

A NEW BEGINNING

IGNORING THE STARING CROWDS on Monday morning, Malene alighted from the wagon with Jake's help. Taking Nate's hand, she made her way as quickly as possible up the steps of the courthouse and into the small anteroom once more.

Despite her feigned indifference to the assembled jurors and lawyers, she watched from the corner of her eye as Don Lockridge slowly made his way down the hall. He lifted his chin in acknowledgment and gave her a quick smile. Lori Beth was all right. She breathed a sigh—which she had held in for the past two days. Nothing else about the trial would matter now. No verdict could bring Clint or Leah Belle back to her. But, at least, Lori Beth was safe. Her mother would see to that now.

Slipping away from his mother for a drink of water, Nate was poised over the fountain as Willie—flanked by two marshals—passed by. Looking first at the empty seat beside Malene, Willie turned quickly to Nate. "Lori Beth sick?" he asked.

"She's gone, Willie," Nate answered, wiping a drop from his chin with the back of his hand.

"Gone where?" Willie questioned.

"I don't know," Nate shrugged. "Mamma didn't say. She left Saturday before I got up."

"When's she gonna be back?" Willie continued. "I mean, it won't be long afore the baby's born," he added.

"Can't say," Nate shrugged again. "Gotta go, Willie," he added before running back to his seat.

"Willie was askin' 'bout Lori Beth, Mamma," Nate announced as he sat down again between Jake and Malene.

"What did you tell him?" Malene asked.

"That I don't know nuthin'," Nate answered. "Like you said to. But why can't you tell me where she is, Mamma?"

"Trust me, Nate," Malene answered, squeezing his hand. "It's better if you don't know nothin'."

"But, Mamma, everybody's leavin'," Nate complained, looking at his mother with his earnest blue eyes—so like Clint's. "An' now it's just you an' me an' Jake."

"And we'll do just fine," Malene asserted, turning her head to conceal the tears in her eyes.

● ● ●

ALL RISE," THE bailiff ordered as the jury filed back into the jury box.

"Mr. Foreman, is the jury ready with a verdict?" the judge asked.

"We are, Your Honor," the heavy-set man with the thinning hair and wire-rimmed glasses began—as a buzz ran around the courtroom. An audible gasp escaped Leah Belle's lips. Anna Phelps grabbed hold of her arm as several onlookers turned to stare at the young woman.

Malene—seated on the opposite side of the room—did not turn. Her daughter belonged to the Phelpses now. There was nothing she could say or do to change that. No decision of the jury would make any difference now in their relationship. Lori Beth's condition and accusations and Willie's arrest had broken all ties between the two families. Leah Belle had gone from her just as surely as had Clint. And neither Willie's guilt nor innocence would bring either of them back to her.

Perhaps, the same might be said of Lori Beth, Malene thought, as a pain shot through her heart. Despite the efforts of Mack Bentson and Don Lockridge, they were no closer now to finding the author of the note than they had been when Lori Beth had left. Malene knew she could never allow her to return as long as there was danger for her in town.

Don Lockridge had been a Godsend as he journeyed to Roanoke Rapids each weekend—insisting that he enjoyed the drive. He had been more than willing to take letters and parcels to Lori Beth and had cheerfully brought back word of her condition each time. Malene knew she could never repay him, as she watched him stack his papers on the long walnut table and replace them in his leather briefcase. Win or lose, he'd presented a good case. She must tell him so, she decided, as she—and the rest of the crowded court-room—waited for the foreman to clear his throat.

"The jury finds the defendant, William Phelps, 'Not Guilty' in the shooting death of Clint Causey," the foreman announced.

All eyes turned to Willie, who stood at the front table on the other side of the room. A grin spread over his face as William Green clapped him on the shoulder and proceeded to shake his hand.

Squeezing his mother's hand tightly as they listened to the ver-dict, Jake turned to see her chin thrust defiantly upward—her eyes forward. Whatever tears might be shed later, he knew they would not spill over here.

"Order in the court!" the judge bellowed, slamming his gavel down to silence the sudden din of voices. "The jury has declared the defendant 'Not Guilty' in the murder of Clint Causey. The defendant, Willie Phelps, is hereby released from the court's custody and will be restored all rights as befitting a citizen of this state," he added.

As the judge rose and left the bench, Leah Belle rushed from her seat. She threw herself into the arms of a clearly-embarrassed Willie, who paused to hug her before motioning her to return to her seat and retrieve her coat and purse.

Slowly, Willie turned, his gaze seeking out Malene on the other side of the room. For a moment, their eyes locked. Then, pausing to shake his lawyer's hand one final time, Willie made his way up the aisle of the courtroom. As he passed Malene's bench, he whispered, "Give Lori Beth my best, Miz Causey. An' . . . , could you let me know—about the baby?"

Malene hesitated a moment—her eyes straight ahead. She could feel the young man's presence beside her as he waited for her answer. At last, without turning, she nodded—the movement of her head barely perceptible as she wrestled with her conflicting feelings.

Willie had come between her two daughters and had cost each of them dearly. For that, she would never forgive him. But it was she and Clint who had forced his marriage to Leah Belle—to save their own pride—and had broken up Willie's relationship with Lori Beth. Then, too, she knew Clint's threats—accompanied by his shotgun—could not have been ignored by anyone.

Even if Willie had pulled the trigger that long-ago afternoon, she knew they all shared some of the blame. Malene could no longer feel any anger—only compassion. She was sorry for Leah Belle—pulled, as she must have been, in two directions at once. She felt for Willie, too, in having to face the town now, with the stigma of a murder trial on his head—despite the verdict.

Her heart bled for Lori Beth in having to face childbirth alone and rear an illegitimate child. She regretted that Jake—at his young age—must take on the responsibilities as man of the house. And she wept for little Nate in having to grow up fatherless and for herself in having lost two daughters and a husband in a little over a year.

Life had not been kind—to any of them. There was no longer room for hatred. It was over. It was time to pick up whatever pieces remained and try to go on living, she decided. As she stubbornly blinked away the stinging tears behind her lids, she felt a hand on her elbow.

"Mrs. Causey, I'd like to talk to you, if I could," Don Lockridge began. He brushed his dark curls from his forehead—his blue eyes serious as he searched her face.

"It's all right, Mr. Lockridge," Malene answered, turning to him with a slight smile. She reached out to shake his hand. "I know you done all you could, an' I want to thank you—fer everything."

"I wish things could have been different," Don apologized, holding onto her hand and looking into her eyes. "It was my first case, and maybe I overlooked something . . . But with no witnesses and no murder weapon . . . Well, I just couldn't convince the jury 'beyond a reasonable doubt.' I'm so sorry."

"It's over now," Malene answered softly. "Clint's dead, an' no verdict's gonna bring him back to us. Right now, we gotta put this whole trial behind us, pick up the pieces, an' go on livin'. Don't nobody blame you, Mr. Lockridge," she smiled wanly. "An' I'll always be grateful fer what you done fer Lori Beth. I expect, though, now that the case is over, we shouldn't be askin' you to deliver our messages . . . ."

"Mrs. Causey, now that the trial is over, I'd like to talk to you a moment . . . about Lorinda," Don interrupted.

"She's all right, ain't she?" Malene responded quickly. "You ain't keepin' somethin' from me, are you?"

"She's very much all right," Don smiled. "But why don't we go out into the hall to talk so they can clean up in here," he continued. With no further word, he took Malene's arm and led her into the small anteroom, where she had waited so many mornings since the trial began.

"Mrs. Causey," he began as soon as they both were seated facing one another, "I know what an ordeal this trial has been—for your whole family. And I'm so sorry about the outcome. It's been an ordeal for me as well—as my first case as a prosecutor.

"In law school, the mock cases were between characters in a text book. They were only names on a piece of paper. Once I took this case, however, . . . Well, I'll admit, I never expected to allow myself to become as involved as I have become—with all of you . . . ."

"We're most grateful fer everything you've done, Mr. Lockridge," Malene nodded. "An' if there's ever anything we can do . . ."

"I hope you mean that," Don interrupted, smiling, "because I do have a very important request to make of you."

"I'll do what I can," Malene returned his smile.

"Well, the truth is that I also never expected to become as involved with one person as I have become with your daughter, Lorinda," Don continued. "She's every bit as beautiful and courageous as you are, Mrs. Causey, and she's suffered so much. My heart went out to her the first day I saw her at the trial with her head held so high—ignoring all the stares and gossip around her.

"She's a wonderful woman," Don continued. "She deserves to be happy, and I'd like to see that she is—for the rest of her life. What I'm trying to say is that I'm in love with your daughter. If you'll agree, I'd like to marry Lorinda—as soon as possible—and give my name to her baby."

"Have you talked to Lori Beth about this?" Malene asked, incredulous.

"Last weekend," Don nodded. "She wanted me to ask you immediately. But I wanted to wait until the trial was over. I wasn't sure how you'd feel about me—if I lost the case."

"Well, Mr. Lockridge, if Lori Beth wants this, too, you both have my blessing," Malene smiled.

"Maybe you should make it 'Don' if I'm going to become part of the family," he corrected her. "And I have one more request from Lorinda. She wants to be married in her own church—here in Clint's Bend—with you, Jake, and Nate there."

"But, Don, I never told her about the note. She don't know how dangerous it could be fer her here. The trial's over, but Willie's free now, an' we still don't know who it was who sent that note . . . ," Malene began.

"Why not leave everything up to me," Don smiled. "I've already talked to the minister. He's promised to perform the ceremony very early Saturday morning and to tell no one else. I think I can get Lorinda into town quietly enough. And we'll leave again right after the ceremony.

"I also want you to know that I have applied for a position with a firm in Raleigh," he concluded. "I'll be leaving to take Lorinda there as soon as I can close up my practice here. Once we get relocated, it will be difficult to trace her. Now, if I may, I'd like to escort you outside—and back to your home for a little celebration."

• • •

JAKE, I'M SO glad the trial's over at last," Carrie Sue began as she saw Jake approaching down the familiar path under the bare branches of the towering oak trees. "I never thought it would end," she added, burying her face in his heavy wool jacket and taking in the smell of hay and horses she had grown so accustomed to. "I . . . I feel so torn. I'm happy fer Willie, of course. He says he didn't kill yer pa, an' I believe him. But I'm so sorry fer all of you. Yer pa's killer may still be out there, an'. . . Do you think things can ever get back to normal?"

"If you mean normal enough fer us to start seein' each other openly, I doubt it," Jake answered, stroking her back and breathing in the sweet scent of her hair. "Yer folks won't never approve o' us being together—after all that's happened. You see how they've been keepin' Leah Belle from visitin' us. Wouldn't even let her speak to Mamma at the trial.

"We'll have to run away, Carrie Sue. But it can't be right away. I can't leave Mamma alone with the farm—not after all that's happened. Maybe when Nate's a little older. . . ," Jake continued.

"But, Jake, it all seems so hopeless," Carrie Sue sighed, tears beginning in her eyes.

"Nothing's totally hopeless, an' I can prove it," Jake added, reaching out a finger to wipe away a tear on her cheek. "Can you keep a secret?" he asked.

"Of course," Carrie Sue brightened. "Tell me."

"Lori Beth's gittin' married. The baby's gonna have a name," Jake said, smiling. "Ain't that the best news?"

"How wonderful. I'm so happy fer her. Who's she marryin'?" Carrie Sue asked, her eyes alight.

"Can't say," Jake answered, shaking his head. "It's happenin' on Saturday—so's they can get it done afore the baby comes. Who would have thought? So, you see, nothing's really hopeless. Our time will come, too. You'll see," he added, as he pulled her to him again and looked over her head at the cloudless winter sky—a prayer on his lips.

● ● ●

CARRIE SUE, WHERE you been?" Anna Phelps accused, reprimanding her daughter as she entered the back door. "Yer brother just acquitted o' murder an' comin' home fer a celebration, an' you not even here to welcome him."

"I thought he'd wanta spend his time with Leah Belle an' the baby 'stead o' his sister—since we two ain't never seen eye-to-eye as it is," Carrie Sue answered.

"Well, he's been askin' 'bout you," Anna responded.

"Then, I'll go find him," Carrie Sue offered. "Where'd he go?"

"He's out behind the wood shed helpin' yer pa to get them last logs cut afore the snow flies. It's been real hard on yer pa while Willie's been gone. 'Course the judge didn't think nothin' o' that before puttin' a man in jail fer a crime he ain't committed," Anna added bitterly.

"Well, it's all over now, Mamma. Willie's home again, an' everything's gonna be just fine," Carrie Sue answered, planting a brief kiss on her mother's face as she turned and walked out the back door.

"Won't nobody in town speak to us now; the whole business is goin' to pot; an' she says things is gonna be all right!" Anna Phelps scoffed under her breath as the door slammed behind Carrie Sue.

● ● ●

SO HAPPY ABOUT the trial, Willie," Carrie Sue smiled, approaching Willie beside a pile of logs and kissing his cheek. "I'm glad it's finally over an' you're back home."

"I may be home, but it ain't never gonna be over," Willie answered bitterly, bending to pick up a piece of wood and throwing it angrily onto the small pile at his feet. "Got any idea how it feels to be accused o' somethin' you ain't done?" he asked.

"There's some that'll always think I'm guilty. Now, little Annabelle's gotta grow up with folks callin' her pa a murderer. An' I won't never git to see my son . . . ," he concluded. He shook his head as he sat down on the pile of logs—wiping an errant tear from his eye.

"But I guess I made my own trouble—tryin' to pull one over on old Clint Causey," he added. "Looks like he got the last laugh after all—even from his grave. Sure do wish I could have changed things, though—'specially about Lori Beth. I sure never meant to cause her all that pain, but there weren't a thing I could do about it," he concluded, burying his head in his hands.

"Want to hear some good news?" Carrie Sue smiled, taking a seat beside her brother on the wood pile and placing her hand on his leg.

"The baby ain't come, has it?" Willie asked, his blue eyes whipping around to catch Carrie Sue's.

"That's two more weeks off," Carrie Sue smiled, shaking her head.

"Poor little tyke. Gonna be hard with no pa," Willie answered despondently.

"That's what I wanted to tell you. He's gonna have a daddy after all," Carrie Sue announced excitedly. "Jake just told me today. It's supposed to be a secret, but I don't see what harm there is in telling you so's you can rest easy 'bout Lori Beth an' the baby . . . ."

"What're you talkin' about?" Willie demanded, grabbing Carrie Sue's arm and pulling her around to face him. "I thought Nate said she'd run away an' nobody knew where she was."

"I'm sure the Causeys know where she is, 'cause Jake told me she's gettin' married on Saturday," Carrie Sue responded. "Ain't that great news?"

"Married? Who'd marry Lori Beth—lookin' like she does right now an' carryin' another man's child?" Willie demanded. "She can't just go off an'. . ."

"Of course, she can, Willie. She can marry whoever she wants. You wouldn't take no responsibility fer the baby—wouldn't even admit that it was yers," Carrie Sue admonished. "An' now she's found someone who wants to marry her an' give that little baby a name . . . ."

"Who is it?" Willie asked angrily. "Is it Billie Johnson or Bubba Thomas? Them two fellas was always droolin' over Lori

Beth. It'd be just like either one o' them two to take her now an' claim what ain't theirs."

"I should think you'd be happy to have someone else take on yer responsibility," Carrie Sue answered curtly, "since you didn't have no interest in doin' it.

"Well, I just come to tell you," she added. "Thought it'd make it a little easier fer you—knowin'," she concluded as she jumped off the wood pile. "You made yer own trouble, Willie, an' most o' ours, too," she added over her shoulder as she made her way back toward the house.

CHAPTER SIXTEEN

A SECOND CHANCE

JAKE, MAMMA SAYS DID you git them flowers all packed into the wagon like she asked?" Nate, dressed in a dark-blue suit with last year's hem marks still visible above each cuff, yelled from the back door. His words hung in clouds on the cold winter air.

"Tell Mamma I fed the chickens and the cows, and I packed everything she told me," Jake called from the barn door as he pulled the protesting old brown mare into the frigid air. He stopped to blow on his hands a moment before leading the horse to the wagon and picking up the traces.

"But you tell her it's pretty darn cold out here. If you two don't git out here soon, them inside flowers she gived me is gonna be froze harder'n the water in this pail," he called back, pausing to kick an ice-filled pail up beside the barn for emphasis.

"She's still puttin' the hem in the weddin' dress she done made fer Lori Beth. But she says she'll just be a minute more," Nate answered, letting the screen door slam shut as he walked back inside.

"Tell her to make it quick. This summer suit ain't made fer this weather," Jake called back, attempting to pull his heavy coat more closely about him. "Don and Lori Beth should be at the church right now," he continued.

"We're ready, Jake," Malene called from the back porch. "Nate, pull that door closed tight behind you. It'll be cold enough when we get back," she ordered before making her way down the two short steps. Her arms were stretched out in front of her and draped with a delicate ivory dress. Nate followed at her heels—the veil of ivory lace held high above his head to avoid having it touch the ground.

"You look great, Ma," Jake smiled. It was good to see his mother happy again.

"It's last year's coat an' hat," Malene smiled back, looking down at the deep-blue wool cloak. "But I think the Lord an' yer pa will forgive me fer breakin' my mournin' just this once. After all, you can't wear black to a weddin'," she added, handing over her bundle.

Taking the dress from Malene, Jake laid it gently across the back of the wagon and placed the veil beside it before helping his mother onto the seat.

"Careful o' the dress! And mind yer suit, Nate," Malene cautioned as the child stepped onto the wheel and jumped into the wagon behind them. "I done fixed it once already."

"I still can't believe Lori Beth an' Don are gittin' married," Jake remarked as he took the driver's seat and picked up the reins— leading the horse down the drive. "After all that's happened, who would've thought . . ."

"The Lord works in strange ways," Malene added. "I just hope we're doin' the right thing, though, in lettin' Don bring Lori Beth back here," she whispered—keeping her voice low enough so that Nate didn't hear.

"Next, it'll be Jake an' Carrie Sue!" Nate called loudly from the back.

"Hush, Nate," Jake admonished.

"But, Jake, I seen you two . . . ," Nate began.

"Jake, you still seeing Carrie Sue—after all that's happened?" Malene asked, turning to her son.

"I love her, Mamma, an' she feels the same about me," Jake added honestly, his hazel eyes turned to his mother. "Her pa'd disown her if he knew, though. I didn't think you'd feel the same, but—with the trial an' all—we didn't want to upset you any more. Do you mind?"

"She's a lovely young woman, an' she risked a lot by comin' to yer pa's funeral," Malene answered. "I'd welcome her into the family. But I know how her family feels 'bout all o' us Causeys since Willie's arrest. What will you two do?"

"We'll have to wait fer the time being," Jake answered. "Way I look at it, we ain't got much choice. Right now, her family needs to git back to normal—if that's possible. Any mention o' our family sure ain't gonna help that. An' you an' Nate need me here—on the farm. Ain't no secret 'bout that. But I'd like to go on seein' her—long as you don't mind."

"I don't mind a bit, Jake. You got my blessin'. I just wish there was another answer fer the two o' you," Malene responded, shaking her head. "Don't know how all our lives got so messed up," she continued sadly.

"Well, Lori Beth's 'bout to fix hers, so maybe some day . . . ," Jake sighed as he guided the horse onto the main road and began the short journey to the church.

● ● ●

A THIN, WHITE haze of frost gilded the dry grass and patches of gray dirt beside the road, and the whole world seemed sugarcoated under a pale winter sun. The steady clop-clop of the horse's hooves and an occasional snort were the only sounds to break the dawn stillness—as both Malene and Jake quickly scanned the barren countryside. Seeing nothing, however, as they pulled onto the main road, Malene settled back to enjoy the winter morning.

God was good. She had to remember that. He'd answered her prayers. And now Lori Beth would be able to lead a normal life with a husband and new baby.

Don had said he loved Lori Beth. From what she knew of the young man, he would love the baby as well. They would have other children he could call his own. It was a perfect solution—even more perfect than she could have hoped for. Clint would have been very happy. She knew he would have loved Don Lockridge.

As the lone wagon drew to a halt before the small, white church—beside Don's black auto—Jake helped Malene down and handed her the precious dress. It was good to see his mother smile again. It was a glorious morning for all of them.

Nate ran ahead excitedly to the church door as Jake and Malene followed, looking for Lori Beth. No one even thought to glance at the hill behind the church, where an identical wagon now waited—hidden behind the gnarled branches of an old, bare oak.

● ● ●

MALENE LOOKED AROUND the tiny, whitewashed church with its dark, wooden pews. Thin rays of morning sun were just peeping through the two stained-glass windows on the east side. They threw a rainbow of colors onto the dark, wooden floor at her feet and highlighted the two violet plants she had brought to brighten the sanctuary.

Had it been only six months ago she had sat in this very same place—her heart breaking as she watched Clint's casket being carried out? How much he had missed . . . . He would have been so proud to have walked Lori Beth down the familiar aisle and to have seen her as happy as she was today.

Malene smiled as she watched Jake offer his arm to Lori Beth. Her long, honey-colored hair was swept up into a cascade of curls, and she was dressed in her new ivory dress. She looked beautiful—despite the obvious swelling beneath the lace bodice. One look at Don Lockridge—his face aglow as he waited at the front of the church for Jake and Lori Beth—, and it was obvious how much he cared for her. Only a week ago, she had thought her daughter doomed to raise her child alone.

She squeezed Nate's hand as he sat beside her and closed her eyes for a moment. She remembered the overflowing crowd that had attended Leah Belle's wedding. After all, the town had been named for Clint's grandfather, and most folks in it could trace their ancestry to the grand plantation old man Clinton had once owned. And, aside from the animosity toward Joe Phelps, Clint had called everyone else in town "friend."

Over the past several months, though, she'd learned how fickle those former friends had become when the word "murder" had been uttered. Maybe it was a blessing then that Clint had not lived to see this day, she thought. But she was happy for Lori Beth and Don. They had each other, and that was enough. They didn't even seem to notice the empty pews.

"You may kiss your bride," Reverend Saunders announced, his blue eyes twinkling, as Don took Lori Beth in his arms for a moment before they both turned—beaming at their small congregation of three.

"Mamma," Lori Beth cried, throwing herself into her mother's arms at the end of the ceremony. "It was so perfect, an' I'm so happy. Thank you fer lettin' me come home fer the weddin'.

"Did Don tell you? We're gonna be moving to Raleigh as soon as the baby's born. He wants to be near his parents. We've picked out a name, too. If it's a boy, we want to call him 'Philip' after Grandpa Blaine. It'll make Grandma Blaine so happy," she bubbled.

"A new son-in-law an' a grandbaby all at once! I can't believe it. I'm just so happy fer you both," Malene smiled, tears rolling down her cheeks. "You deserve some happiness. An' after you're settled, Jake an' Nate an' I'll come to see the two o' you—an' the baby. You have a wonderful, new life ahead o' you, Lori Beth. Soon you'll forget all the pain o' the past few months."

"Thank you, Malene," Don offered, embracing her after he had shaken the minister's hand and slapped Jake on the back in excitement. "Now, I'd better take the 'little mother' back to Roanoke Rapids. We'll be spending the rest of the weekend there, but I'll be back in Clint's Bend on Monday morning. I still have a few things to clear up here," he added as he put his arm around Lori Beth and turned her toward the double oak doors at the back of the church.

"Hey, Don," Nate called, running a few steps after them, "you still owe me a ride in yer car!"

"I haven't forgotten," Don called back. "I'll see you Monday afternoon. Maybe I'll even pick you up after school and drive you home," he smiled at the little boy.

"Wow! Wait until Bobby Joe sees that!" Nate called excitedly as he ran back to Malene and Jake.

Jake leaned over and ruffled Nate's spiky hair. What he wouldn't give to be eight years old again and have nothing more to worry about than a ride in an automobile. Thank God they had managed to spare Nate most of the worry of the past few months.

It was finally over. Maybe now life could get back to normal. Of course, it wasn't going to be easy without Pa, but they'd manage. And, there was always Carrie Sue—who was probably waiting for him right now down at the river. He hadn't been able to tell her the time or place of the wedding. You never knew who she might tell.

Offering a smile to his mother, Jake gallantly turned and offered her his elbow. As the two began to walk down the aisle— Nate skipping behind—a loud "bang" rang out just beyond the open doors of the church, and a piercing scream rent the air. Dropping his mother's arm, Jake began to run to the door with Malene on his heels.

A second "bang" followed the first in quick succession. Then, all was quiet. Stopping short at the door and looking outside, Jake held out his arms and blocked Malene's progress. "Don't come out here, Mamma!" he shouted, as Reverend Saunders pushed past him and stopped as well.

"Oh, my God! Jake, go get Doc Mason right away," the minister yelled, as he dropped to his knees over the fallen couple, raised his eyes to the sky, and began to chant, "Our Father, who art in Heaven . . ."

CHAPTER SEVENTEEN

'TIL DEATH DO WE PART

Running toward the wagon, Jake watched in horror as their horse—having heard the noise—reared into the air. The sudden movement unwrapped the loosely-wound bridle, and the horse took off on a run with the empty wagon bouncing along the frozen ground behind him.

"Don's car!" Reverend Saunders called, pointing across the parking lot at the shiny, black auto. Without thinking, Jake rushed to the car, pulled open the door, turned the key—which was still in the ignition—and ground the motor to a start. He'd watched Don several times. He could do this. He had to, he decided. With one backward glance at the carnage beside the church door, he spun off down the main road to town.

"Lori Beth, Don! No!" Malene screamed from the doorway of the church as she began to run toward the couple. Lori Beth lay still on her back on the frost-covered parking area beneath the equally-still figure of Don Lockridge, who had obviously tried unsuccessfully to block his bride from the bullet.

"My God, they're not both . . . They can't be . . . ," Malene screamed to the kneeling Reverend Saunders. Reaching for Lori Beth's wide-flung hand, she chafed at the cold skin and ran her hand over her daughter's tangled hair—still entwined with baby's breath. "Can't somebody do something?" she screamed, looking wildly around.

"Jake's gone for Doc Mason. We shouldn't move them until he gets here," Reverend Saunders answered. Shaking his head at the two still figures, who had been so full of life only moments before, he, too, looked around the empty parking lot for help.

"They could bleed to death by the time Jake an' the doc get back," Malene pleaded, pointing to the two pools of blood now commingling on the gravel driveway. "An' we gotta get them warm."

"I suppose we can at least do that," Reverend Saunders sighed. Looking back toward the church, he noticed Nate—the little boy's eyes wide with horror as he peered from the church doorway. "Nate, run to my house as fast as you can," Reverend Saunders called. "Tell Mrs. Saunders to give you all the blankets she can find. It's cold out here, and we need to keep Lori Beth and Don warm." He watched as the little boy turned and ran to the other side of the church toward a small stone house with blue shutters.

Nate returned a few minutes later behind Kate Saunders—a kindly, middle-aged lady with graying brown hair. A heavy, red and black plaid jacket—obviously belonging to her husband—was thrown carelessly over her shoulders above a calico dress and white apron. Gasping as she saw the tragedy, Kate, nonetheless, contin-ued to walk toward her husband—the stack of blankets held out like a peace offering.

At her husband's direction, she threw a blanket over Don's back and then bent to tuck another around Lori Beth's outflung legs. Then, turning to Malene with tears in her eyes, she laid her hand gently on Malene's arm.

"Come on back to the house with me, Malene," Kate Saunders whispered. "It's too cold out here. We'll hear the cars when Jake returns."

"My little girl needs her mamma right now, Kate, an' I can't leave her," Malene answered, looking up—her eyes filled with tears. "But would you take Nate fer me, please?" she pleaded—her words hanging in a cloud of steam on the frosty air. "This ain't no place fer him," Nodding silently, Kate rose and reached for Nate's hand, pulling him toward the house as he continued to stare behind him without a word.

Three automobiles pulled simultaneously into the gravel lot. Pebbles spit from under their tires as they spun into position and stopped suddenly beside Reverend Saunders and Malene. Doc Mason reached into his back seat, removed his medical bag, and jumped from the car as soon as he had killed the engine.

"Doc, they're not . . . Tell me they're not . . . ," Malene screamed, the tears pouring down her cheeks as she looked into the doctor's eyes.

"Malene, I'll have to get in there to examine them before I know anything," Doc Mason answered. "If you'll just move aside now," he added gently, as he moved into position beside her. "Jake, spread one of those blankets over here and help me move Don," he ordered, as Jake gently picked up Don's legs and helped to slide him off of Lori Beth's body and onto his side, while Doc Mason opened his bag.

"Anybody see what happened?" Sheriff Bentson called over his shoulder, as he walked back to his car and pulled a leather folder and pen from it.

"We was all still inside," Jake answered, shaking his head.

"They was so happy. They had so many plans. They'd just left the church," Malene wailed, wringing her hands as she watched the doctor work.

"There was two gun shots—from somewhere right outside," Jake offered, looking at the sheriff for a moment before kneeling to help Doc Mason.

"Anybody else at the ceremony?" the sheriff continued, as Malene shook her head. "Thought I'd advised you not to bring Lori Beth back to town. Could've predicted something like this would happen after that note you got," he added, shaking his head. "An' with Willie free now . . ."

"Don thought he had it all planned out. They was gonna leave right after the ceremony. Nobody else in town knew . . . ," Malene sobbed, looking at the deep-red stain on the ivory bodice.

"Someone did," Mack answered ruefully. "Any way Willie could have found out?"

"Come on, Sheriff. You've got no proof it was Willie," Reverend Saunders spoke up quickly, catching Mack's eye as he, too, stood to give the doctor room. "It could've been anyone."

"How are they?" Malene interrupted, turning as Doc Mason finished examining the gaping wound in Don's back and turned him over, checking for a heartbeat.

"He didn't suffer any," the doctor whispered sadly a moment later, shaking his head as he pulled one of the blood-soaked blankets over Don's face.

"An' Lori Beth?" Malene gasped, holding her breath as the doctor turned to her daughter, probed the wound in her chest, and listened for a heartbeat.

"She's lost a lot of blood, but she's still alive. Thankfully, she's unconscious," Doc Mason replied, feeling her pulse and then sitting back on his heels and looking up at the others. "I'll need to try to stabilize her as soon as possible. And we've got the baby to consider . . . . But it's much too cold out here.

"I need to get her to my office immediately," he added, looking around the parking lot. "But we shouldn't move her any more than necessary. We don't know where the bullet is lodged, nor what the fall did to the baby. I don't think we should try to squeeze her into one of the cars."

"I've got a wagon," Reverend Saunders offered. "Jake, it's in my barn—beside the house. If you'll get it, I'll get my horse. We can put some of these blankets inside to cushion it for her," he added, running toward the house and the barn beside it.

● ● ●

IT WAS THE longest ride to town Malene could ever remember as she sat in the back of the wagon, Lori Beth's head cradled in her lap and the cold wind whipping in her face. At least, Kate had offered to keep Nate for her. She had no energy now for anything else other than her effort to will life back into Lori Beth—and the baby.

She tried to focus on Lori Beth's pale face and not to look at the blanket-wrapped figure beside her. Lori Beth had to survive. God couldn't be that cruel! "Please, God," she begged, her eyes raised in supplication as her hand subconsciously stroked Lori Beth's hair from her eyes. Maybe it was God's blessing that she was not aware of what had happened. She looked so peaceful, wrapped in the pale-blue blanket—if one didn't look at the red stain creeping through the wool.

Oh, why didn't that horse hurry! They were losing precious time with every second. And what about that innocent life that hadn't even had a chance to begin yet? She would will that child to live, she decided, her chin set defiantly as she looked at the swelling beneath the blanket. There had been no injury there. Surely, the doctor could save that poor, innocent baby. And she— no, she and Lori Beth—would raise that child together. A baby needed its mamma. God would allow them all a brand new start, she assured herself as the wagon drew to a halt beside Doc Mason's small, yellow frame house with the added wing where he held his medical practice.

"We'll take her now, Mamma," Jake spoke softly, breaking Malene's reverie. Climbing over the front seat into the back of the wagon, he gently slipped an arm under Lori Beth's shoulders and knees and lifted her from her mother's lap.

● ● ●

MAMMA," LORI BETH called weakly. She looked around the unfamiliar room until her cloudy gaze met her mother's concerned eyes as Malene hung over the table where Jake and Doc Mason had placed Lori Beth. "What happened? The baby . . . ," she gasped, placing one hand on her stomach and wincing when she moved her arm.

"Hush, Sweetheart!" Malene crooned, grabbing her daughter's cold hand and holding it in her own warm one. "You're both gonna be fine. Doc Mason is right here to take care of you," she added, as she moved aside to give the doctor room.

"We're going to get this young'un here before you know it," Doc Mason offered, looking from Lori Beth to Malene. "And you couldn't be in better hands with your mamma here to help, too. I hear you already have a name picked out," he said gently, as he pulled the blanket aside and began to probe Lori Beth's abdomen.

"Don an' I picked it together," Lori Beth smiled faintly. "We're going to call him 'Philip' after my grandfather. Where is Don?" she asked then, lifting her head slightly and looking around the room.

"You know we don't let fathers into the birthin' room," Doc Mason countered. He attempted a smile as he cut his eyes at Malene, who turned her head to prevent Lori Beth from seeing the tears in her eyes. Time enough later—when she was stronger—to tell her the truth, he decided, as he continued his examination.

Unless he'd missed his guess, the shock—coupled with her fall—had brought on Lori Beth's labor. There was nothing he could do to forestall it. But she'd lost a lot of blood, and he would have preferred that he'd had time to stabilize her fully before she went through the birth. It was clear to him that she might not survive the ordeal, but he couldn't tell Malene. He'd need her help—if there was to be any hope at all.

● ● ●

IT'S A BOY!" Doc Mason called proudly, as Malene beamed beside him. They had lost one life today, but there, squalling in the doctor's hands as he held him by the feet and slapped his little rump, was the most perfect baby she thought she had ever seen. His tiny fists were drawn up tight, his eyes closed, and his lungs— well, they would have done justice to a tobacco auctioneer, she smiled.

She was sure it would devastate Lori Beth when they told her about Don. They had both been so happy and so full of plans for the future. But Lori Beth was young and strong. She could get through this. She had to—for their baby's sake. And, Malene swore, she'd be there for both her daughter and grandson—even if she had to move to Roanoke Rapids as well. They'd raise that baby together, she decided, as she handed the doctor a blanket to wrap the tiny child.

"Doc, can I see my son?" Lori Beth asked, her voice weak and raspy as she tried to raise her head from the table. Why had no one told her how painful giving birth would be? Her chest and arm hurt so much, too. And where was Don? He'd promised to be there. She couldn't wait to show him their "little Phil." He'd promised to love him as his own, and the child would bear his name . . . .

"He's beautiful," Doc Mason cut into her thoughts as he placed the small bundle into her arms and watched as a smile broke over her pale face.

"I'll need a name," Doc Mason said, smiling back as he picked up a paper and pen from his desk and slid a rolling stool beside the table.

"It's 'Philip—Lockridge,'" Lori Beth whispered, running a finger across the damp, blond head of the tiny baby and turning to her mother. "You can ask Don to come in now," she nodded. "I want to see his face when he sees little Phil."

"Don can't come right now, Lori Beth," Malene began, looking at the doctor and willing the tears away. "He's gone on to Raleigh. He wanted everything to be perfect for you both when you were ready to travel," she lied.

"But he promised to be here," Lori Beth called weakly. "And I want him to see our son . . . ."

"I'm sure he meant to be here," Malene nodded, biting her lip to stop the tears. "But you surprised us all by goin' into labor so soon," she added.

"I'm so sleepy, Mamma," Lori Beth answered. She closed her eyes and dropped her arm with the baby in it back onto the table as Malene rescued the tiny infant and cradled it in her own arms.

"It's the Lord's way of making you rest. You've been through a lot," Doc Mason put in, taking Lori Beth's hand in his and feeling her pulse. "She needs her rest," he added, motioning for Malene to leave the room.

"How is she, Mamma?" Jake asked, rising as the door opened. He hurried to Malene's side as he saw the tiny baby nestled in her arms. "Boy or girl?" he whispered, smiling down at the infant.

"It's a boy, an' he's perfect," Malene smiled back. "His name's 'Philip.'"

"Don said he wanted a boy," Jake sighed. "I hope somehow he knows," he added sadly. "An' Lori Beth?"

"She's lost a lot of blood," Malene answered, shaking her head, "The birth took a lot out o' her, too. She's so young to go through all this, Jake," she sighed, wiping away a tear. "We can only pray—an' wait."

"We have one miracle," Jake answered, looking down at the sleeping infant. "We can hope fer another."

"Malene," Doc Mason whispered from the doorway, motioning Malene over to him. "She's sleeping now. We shouldn't move her. Why don't you get Jake to drive you and the baby on home. I can send for you if things change. Do you have all you need for the baby at home?"

"We've still got an old cradle in the attic," Malene nodded, "but I didn't think I'd need it . . . ."

"Bundle the little fellow up good," Doc Mason smiled. "It's cold outside, but I don't think you'll have any problems."

"Will . . . I mean . . . Is Lori Beth gonna make it?" Malene whispered, her eyes searching the doctor's.

"That's in God's hands," Doc Mason answered. "All we can do now is pray. She's young. She's got that much going for her," he added sadly.

● ● ●

Miz Causey, I'm so very sorry about all that's happened," Carrie Sue called, running breathlessly in through the kitchen door as Jake held it open for her.

"Carrie Sue's been down to the river waitin' fer me fer hours, Mamma," Jake explained as he put his arms around her and guided her to the fireplace.

"I knew somethin' was wrong when Jake didn't come," Carrie Sue added, her body shaking involuntarily with a chill. "You don't . . . I mean, I'll understand. If you want me to, I'll leave. It's just that I . . . I thought, with Lori Beth so sick an' all, maybe I could help a little. I could stay with the baby while you go back to Doc Mason's to be with Lori Beth," she added, watching Malene's face for a reaction.

"Of course, I don't mind yer offerin' to help, Carrie Sue. It's really very sweet o' you," Malene added, attempting a smile. "It's just that, well, you don't know what all's been goin' on . . . ."

"I told her, Mamma," Jake admitted. "I had to . . . I needed someone. Carrie Sue won't tell anyone."

"Jake says the sheriff thinks Willie shot Don an' Lori Beth," Carrie Sue went on, taking the chair Jake now pulled out for her. "Willie wouldn't do that, Miz Causey. I know him better 'n that. He was so excited 'bout the baby—made me promise to tell him as soon as it come. He wouldn't hurt it or Lori Beth. I just know it."

"I understand how you feel about yer brother, Carrie Sue, but I wish I could be so sure," Malene answered. "Fer now, it don't matter none. All that matters now is fer that baby upstairs to have his mamma. I gotta use all my strength to pull Lori Beth through this. Sheriff Bentson's gotta do his job, an' I gotta do mine," she concluded, giving Carrie Sue's hand a pat as she rose from the table. "An' if you mean it, I sure could use another hand 'round here," she smiled as she pushed open the dining room door and let it slam behind her.

● ● ●

She's very weak, but she's been asking for you," Doc Mason greeted Malene at the door the next morning as she alighted from the old wagon. "How's the little tyke?"

"He's home with Jake—an' Carrie Sue Phelps." Malene smiled as she noticed the doctor's eyebrow raise slightly at the mention of Carrie Sue's name. "He's a strong baby," Malene continued. "He'll be just fine as soon as his mamma gits home."

"Well, that might be a while," Doc Mason hedged. "Margaret and I moved her to our spare bedroom this morning. Thought cheerier surroundings might help her recovery. I'll need to watch her for several more days—maybe longer. Margaret has been with her. Come in, and you can see for yourself," he offered, holding the door for her.

"Mamma," Lori Beth called weakly from the bed as Malene entered. "How's Little Phil?" she asked, her tired eyes searching her mother's face for any news.

"Never saw such a strappin' baby," Malene smiled, grasping Lori Beth's hand. "Cried all night fer his mamma, though. So you gotta git better an' git home to take care o' him."

"An' Don? Have you heard from him?" Lori Beth asked, turning from Malene to Doc Mason.

"He's not due back 'til the end o' the week," Malene hedged, avoiding Lori Beth's eyes.

"Couldn't Jake go get him?" Lori Beth pleaded. "I mean . . . He could go to Raleigh an' try to find Don. Little Phil's gonna need his papa, too."

"We'll see what we can do," Malene promised, exchanging glances with Doc Mason as he walked into the hall and gently closed the door.

"Mamma, I don't just want Don here fer Little Phil," Lori Beth confided as Doc Mason left the room. "I want him here fer me, too," she continued, tears cascading down her cheeks and into the long, dark-gold hair covering the pillow.

"I know you do, Sweetheart," Malene nodded, her own tears flowing freely as well. The thin, ashen figure on the bed bore almost no resemblance to the beautiful, healthy, headstrong little girl she loved so much—except for those deep, gold-green eyes now swimming in tears.

"I ain't bein' selfish, Mamma, if that's what you're thinkin'," Lori Beth began again. "I just need to tell him I love him an' ask him to take good care o' Little Phil. He will, won't he, Mamma? I mean, he knows Phil isn't really his, but he did promise to be his papa . . ."

"I know, Lori Beth. Little Phil will be just fine. We'll all see to that. You just concentrate on gittin' yerself well now an' gittin' home . . . ," Malene began.

"But, Mamma, I'm not comin' home. That's why I need to see Don," Lori Beth continued, her eyes earnestly watching her mother.

"Some things you just know. I ain't got the strength to git through this," she gasped, the tears pouring down her face and soaking the pillow beneath her head.

"Don't be sad, Mamma," she added, as Malene choked back a sob. "I ain't scared, but I just gotta be sure my baby will be all right."

"He'll be all right, Lori Beth," Malene sobbed, holding onto Lori Beth's hand tenaciously as if willing her own life into her daughter. "I promise. We won't never let anything happen to him. He's gonna grow up to be a fine, upstanding man—just like his new pa—an' his grandpappy. Someday, we'll all be very proud o' him."

"I just wish Don would hurry," Lori Beth sighed, her eyes clouding over as they rolled toward the ceiling. "I want to hold on, but . . . ," she stopped, breathing heavily.

"It's all right, Lori Beth," Malene called softly at last. "Don's waitin' fer you," she added, reaching out a hand tentatively to stroke the matted hair from her daughter's forehead one last time.

"Malene . . . ," Doc Mason called softly, opening the door a crack and sticking his head around it.

"She's found her Don," Malene whispered back, letting go of the limp hand at last and planting one last kiss on the pale cheek beneath her.

CHAPTER EIGHTEEN

NO END TO TRAGEDY

LEAH BELLE!" JAKE CALLED, his surprise evident in his voice as he opened the back door. "What're you doin' here?" he asked when he had recovered a bit.

"Can't a body come home wantin' to see her own flesh an' blood without folks wantin' to know what she's doin' there?" Leah Belle asked, her pale-blue eyes searching Jake's face. "I just heard what happened over to the church, an' I come to see Lori Beth," she continued, tucking her long, thin, brown hair behind her ear and pulling her tweed coat more closely about her.

"It's cold out here, Jake. Ain't you at least gonna invite me in?" she continued.

"I would, Leah Belle, but Ma ain't here, an'. . . ," Jake hedged, looking quickly over his shoulder and avoiding Leah Belle's eyes. If Joe Phelps found out Carrie Sue was here . . . Well, there was no telling what he might do. And Jake couldn't tell where Leah Belle's loyalties lay nowadays.

"I ain't come to see Mamma. I told you, I come to see Lori Beth," Leah Belle responded angrily, craning her neck to see past her brother into the dark kitchen.

"Well, Lori Beth ain't here, either," Jake answered, continuing to stand between the door and the kitchen.

"Then, where is she?" Leah Belle demanded. "Seems to me Doc Mason's reaching his dotage if he's let her travel so soon—'specially with the baby due an' all. An' I 'spect Mamma's had somethin'. . ."

"Can't say?" Jake shrugged.

"Jake Causey, you know durn good an' well where Lori Beth is," Leah Belle bellowed. "I have a right to see my own sister—fer God's sake!"

"When Lori Beth gets home, we'll send fer you," Jake replied, unabashed.

"Do I have to remind you that the child she's carryin' belongs to my husband?" Leah Belle shouted.

"Not from where I'm standin'," Jake added, shaking his head. "Seems to me Willie never did live up to any part in makin' that child."

"Jake Causey, what's gotten into you? You'd think I was the enemy—or somethin'," Leah Belle added, softening her tone. "I come all the way over here this mornin'—catchin' my death in all this cold—just so's I could see my own little sister an' bring her a little gift," she continued, holding up a quilted, cloth market bag with a red and blue patchwork square on each side. "You act like I was fixin' to poison her or somethin'."

"To tell you the truth, Leah Belle, you ain't exactly been real friendly to any o' us since Pa died," Jake continued, stepping out onto the back step. He gently closed the door behind him—not allowing Leah Belle to advance any further. "You didn't come to the funeral, an' you didn't even speak to one o' us during the trial. It really hurt Mamma, Leah Belle. I don't mind tellin' you. You ain't seen her cryin' like I has each time she walks past yer empty room or seen her face each time you ignored her at the trial.

"Mamma's been through a lot this last year. If I can spare her just a little hurt, then I'm gonna do it—even if it means turnin' away my own sister. I'll tell her you was here—an' Lori Beth, too, next time I see her," Jake concluded.

"Jake, where did you . . . ," Carrie Sue began as she opened the kitchen door—the savory smell of frying chicken wafting into the cold morning air. "Oh, hello, Leah Belle," she smiled as she noticed her sister-in-law. "What're you . . ."

"If you're askin' me what I'm doin' at the door to my own home . . . ," Leah Belle retorted angrily, "I'm bein' turned away, that's what, when alls I wanted to do was to see my family.

"But now I see how it is. Mamma's gone, an' you two are here alone. That's pretty convenient. Bet Pa Phelps'll be pleased as punch to find out where you've been spendin' so much o' yer time, Carrie Sue. I'll be sure to tell him you said, 'Hello,'" Leah Belle called over her shoulder as she turned and walked back down the dirt road, the red and blue cloth bag bouncing against her hip as she went.

"Jake, you don't really think she'll tell Pa I was here, do you?" Carrie Sue wailed, her large, blue eyes searching Jake's face as he held the door for her and ushered her back into the warm kitchen.

"I don't know, Carrie Sue," Jake admitted, shaking his head. "I used to think I knew Leah Belle, but she's been actin' like a stranger ever since Pa's death. I tried to keep her out—fer you an' fer Ma. Ma's been through enough lately. She don't need no more hurt right now."

"I've never seen Leah Belle so angry," Carrie Sue admitted. "If she tells Pa I've been seein' you, Jake, he'll take me out to his woodpile. I know he will. He'll bust one o' them big planks o' his over my butt first, an' then, he'll probably disown me an' throw me out o' the house after that.

"He thinks every problem that's ever come to our family is due to one o' you Causeys. He's forbidden any of us to even speak to you. That's why Leah Belle's been actin' like she has. She's scared to death o' him, Jake. We all are, an' that's the truth. If Leah Belle tells Pa where I've been . . . I can't go home, Jake, I just can't!" Carrie Sue cried, burying her head on Jake's shoulder.

"Mamma," Jake called a few seconds later—backing away from Carrie Sue as the door opened slowly. Malene walked quietly into the kitchen and sat down in one of the kitchen chairs—her head buried in her hands. "Mamma, what's wrong? Is it Lori Beth?" Jake called in alarm as he went to her side and put his arms around her shoulders.

"Miz Causey, has somethin' else happened?" Carrie Sue asked, coming to stand beside Jake.

"It's Lori Beth," Malene began, choking on her words—the tears flowing freely at last.

"She's all right, ain't she?" Jake begged, pulling out a chair beside his mother, sitting down, and grabbing her hand.

"She . . . Jake, she didn't make it!" Malene gasped, shaking her head. "I went to see her at Doc Mason's, an'. . . she knowed it, Jake. She knowed it. She said she weren't scared, an' she just asked me to take care o' her baby fer her. She was so worried about him.

"Oh, Jake, she was so young. They was gonna be so happy. An' now . . . the baby, Jake, that poor, motherless baby. Oh, what're we gonna do?" Malene sobbed.

"We'll get through this, Mamma. We have to," Jake answered. "You, Nate, an' I can raise him together. We're his family, an' if we love him . . ."

"An' I'll be here," Carrie Sue interrupted quietly. "I can help with the baby, too."

"But, Carrie Sue, what about yer pa?" Jake added, looking up with tears in his eyes.

"I want to be here. I'm doin' it fer Lori Beth," Carrie Sue answered. "An' if my pa don't understand, then . . ."

"Carrie Sue, that's so sweet of you, but we can't let you git into trouble at home," Malene answered, looking at the earnest young woman through red-rimmed eyes. "Oh, everything's gone so wrong the past few months," she wailed, burying her head in her hands once again.

"Mamma, Leah Belle was here," Jake spoke slowly, ignoring the warning in Carrie Sue's eyes as she touched his arm.

"Leah Belle? What'd she want?" Malene looked up, startled.

"Said she wanted to see Lori Beth," Jake shrugged.

"How'd she know she was in town?" Malene asked.

"Miz Causey, if you'll pardon me," Carrie Sue added gently, "the shootin's just about the biggest thing that's ever happened 'round here. Everybody's heard by now. An' Sheriff Bentson was at our house last night askin' Willie lots of questions—'bout where he was yesterday mornin' an' all."

"You didn't tell me that, Carrie Sue," Jake accused, turning to her.

"I didn't think it mattered," Carrie Sue shrugged.

"Didn't matter?" Jake added, his voice rising. "My sister an' her husband both git gunned down in broad daylight in front o' the church, an' you think it don't matter?"

"That's not what I meant, Jake," Carrie Sue added calmly. "I didn't think it mattered because Sheriff Bentson didn't charge him with anything. Willie says he was at the lumber yard workin' all mornin'. An' Pa an' the other hands swear they saw him there."

"So, where does that leave us?" Jake asked. "Pa's murderer's still runnin' free, an' now we got two new murders an' no one to blame for them, either."

"An'," Malene added, "we don't know who's gunnin' fer all o' us now. My God, we could all be in danger!"

"What do you mean?" Carrie Sue asked. "Have you had threats?"

"In a note," Jake nodded. "Someone threatened both Lori Beth an' the baby two months ago—while the trial was still going on."

"Jake, how awful. You never told me . . . ," Carrie Sue gasped. "No wonder . . . "

"Don and Sheriff Bentson were investigating the case," Jake answered. "They thought it was Willie. That's why we sent Lori Beth out o' town."

"Where she should've stayed," Malene interrupted, shaking her head. "Oh, why did I ever listen to Don an' agree to let Lori Beth come back here?"

"We didn't know, Mamma," Jake added, putting his arm around his mother again. "Nobody did. Don thought he could protect her."

"Mamma!" Nate yelled as the kitchen door swung inward and hit the wall. He ran to put his arms around Malene. "I thought somethin' had happened to you," the little boy sobbed as he climbed into her lap.

"I'm sorry, Malene," Reverend Saunders spoke softly from the doorway. "Kate and I would have kept him longer, but he was so worried about you. He kept cryin' to come home. We decided his imagination might be worse than reality, so I agreed to bring him over. If it's too much for you . . ."

"No, no," Malene called, shaking her head as she held Nate to her and stroked his hair. "You was right to bring him home. I need what little family I got left right now," she added, as tears filled her eyes.

"Doc Mason was out, Malene. We heard," Reverend Saunders added, reaching over to grasp her free hand. "Kate and I are so sorry. I want you to know you don't have to worry about a thing.

Doc Mason and I will handle all the arrangements. I assume you'll want them both in your family plot?"

"I guess . . . Yes. Oh, my God! We ain't even tried to let Don's parents know yet. They'll be so broken up. An' they may want to take him somewhere else . . . ," Malene answered.

"Sheriff Bentson has already notified them," Reverend Saunders said softly. "They'll be here in the morning. Can you all be at the church at ten o'clock?"

"We'll be there," Malene nodded. "An'. . . thank you. Thank you all," she whispered through her tears.

"God is with you, Malene. Never doubt that," Reverend Saunders added. "He just had other plans for Lori Beth and Don. But you can rest easy knowin' they're together now—as they wanted to be. Remember, I said 'until death do they part,' and God was kind enough to keep them together even then. They've found their peace. We just have to find ours. I'll see you in the morning.

"Jake, come for me any time if your mother needs me," he added conspiratorially to Jake as he walked out the door.

"Mamma, is Lori Beth really dead—like Pa an' Don?" Nate asked, raising his tear-stained face to look into his mother's eyes.

"She's up with God now," Malene nodded.

"An', Pa an' Don, too, right?" Nate persisted.

"They're all together," Malene tried to smile.

"Pa'll like Don, won't he?" Nate asked.

"A lot, I'm sure. We all did," Malene agreed. "An', Nate, we're gonna need yer help around here."

"What can I do, Mamma?" the little boy asked earnestly.

"Nate, I want you to promise me somethin'," Malene replied, looking into the child's eyes. "There's a little baby upstairs who's gonna need a lot o' love an' carin'. . ."

"A baby?" Nate questioned. "You mean Lori Beth had her baby afore she went to see God?"

"His name is Phil," Malene nodded. "An', so far, he don't know very much about the world. With no mamma or papa, he's gonna need someone to look after him. I just thought, with bein' a little boy not so long ago, you might be able to teach him a lot o' the things he'll need to know."

"Could I, Mamma? Could I really? Jake an' I could teach him to fish an' to swim . . . ," he began.

"An' to milk cows," Jake added with a slight smile. "Unless you want to keep yer job a while longer."

"Could I see him, Mamma?" Nate asked excitedly.

"I don't see why not," Malene added, shaking her head sadly as she placed Nate on the floor and stood up—taking his hand in hers. "I suppose it's time somebody looked after the poor little orphan. He's gonna have a tough road ahead o' him."

● ● ●

EARLY MORNING FOG shrouded the dry, brittle grass beneath the spreading branches of the bare oak tree. It rose in two identical clouds from the newly-dug, gaping holes surrounded by wet mounds of dirt as the small procession made its way out of the front door of the church and up the slight incline. The smaller casket was borne on the shoulders of Jake, Sheriff Bentson, Doc Mason, and Reverend Saunders—for lack of another male. The larger one was borne on the shoulders of a much-older, dark-haired man, and three younger men with the same dark, curly hair.

Malene walked sadly behind with a handkerchief clutched to her eyes with one hand, while Nate hung onto her other—attempting to hide his face behind her cloak. Alone, beside Malene, walked a tall, slim woman dressed all in black—her white hair piled regally on top of her head and a white, embroidered handkerchief held to her streaming eyes. Behind these three, her dark-blue cloak almost completely covering the tiny bundle in her arms, walked Carrie Sue. Her blond curls were hidden beneath her hood as she hung her head and openly wept.

At a distance followed Kate Saunders and Margaret Mason—their eyes facing straight ahead as they followed their husbands with their sad burden. No one else was visible on the tiny church-yard grounds. Along the nearby road, however, curtains were pulled back just enough to allow occupants a glimpse of the small procession at the crest of the hill—overlooking the placid Roanoke River.

Out of sight of the mourners—on a small log raft tucked beneath a spreading oak tree on the fog-covered bank of the river—a lone figure stood sentinel. Grasping a low-hanging branch to steady himself, he wiped a lock of white-blond hair from his fore-head as he watched the procession pause above him.

Across from the church—shrouded in mist behind the trunk of a large pine tree marking the crossroads—a tiny figure in a tweed coat stood on tiptoe. She peered from watery blue eyes at the ceremony, pausing to tuck a wisp of dry, brown hair behind her ear.

● ● ●

MAMMA," NATE CALLED softly as he climbed up onto the wagon, "someone's left us a note."

"A what?" Malene asked distractedly. Her head was still turned to the cemetery where Jake and the other men were silently at work shoveling the wet dirt back into the steaming holes. She winced as each shovelful splattered onto the hollow caskets and reverberated in the damp, morning air.

"A note," Nate repeated. "Want me to read it?" he asked, beginning to unfold the paper.

"Read what?" Carrie Sue called from beside the wagon—noticing Malene's grief and taking charge. She placed the baby in the small cradle nestled in the back of the wagon and crawled up on the seat beside Nate.

"This note I found on the wagon seat," Nate answered, holding the paper out for Carrie Sue to see.

"I expect it's fer yer mother," Carrie Sue remarked, glancing down at the paper. "She'll probably want to read it herself," she continued, taking the note gently from the little boy's hand.

"Miz Causey?" she questioned, holding the paper out to Malene, who still watched as the last shovelful of dirt was thrown in. Jake gently laid down the shovel and knelt to smooth the dirt over the grave. "Miz Causey," Carrie Sue spoke again in an attempt to distract Malene from her vigil. She'd promised Jake . . .

"What is it, Carrie Sue?" Malene asked at last, turning toward the wagon.

"Someone's left you a note. I thought you might want to read it," Carrie Sue continued, placing the folded paper in Malene's hand.

"Cowards . . . That's what they all is," Malene hissed angrily, crumpling the note and stuffing it into the pocket of her cloak. "They wouldn't—none of 'em—show their faces at the funeral. Now they think sendin' a note is gonna make it right. Well, we don't need 'em. We Causeys has always looked after ourselves, an' we'll keep right on doin' it."

"Mamma, Mr. and Mrs. Lockridge want to say goodbye," Jake remarked, brushing his dirt-encrusted hands off on the seat of his slacks.

"Look after Nate an' the baby, will you, Carrie Sue?" Malene asked then, waiting for Carrie Sue's nod before following Jake to the large automobile parked at the end of the parking lot. Sadly, she took the outstretched hands of Bill and Elizabeth Lockridge and their three sons as they stood beside their auto.

"There's so little to say . . . ," Elizabeth spoke softly, tears flowing freely. "Don really loved your daughter, Mrs. Causey. I've never seen him so happy. He had so many plans. Thank you for allowing them both what little happiness they had."

"If you ever . . . ," Bill began—as the three turned, startled at the sound of wagon wheels behind them.

"Carrie Sue!" A male voice boomed as a long wagon filled with bound logs pulled into the church parking lot and came to a stop beside the Causey wagon. "Yer Ma tole me this is where you'd be, but I didn't believe her!" Joe Phelps called. He pulled his stocking cap down further over his grizzled hair as he jumped down from the wagon and ran over to stand beneath Carrie Sue and Nate.

"You git down from that wagon right now an' git on home where you belong," he continued, grabbing Carrie Sue's arm and roughly pulling her from the wagon until she staggered at last onto the gravel driveway.

"You're hurtin', Pa!" she whimpered, trying to pull her arm from her father's grasp.

"I ain't hurtin' you near as much as I'm gonna do when I git this lumber delivered an' git back home," Joe called loudly. "I promise you ain't gonna be able to sit down fer a week when I git finished with you. I done tole you them Causey's ain't no good— an' you no better—hangin' out with 'em. Fer all their high an' mighty airs, they're nuthin' but trash . . . ."

"Papa, I won't let you talk about them that way. They're good, decent people . . . . ," Carrie Sue retorted angrily, backing away from her father's grasp.

The crack of Joe's hand across Carrie Sue's mouth resounded across the entire parking lot. Jake turned and began to run toward the wagon. At the same moment, the front door of the church opened and Reverend Saunders strode directly toward the wagon, grabbing Joe Phelps by the collar of his plaid jacket.

"Joe Phelps," he ordered, "you let go of that child this instant, or I'll call Sheriff Bentson. He's just out back by the barn, and he's itchin' to arrest someone after all that's gone on in this town lately. And I don't think I need to remind you of whose house this is or who is witnessing this whole event," his voice boomed as he motioned toward the church.

At Reverend Saunders's words, Joe Phelps meekly let go of Carrie Sue's arm and began to back away. "You got no right comin' between a pa an' his kid," he asserted at last as he reached his own wagon. "Little snip needs a good board 'cross her backside—leavin' her ma with all the work in the house while she runs around town like a strumpet.

"I'll see you when you git home, young lady!" he added, wagging his finger at Carrie Sue. "Can't nobody—includin' yer Almighty—mess with what I do in my own home," he continued to Reverend Saunders as he climbed back up onto his wagon seat.

Without another word, Joe picked up a leather whip from the floor and angrily brought it down on the horse's back. Startled, the horse sprang forward, jerking the wagon and its contents and threatening to throw Joe and his load of logs onto the gravel drive. Skillfully manipulating the reins, however, Joe managed to right his load and turn the wagon back toward the main road—as the small group of mourners watched in shock.

CHAPTER NINETEEN

THAT OTHERS MIGHT LIVE

THE WAILING OF AN infant and the sobbing of Carrie Sue broke the churchyard silence as Joe Phelps finally swung his wagon out of the parking area. Malene rushed back to her own wagon to lift the child into her arms and cradle him beneath her cloak, while Jake pulled Carrie Sue to him, cradling her head against his chest as she continued to sob uncontrollably.

Slowly, and with several backward glances, the Lockridge family climbed into their car. It was over. There was nothing left to say. "What must they be thinking?" Malene wondered as she cooed to the whimpering child and watched their car back from the parking space. The gravel crunched beneath the tires as the car pulled onto the main road away from town—disappearing into the fog. Raleigh was a world away.

As the muffled sound of the motor died away, Jake gently pushed Carrie Sue from him and placed a finger under her chin. He tipped her face upward—running the index finger of his other hand gently over the deep-red marks left by several of Joe's fingers on her left cheek. "I'll kill him!" Jake muttered, subconsciously balling his hand into a fist as he looked back toward town in the direction Joe had gone.

"There's been too much o' that already," Malene said sadly, reaching out with her free hand to grasp Jake's fist and gently unfold the fingers.

"But, Mamma, he can't git away with what he done to Carrie Sue!" Jake exploded, pulling his hand from Malene's grasp.

"She's his daughter," Malene explained, shaking her head. "A man can deal with his children any way he wants. Ain't a court in the land gonna tell a father how to run his family. You know that."

"She can't go back there. We can't let her. He'll kill her if someone doesn't do something!" Jake answered, pulling the sobbing Carrie Sue into his arms once more.

"Then, she'll stay with us," Malene answered defiantly. "Lord knows we got the room now," she added quietly, looking back involuntarily over her shoulder at the fog-shrouded cemetery and the two steaming grave sites.

"Malene," Reverend Saunders offered gently, stepping toward her, "you saw Joe Phelps, and you heard what he said. Neither you nor Jake are any match for him. If Carrie Sue doesn't return home, your house is the first place he's gonna go looking for her. If he finds her there, there's no telling what he'll do—to all of you and to Carrie Sue. I can't let you take that chance.

"Carrie Sue," he offered, reaching out to take the young woman's hand, "Kate and I could use someone to cook and do a little cleaning for us. Now that our kids are grown, it's kind of lonely in the house, too. We'd both be mighty pleased if you'd come to live with us."

"I couldn't do that, Reverend Saunders," Carrie Sue sobbed. "Don't you see? My pa's gonna find me wherever I go. I couldn't put you an' Miz Saunders in that position."

"Why not let us worry about that," Reverend Saunders answered. "After all, we got one mighty powerful ally right up there," he smiled, pointing to the church roof, where a large, white cross rose above the ground fog and glowed in a faint ray of sunshine.

"Now, you just come on along with me," Reverend Saunders offered, putting his arm around Carrie Sue's shoulders and turning her toward his house. "You must be starved, and I think Kate probably has breakfast ready about this time. Don't worry, I'll deal with your pa when he comes back here.

"Malene, Jake, you've had too much to deal with already," he called over his shoulder. "Carrie Sue'll be just fine with Kate and me. I'll send word to you later. Right now, you'd better get that young'un home. This cold can't be good for him. And I think Nate needs a good breakfast, too. Don't you, Old Man?" he questioned, reaching over playfully to punch the silent little boy in the ribs.

"Thank you, Reverend Saunders," Jake offered. "It'll be all right, Carrie Sue," he said, attempting a smile. "I gotta git Mamma an' the kids home now, but I'll be back later—that is, if it's all right with Reverend Saunders," he added.

"The Lord's house is open to you both—any time," Reverend Saunders smiled—one arm still around Carrie Sue and his other arm raised in a farewell. The two watched as Jake helped Malene into the wagon with the baby, jumped in himself, and silently turned the horse toward the road.

● ● ●

MAMMA, I'LL TAKE the baby upstairs now," Jake offered as he stood up from the fireplace, brushed his hands off on his trousers, and paused to watch the new log catch and flame. "Nate's feedin' the chickens. He'll be inside in a while," he added as he took the sleeping infant from his mother's arms. "Now, you just sit down here by the fire an' git warm. Soon's I git back, I'll fix us all a cup o' tea."

Malene nodded silently as she paused to tuck the blanket more closely about the tiny child before collapsing into the nearest chair— cloak and all—her head in her hands. Funerals were so final. There was no longer anything left to do—no words left to say, she thought as she looked around the empty kitchen—once so full of life. Oh, what she wouldn't give for Leah Belle to come banging in through the door complaining about something Lori Beth had done or Clint yelling from the barnyard for someone to milk the cows or feed the chickens . . . .

But she had to face reality. This was the way it would be from now on—the empty bed, the empty bedrooms, the silent kitchen— just her and the boys. They had all been through so much. They would have to pull together now. They had a new life to think about. That poor little baby upstairs deserved the best that they could give him. And he was a part of Lori Beth. The Lord had given her that much—at least. But she was tired—so tired—of the worry, of the heartbreak, of the emptiness, she thought as she rose quietly, slid her cloak from her shoulders, and walked over to the wall to hang it on the peg.

As she hung up the cloak, something rustled in the pocket. The note—she'd forgotten all about it. At least someone in town had cared enough to respond to her grief, even if no one had shown up for the funeral, she thought as she reached into the pocket and removed the folded piece of paper. Returning to the fire, she opened the paper and began to read.

"Jake!" Malene shrieked, her voice rising in hysteria. "Jake, git down here now, please!" she begged. Her hand began to tremble, and the note dropped to the floor.

"Mamma, Mamma, what's the matter? What is it?" Jake called, pushing open the dining room door and rushing to her side. "Mamma, I just got Little Phil in bed," he explained, catching his mother by the shoulders as she collapsed into his arms. "What's happened?" he tried again.

"The note, Jake! It's not over yet!" Malene cried, her body shaking as she pointed to the crumpled paper on the floor.

"What note?" Jake asked, confused, bending to retrieve the paper lying face down on the hearth.

"Carrie Sue found it in the wagon when we returned from the cemetery," Malene explained. "Read it, Jake. Read it to me again," she sobbed.

"But, Mamma, it's just like the last one!" Jake breathed. He looked at the mail-order letters, which had been cut and pasted on the page, and then back at his mother.

"Read it, Jake," she ordered again.

"It says, 'The baby is next,'" Jake answered, his finger following the crudely-pasted letters down the page. "Mamma, it can't be. Who'd want to harm an innocent baby?"

"It's a curse—a curse on all o' us!" Malene cried hysterically. "An' it's never gonna be over—never—'til the whole o' us Causeys is in the ground along with Clint an' Lori Beth an' . . ."

"Mamma, Mamma, stop it!" Jake ordered, taking his mother by the shoulders. "Carryin' on like that ain't good fer you. It's not a curse. It's just one vicious person. All we need to do is show this to Sheriff Bentson an' . . ."

"He couldn't trace the other note," Malene added, shaking her head, "an' look what happened. Jake, we can't take that chance. We owe it to Lori Beth an' to that poor, innocent baby upstairs. We gotta do whatever it takes to protect him now."

"But what more can we do?" Jake asked, collapsing into the seat beside his mother. "We can try to protect him, but there'll be times . . ."

"We have to git him out o' town—as far away from Clint's Bend as possible," Malene answered, drying her eyes and taking charge.

"We can't make the same mistake we done with Lori Beth. No one can ever know where he is. An' we can't bring him back here—ever!"

"But, Mamma, where will we go?" Jake questioned. "We don't know nowhere but Clint's Bend, an' we all can't just up an' leave the farm . . . ."

"We all can't, but you an' Little Phil can," Malene replied, calmly.

"Me? What would I do? I ain't got no money, an' I don't know nothin' 'bout takin' care of a baby," Jake protested.

"Carrie Sue does," Malene continued. "She's been helping Leah Belle with little Annabelle. You wanted to git her away from her pa anyway, didn't you?"

"I can't just take her an' the baby . . . ," Jake tried again. "I mean—it ain't right, taking a girl I ain't married to . . ."

"You want to marry her, don't you?" Malene asked, her eyes holding Jake's.

"Of course, some day, but . . . ," Jake whispered.

"Go to Reverend Saunders, Jake," Malene continued. "Tell him what's happened. He saw Joe this mornin' at the church. He'll understand. An' he can marry you right away—if it's an emergency."

"But I can't leave you all alone here with the farm . . . ," Jake protested.

"It won't be easy, but Nate an' I'll manage. Yer pa left a little money. We can hire a hand or two. An' I'll rest a lot easier nights knowin' you an' Carrie Sue an' Little Phil are safe. They need you, Son, more than me. It'll be like cuttin' off my right arm to lose you. You know that. You always knowed how I felt about you. But it's the only way. Don't you see?" she concluded, her voice breaking as she looked away.

"You can't tell me where you're going, an' you can't write. We can't take that chance—not fer Carrie Sue or the baby's sake.

But you'll be happy, Jake. You an' Carrie Sue deserve that," she added, rising and going to the long, mahogany sideboard beside the dining room door. Raising the top, she reached inside and removed a small wooden chest.

"Here," she offered, handing the box to Jake, "take my wedding silver. Lord knows I ain't got no use fer it now. Go to Raleigh—where no one knows you—an' sell it. It should bring enough money to git you an' Carrie Sue wherever you want to go an' give you a start."

"Mamma, this is insane! I can't do that," Jake answered, finding his tongue at last as he set the heavy chest down on the table in front of him.

"It's the only way. Don't you see that?" Malene whispered, turning her face away to hide the tears. "Fer God's sake, listen to me, Jake. Git the baby. Go now . . . , an' hurry! We can't afford to wait. Go now, while I still have the strength to send you away."

"All right, Mamma, I'll go, if that's what you want. I'll take little Phil an' Carrie Sue away," Jake answered slowly, reaching up to wipe his mother's tears away and hug her to him, "but only until Sheriff Bentson gets enough evidence on Willie . . ."

"I don't think so, Son," Malene shook her head. "Somehow, I don't think he's the one behind this. I saw him at the trial when he asked about the baby. I don't think he'd want to hurt it—no matter what his feelings are to all o' us."

"I'll find some way to keep in touch," Jake promised, bending down to kiss Malene's cheek. "Don't worry, Mamma, this'll be over soon, an' we can all be together again," he answered as he took his coat from the peg on the wall and picked up the chest. "I'll go git the wagon ready if you'll git Little Phil fer me."

● ● ●

THE SMELL OF baby powder emanated from the room as Malene opened the door. It had been too long since there had been a baby in the house. Lori Beth's baby . . . They had had so many plans.

The faded, pink wallpaper swam before Malene's eyes as she entered the darkened room. Flowers would never do for a little boy. She had planned it just that morning—she and Jake would paint the room a pale blue. There would be teddy bears and toy soldiers . . . . But she mustn't go on this way. There was work to be done, Malene sighed.

"I'm sure Carrie Sue will have other ideas. She'll be a good mother," she thought as she opened the top drawer of the dresser and began to fill the small valise on her arm. Diapers—they would need lots of these. And booties . . . Lori Beth had been so proud of the several pairs Grandma Blaine had knitted for the new baby. A tear fell on the tiny, yellow sweater Malene, herself, had knitted for her new grandchild—not knowing if it would be a boy or a girl. And blankets. Lord knows, after four children of her own, she had plenty of these. But it would be cold on their journey. You could never have too many blankets.

As she lifted the last blanket, her eyes fell on a small copy of Lori Beth's photo lodged in the corner of the drawer beneath a large looking glass. "And what would make little Lori Beth smile? Why a chance to look as beautiful as her mamma—and to get a keepsake of it to carry with her always." Clint's words echoed in her ear. How well he had known their daughter. And, now, that keepsake photo would be all little Phil would ever have to remember the beautiful little girl who had been so full of life and who had given her own life to give him his.

Using the corner of the blanket, Malene attempted to stem the flood of tears. Then, taking one last look at the peaceful infant in his tiny cradle, she tucked the small photo into the pocket on the front of the valise and closed the latch—draping the handle over her arm. Picking up the sleeping child, then, she cradled his head against her breast and pressed her cheek to it. Softly, she began to hum, "Hush little baby, don't you cry. . . ." It was time.

● ● ●

THE RUMBLE OF wagon wheels died away at last on the cold, crisp air; yet, Malene continued to stand, unmoving, on the back porch— her hand still raised in a final farewell.

"Where's Jake goin' in such an all-fired hurry?" Nate demanded, running around the house and up onto the back porch— stopping short when he saw his mother's face.

"I don't know," Malene answered honestly, making no attempt to stop the tears coursing down her face.

"Well, when's he comin' back, then?" Nate persisted, raising his candid blue eyes to meet his mother's red-rimmed ones.

"He's not ever comin' back, Son," Malene whispered, shaking her head. "Come back inside now, Nate. You'll catch your death if you stay out here much longer," she continued at last, wrapping her arm around the little boy's shoulders and turning him toward the door.

"But Mamma, everybody's gone now. Who's gonna take care o' us?" Nate asked, the tears standing in his eyes as he looked after the disappearing wagon.

"I guess you'll have to be the man o' the house," his mother answered, a sad smile on her face. "It's just you an' me now, Son. But we'll manage. We always have."

PART II

CHAPTER TWENTY

THE LEGACY

GAINESVILLE, FLORIDA, SEPTEMBER, 1960

HE SUPPOSED THE FIRST day of college was always a bit overwhelming, but to Dick the transition was about as subtle as if he'd been suddenly whisked into space on the Russian rocket "Sputnik." What had ever convinced a kid from the flat cornfields of the Midwest that he could feel at home for the next four years amidst the rolling hills, live oaks, and stately pine trees of North Florida?

And what had ever inspired his mother or him to believe the college clothing displays in their hometown department stores? In Ohio, the leaves were already changing and students were in pullover sweaters. Here, he would gladly have paid next week's meal tickets for one short-sleeved shirt.

To top it off, nobody down here had ever had the sense to design straight paths. Instead, all roads and walks at the University of Florida seemed about as organized as a bowl of spaghetti noodles, he fumed as he stopped on the path leading from the Student Union and pulled out his campus map to check his bearings. Finding the building for his first class at last, he folded the map and slipped it back into his pocket—then paused to look around the campus that was to be his home for the next four years.

Early rays from the late-summer sun slid sideways through gray fingers of Spanish moss—swinging from gnarled live oak branches like tired children on a jungle gym—and gilded the surface of the gray-green, algae-covered lake at the end of the path—across from the red-brick carillon building. Perceiving the lake as the only placid spot on the already teeming campus, Dick stepped off the path for a moment and pulled the remains of a soggy egg sandwich from his pocket. He had a few moments, and it wouldn't hurt to catch his breath before heading to his first class.

As he took his first bite, an almost imperceptible movement from the far side of the lake caught his eye. There he was—Albert, the campus mascot. Dick had read about him, but this would be their first meeting. Crouching, he held out the remains of his egg sandwich and watched as the ungainly creature slid silently off the bank and into the water—his eyes his only visible feature as he slowly approached the bank where Dick stood.

"Be careful!" a young woman's voice rang out from just behind him as a hand suddenly reached out—grabbing his wrist and knocking the remains of the egg sandwich to the ground. Astonished, he turned and blinked into the blinding, early-morning sunlight. It was difficult to focus on his unexpected companion's face—which was, at the moment, obscured by a sweep of fine, honey-colored hair as the young woman stood immobile—watching the alligator.

As the creature turned at last and floated effortlessly back to his sunny bank, she turned with a sigh. "I'm sorry. I didn't mean to be so forward . . . ," she apologized, blushing as she turned a pair of riveting gold-flecked green eyes to Dick. "I was just so worried when I saw you so close. Alligators may look docile, but they can be very dangerous. A friend of mine was attacked by an alligator—on the New River in Fort Lauderdale, where I'm from," the young woman went on. "Is this the first time you've seen one?" she inquired as Dick continued to stare at her—unable to say a word. "I mean . . . With your fair skin . . . You're not from around here, are you?"

Chanel Number Five at seven-thirty in the morning! It wasn't fair, he decided as he breathed in the heady fragrance and took in the beauty beside him. Realizing at last that she was waiting for a reply, he nodded. "I'm from Ohio. It's my first time in Florida. I've heard about alligators all my life, but I've never seen one before. I don't think this one's dangerous, or they wouldn't have him around," he added, looking back at the placid lake surface.

"I'm not sure the university has a choice. There are alligators in almost every lake in the state," the young woman laughed. "But don't let him fool you," she went on, shaking her head. "Alligators may look innocent, but they can attack in seconds and pull you into the water before you know what has you. My father says they're a lesson to us that the most innocent-appearing creatures can sometimes be the most vicious. I . . . Well, I just thought you ought to be warned before you go swimming or boating in any of the rivers or lakes around the campus," she added—as the carillon in the brick tower across the lake sounded the half hour.

"Oh, it's late," the young woman announced, looking at her watch, "and I wanted to get to my first class early. Nice to have met you," she added with a smile and a wave as she hurried off.

"Wow!" Dick whistled as he watched her disappear into the crowd hurrying from the Student Union. If the women at the University of Florida were all that gorgeous, he'd really made the right decision. Wait until he wrote his younger brother Bob, who had chided him unmercifully all summer about his decision to leave home and not attend Ohio State. But he'd have to be more alert next time. He'd just met the most gorgeous girl he'd ever seen— and he hadn't even thought to get her name.

• • •

THE DOOR TO the chemistry classroom stood open to reveal seven rows of long, black, scarred tables. It was still twenty minutes before class time; yet, as he looked over the classroom, Dick was surprised to see that someone had actually gotten there ahead of him—although that person was nowhere in sight at the moment.

"Lorinda"—the beautiful, old-fashioned name was neatly emblazoned in black ink across a blue spiral notebook deposited at the end of the front table. Unusual name, he mused, turning the notebook over in his hands. And an unusual class for a female. But since chemistry had the ungodly distinction of being taught at eight o'clock on Tuesday, Thursday, and Saturday mornings, a female lab partner would not be unwelcome—especially if she turned out to be half as good looking as the girl at the lake.

Looking around the empty classroom for any deterrent to his plans and finding none, he quickly deposited his own maroon notebook—rather haphazardly labeled with "Dick Everett"—on the front table as well and took the next chair.

Within five minutes, the class was nearly filled with male students. Still, there was no sign of the lovely Lorinda—whom he was beginning to equate with Marilyn Monroe or Jayne Mansfield. Finally, to the pealing of the carillon sounding the eight o'clock hour, a young, dark-blond woman in a pale-green shirtwaist dress rushed breathlessly to the door, then stopped—peering over the sea of faces.

Immediately recognizing the young woman from the lake, Dick smiled to himself. He had chosen his seat wisely. It was, indeed, his lucky day. Sandra Dee, he corrected himself—remembering his favorite actress as he noted the neat pageboy, the tiny waist, and a figure one could die for.

Her sudden appearance seemed to have the same effect on every male student. Those who, expecting this to be an all-male class, had neglected to shave or bathe before coming to class slid down quietly in their seats and vowed immediately to clean up—at least every Tuesday, Thursday, and Saturday. Those who had, by good fortune, groomed themselves for the first day of class, however, sat up just a little straighter, hoping for her eyes to land—if only for a moment—on each of them.

Clearly embarrassed as she stared at the roomful of males watching her, the young woman smiled nervously and subconsciously twisted the chain of a large gold locket she wore around her neck. Finally, taking a deep breath and grasping her leather shoulder bag as if it were a lifeline, she slowly made her way down the aisle behind the first table toward the blue spiral notebook.

"Are you following me?" Dick asked at her elbow as she spun around, surprised.

"I think it's the other way around," she smiled—recovering her poise. "It looks like you're following me," she added, pointing to her notebook already lying on the desk beside him. "I think I got here first."

"And almost missed the class," he laughed, pointing to the clock above the blackboard—just as the class bell rang raucously from outside the classroom.

"Daddy says I'll be late for my own funeral," she shrugged. "I did try. You know that. But then I remembered I'd left my class schedule in my dorm room . . . ."

"Well, at least, now I know your name," Dick observed, glancing at the letters on her notebook as she gathered her skirt in one hand and slid into the chair—winding her slim legs in their leather loafers around the metal rung. "'Lorinda.' Pretty name," he mused. "Were you named for someone?"

"My grandmother," Lorinda nodded, twisting at the locket again, her eyes downcast. "My father named me for her."

"And I'll bet you're her favorite grandchild, too," Dick remarked.

"I wish that were true, but I've never known her," Lorinda added sadly, shaking her head. "Neither has my dad. All we know about her is her name—on his birth certificate. But I do have a small photo of her my dad's uncle gave him. Daddy had it put into this locket for me on the day I was born," she continued, inserting a long, pale-pink fingernail into a small indentation on the face of the oval locket. Opening it, she leaned close to reveal the image inside.

Dick could feel the red creeping up his face as she leaned closer, and he could feel the eyes of every other male in the room boring into his back. Yet, not wanting to be rude, he reached out and placed his hand over hers to steady the small image in Lorinda's locket.

Glancing down for a brief second, he suddenly found himself gazing into the same gold-flecked, green eyes which were at that moment watching intently for his reaction. The light-brown hair was parted in the middle and drawn back severely from her face, but the resemblance to the young woman beside him was uncanny.

"It must be sad not to have known her," Dick observed, pressing the locket back gently into Lorinda's hand, He looked around nervously, waiting until the general buzz began again around them—signalling that they were no longer the center of attention. "Dick Everett," he said finally—thrusting out his hand in an effort to end the embarrassing moment.

"I know," she giggled, allowing the locket to drop back against her chest as she pointed to his notebook. "You left your placecard. I'm Lorinda Lockridge."

"Unusual class for a girl," he responded, echoing the thought in every other male student's mind.

"Why?" Lorinda asked, surprised. "I need it—for med school. Actually, it's Daddy's idea. He says I can go into partnership with him—Lockridge and Lockridge. He's been waiting for me."

"But are you sure it's what you want?" Dick asked, confused. He'd never known a woman doctor before. And with her looks— well, he would have pegged her for a drama major. "I mean . . . I just met you, but med school's a tough road," he continued, covering his surprise.

"No tougher than it was for my dad," she shook her head. "If he can do it, so can I. Daddy worked three jobs to put himself through school. He was an orphan and had no one to help him out."

"How sad," Dick answered, thinking how lucky he was to have a father who could pay for his tuition. "But if you're good at chemistry, maybe you can help me out. This class is my mother's idea. I'm no good at science. English is my field. Give me a writing assignment, and I'm in Heaven. Ask me to remember a formula, and my mind dries up."

"Well, I could use some help in English composition," Lorinda smiled. "And I'll be glad to help you with chemistry—any time. It's my favorite subject."

She stopped as a tall, sandy-haired, emaciated man in a loose-fitting tweed jacket with leather patches on each elbow entered the room, took a piece of chalk from the chalk tray, and wrote "Dr. Monroe" in large letters on the blackboard.

● ● ●

WHAT LUCK! I can't believe it," Dick exploded, running into his dorm room after class and finding his roommate, Jim Lawrence, seated at his desk. "'Lorinda Lockridge.' You're from Fort Lauderdale. Do you know her?" he asked breathlessly.

"Golden-haired goddess with eyes you could get lost in?" Jim turned, his dark eyes smiling. "Guess every male within a hundred miles of Fort Lauderdale has pictured her on his arm. Relax, Dick, she's not in your ball park."

"What do you mean by that?" Dick bristled.

"Just that her father is probably the most successful surgeon in the city," Jim answered. "He's worth a mint. You should see her house. It's on the New River—long drive lined with Royal Palm trees, manicured lawn sloping down to the river, two swimming pools . . . They probably can't even remember the names of all their gardeners. All the sightseeing boats stop to point her house out to visitors."

"That bad?" Dick whistled, sitting down hard on his bed.

"Had her debutante party last spring," Jim continued. "Her dad shelled out a fortune for the Glen Miller Orchestra. The invitations were like gold. You'd think anyone who received one had gotten an invite to visit the Eisenhowers at the White House."

"Whew! I guess that does put her out of the league of a Swedish immigrant's kid from Ohio," Dick acknowledged.

"How'd you meet her?" Jim asked, eyeing his roommate curiously.

"Chemistry 101. She's my lab partner."

Now it was Jim's turn to whistle. "How'd you manage that?" he asked, running his fingers through his short, dark hair and looking at Dick with new respect.

"Got there early and picked my spot," Dick shrugged. "If what you say is true, though, it doesn't look like it's going to do me any good."

"I don't know," Jim mused. "Gainesville's a different world from Fort Lauderdale. She's living in a dorm—just like the rest of us. And she's probably just a little bit homesick and lonesome as well right now. Maybe you could work out a study date or something. It's worth a try. If it'll help, you could ask her to double. Cindy and I are going to the Alachua County Fair this weekend."

"I . . . I don't know. I just met her," Dick hesitated.

"And if you wait any longer, at least a hundred other guys will have met her, and you'll be standing in line until next semester. Take my word for it. Better grab your chance while you have it,"

Jim added, opening his book once more and turning back to his studies.

● ● ●

"DICK, THANK YOU so much for lending me your notes," Lorinda smiled, meeting his eyes across the battered Formica table in the Student Union as she handed his notebook back. "I really wouldn't have missed the lab if I could have helped it," she explained. "It's just that . . . Well, Daddy was at a medical conference at Shands Hospital—here at the university. He was in meetings until late last night, so he only had time to see me for breakfast this morning."

"I understand he's a really top-notch surgeon," Dick offered.

"How'd you hear that?" Lorinda asked.

"My roommate, Jim Lawrence."

"Debate captain—Lauderdale High," Lorinda nodded, pausing to take a sip of her cherry cola. "I used to debate against him. Nice guy—even if we did always take opposing sides."

"You went to Lauderdale High?" Dick asked, incredulous. "I would have expected . . ."

"Palm Acres," Lorinda interrupted, shaking her head. "It's a small, private girls' school. After Mommy left, Daddy felt I'd do better in a small school—especially with him working such long hours. I think he was afraid I'd grow up like Topsy, and he was hoping they'd teach me to be a 'lady' at Palm Acres," she laughed. "Daddy's always been a little overprotective, but we're all the family either of us has, so I understand.

"At any rate, I was the debate captain at Palm Acres my senior year. Jim and I met at several meets. I knew his girl friend Cindy, too. They were both on Lauderdale's team."

"Since you already know both of them," Dick began, "how would you like to double on Saturday? The Alachua County Fair is starting this weekend, and Jim and I thought it might be fun to check it out. That is, if you're not already busy," he blurted out—shocked at his own boldness and holding his breath as he waited for her reply.

"I'd really like that, Dick. I've always wanted to go to a fair. But Daddy never . . . ," she stopped, shaking her head. " Anyway, it sounds like lots of fun. And I really like Cindy and Jim. What time should I be ready?" Lorinda asked, waiting as he stared at her, speechless.

CHAPTER TWENTY-ONE

IN SEARCH OF GRANDMA LORINDA

I LOVE THE SMELL of popcorn," Lorinda called—shuffling through the wood shavings at her feet and crinkling up her nose as the foursome made its way across the parking lot toward the brightly-lighted midway.

"I like funnel cakes better," Dick offered, raising his head and sniffing as well. "Who's hungry?" he asked, grabbing Lorinda's hand and pulling her toward the nearest booth.

"Hey, which of you girls wants that big bear over there for your dorm room?" Jim called out, pointing to a large, plush bear hanging above the stacked, wooden milk bottles at the baseball throw. "Come on, Dick. Let's see who has the better arm," he added, picking up a baseball from the table in front of him.

"Oh, Jim, look! There's a fortune teller over there," Cindy called, pulling on his arm as she pointed to a small tent draped in red and purple satin just across the dirt path from the baseball throw. "Can we go?" she asked, her dark-blue eyes under a shock of short auburn curls pleading with him.

Reluctantly tearing himself away from a chance to show off his pitching arm, Jim followed Cindy's gaze. "Why would you want to pay good money to have your fortune told when I can tell your fortune for free?" he questioned, smiling. "You've already met your tall, dark, and handsome stranger and fallen in love. And now you're going to live happily ever after," he added, drawing himself up to his six-foot height and vainly stroking his dark hair—as Lorinda and Dick both laughed.

"Wouldn't it be fun, though, to see if she tells me the same thing, so I'll know for sure?" Cindy teased, pulling on Jim's arm once again. "Come on, Jim. Just this once. You want to go, too, don't you, Lorinda?"

"Not if she's going to meet a tall, dark, and handsome stranger, too," Dick added, playing along.

"Well, two out of three wouldn't be bad," Lorinda smiled, reaching up to run her hand playfully over Dick's short blond 'flat-top.'

"Then, why don't you go ahead and see what she tells you," he answered, giving her a little shove toward Cindy. Maybe a little fortune-telling would play right into his hands, he decided, as he met Jim's sly wink. "Remember, though, I'm still taking you home—no matter who she says you'll meet," he smiled as he followed Jim to the ticket booth and handed the teller a dollar.

● ● ●

THE SCARRED WOODEN chair was hard—its red velvet cushion worn and torn in several places where dirty, gray stuffing was visible. The smell of incense was overpowering. Lorinda thought she might be sick.

From behind the long curtain of shiny plastic beads, she could see the mesmerizing glow of several dozen candles and hear the steady drone of the old woman's voice and the jangle of her many metal bracelets. As she tipped her head back and closed her eyes, trying hard not to breathe in too deeply, she wondered why she had ever let Cindy talk her into this.

"Your turn," Cindy called gaily as she exited the inner room. "Maybe she'll see a tall, handsome, blond Viking whisking you off to his ship," she whispered in Lorinda's ear, her eyes alight. "Go on," she urged as Lorinda hesitated. "It's fun."

Rising, Lorinda followed the direction of the old gypsy—her bony arm thrust from a gauzy red and gold dress to hold back the beads as Lorinda entered the smoky inner room. A cloud of incense rose from a black metal urn in the far corner of the room, and the strains of a tinny gypsy violin emanated from a battered record player—partially visible beneath a small table covered in a red velvet cloth edged in gold fringe.

Motioning Lorinda to one of two chairs drawn up to the table, the old woman took the opposite chair and paused to adjust her thin, organdy veil over her long, gray hair. Then, waving both heavily-jeweled arms slowly above a large crystal ball set in the middle of the table, she began, "The crystal sees all. The crystal does not lie. Tell me what you most want to know."

"I . . . I don't know. I thought you would tell my fortune," Lorinda began, looking around uncomfortably. The pungent incense was making her sick, and the discordant music hurt her ears. She wanted to run, but the old woman's eyes held her captive.

"Your locket has meaning for you?" the old woman asked, as Lorinda nodded. "Whose likeness does it bear?" the woman continued, pointing a bony finger at Lorinda's throat.

"It's a picture of my grandmother," Lorinda answered, slipping a fingernail into the opening and holding the picture close to the old woman's eyes.

"Ah . . . ," the gypsy muttered, gazing at the picture and then down at the crystal ball. "You would like to know something about her?" she added after a moment.

"How . . . How did you know that?" Lorinda asked, incredulous.

"I told you. The crystal sees all," the old woman answered without lifting her eyes from the ball.

"Can you really see my grandmother in there?" Lorinda questioned, leaning forward eagerly, but seeing nothing in the ball herself.

"I'm seeing . . . The image is becoming clearer now," the gypsy nodded. "Her hair is like spun gold. She's wearing a white dress . . . ."

"Like in the picture," Lorinda nodded.

"She's smiling. She is happy—very happy," the woman added, waving her hand above the ball and bending over it more closely.

"Is there anyone with her?" Lorinda asked eagerly, trying to look over the old woman's shoulder.

"I see a young man beside her," the old woman added, peering more closely into her ball.

"Maybe it's my grandfather. Can you describe him?" Lorinda asked. "I know nothing about him."

"He's tall and dark and very good-looking," the old woman answered, giving Lorinda a toothless smile. "He's holding her hand. They seem to be in a church. I see colored windows."

"They must be at their wedding," Lorinda smiled.

"They're walking down the aisle and out of the door," the gypsy nodded.

"No!" she suddenly screamed, throwing one arm across her eyes and reaching out with the other to push the crystal from her—across the table.

"What is it? What did you see?" Lorinda screamed as well. Jumping from her chair, she leaned across the table and tried to look into the crystal ball herself.

"It is red," the old woman shrieked, waving her arm toward the crystal. "The ball is red!" Grabbing Lorinda's arm with her thin fingers, she sought her frightened eyes. "I see blood. There is danger here—much danger. You must look no further."

"But my grandmother . . . Did something happen to her? What did you see? I need to know," Lorinda began, pulling her arm from the old woman's grasp and turning the crystal toward her as she continued to peer into its cloudy surface.

"It is over," the gypsy answered quietly, shaking her head. Her golden earrings caught the candlelight—reflecting it around the room. Her dark eyes bored into Lorinda's. "You must go now. The vision has gone. I can see no more," she added, rising quickly and pulling aside the beaded curtain.

"If I come back later?" Lorinda begged, rising slowly and walking toward the woman. "Please?"

"The crystal is dark now. It is best to look no further," the old woman added, retrieving a deep-purple scarf from the table and quickly covering the ball—while motioning to the next customer— a young woman only a few years younger than Lorinda.

• • •

WELL, WAS I right?" Jim called, putting down the baseball as he saw Cindy emerge from the fortune teller's tent. Crossing the path, he met her halfway—encircling her waist with his arm.

"Right—as always," Cindy nodded solemnly, catching his eye. "Tall, dark, handsome . . . ," she added appraisingly, reaching up to run her fingers through Jim's hair.

"I knew it. A true psychic!" Jim grinned back.

"And father of ten tall, dark, and handsome children as well," Cindy teased, pulling back to observe his shocked look.

"Hey, where'd you leave Lorinda?" Dick asked, looking around Cindy toward the fortune teller's booth and seeing no one in sight.

"Oh, she and the fortune teller were still busy calling up some spirit of her grandmother in the crystal ball," Cindy shrugged. "Her fortune wasn't as clear as mine," she added, smiling at Jim.

"Tough luck, Cowboy. Guess you lose out to Grandma," Jim laughed. He stopped as Lorinda suddenly emerged from the tent across from them—her eyes wide with fear.

"Lorinda, what's wrong?" Dick asked, stepping forward to take her by the elbow as Jim and Cindy discreetly moved away down the path. "You look so upset. Wasn't she able to tell you anything about your grandmother?"

"She saw her," Lorinda nodded. "She said she was happy. My grandfather was with her, too."

"If they were happy, what did she tell you to upset you so?" Dick persisted.

"She said they were in a church. She could see stained-glass panels . . . . Then, she got really frightened. She screamed and pushed her crystal away and wouldn't look at it any more," Lorinda continued, tears filling her eyes.

"What did she see? Did she tell you?"

"She said everything had turned red."

"Sunlight through the stained-glass, I guess," Dick surmised.

"She said it was blood," Lorinda whispered, shaking her head. "She said it meant there was danger . . . ."

"For your grandmother . . . or for you?" Dick asked, intrigued, as he led her across the path—stopping under a floodlight to look at her.

"I don't know. She didn't say," Lorinda answered, wiping her eyes.

"Didn't you ask?" Dick persisted.

"I don't think she knew. I asked her to look again, but she just said her crystal ball had gone dark and she couldn't see any more. I'm not sure I really want to know any more, anyway," Lorinda added with a shudder.

"Hey, we're supposed to be having fun. Remember? But this whole thing really has you upset, doesn't it?" Dick asked, putting his arm around Lorinda and drawing her to him.

He could feel her body shaking. "These carnival booths are all hoaxes. That old woman is probably no more a gypsy than . . ."

"I know. I'm sorry, Dick," Lorinda interrupted apologetically—looking up at him. "I shouldn't have let Cindy talk me into it in the first place. It's just that I do so want to find out about my grandmother, and she seemed to know . . . Let's just try to forget it, though, and go find Jim and Cindy."

"If you're sure you're all right," Dick answered, searching her luminous eyes.

"I'll be fine as soon as you buy me some cotton candy," she said, attempting a smile and playfully pulling him along. "My daddy always used to buy me some at the circus. Cotton candy makes everything all right, don't you think?"

As a large woman with flaming red hair handed Lorinda a sticky cone of pink cotton candy and reached for Dick's coins, he knew—by the fear still written in Lorinda's eyes—that this was one time the magic wouldn't work.

● ● ●

I LOVE IT out here by the lake," Lorinda sighed. Setting her empty soft drink bottle beside the old army blanket, she leaned against the trunk of a spreading live oak tree and gazed toward the reed-enclosed shore of the algae-covered Lake Alice on the southern border of the campus. "It's been a perfect afternoon."

"I still can't believe it's so warm in December," Dick marveled, carefully wrapping the chicken bones from their picnic and depositing them into the paper sack beside him. "I talked to Mom and Dad last night, and they were having snow in Ohio," he added, leaning back beside Lorinda.

"I won't complain about the warm weather, but I do miss the change of seasons. I mean, football just doesn't seem the same at eighty degrees. I can't even imagine Christmas without at least the possibility of snow."

"I've never seen snow," Lorinda added, wistfully. "In fact, I've never been out of Florida."

"Really?" Dick asked, turning to her, incredulous. "I would have thought . . . I mean . . . Hasn't your dad ever taken you on a vacation?"

"I've never gone on a real vacation. Daddy doesn't take much time off," Lorinda shrugged. "A surgeon can't really leave whenever he wants to, you know. It's all right, I guess. We spend a lot of time at our Club. We know everyone there, and there's always something going on.

"My mother couldn't stand it, though. She always wanted to travel. She and Daddy got married right out of college. He was planning to go to medical school, but then the war came along. I had just been born, so Mommy had to take care of me alone until he came back. When he returned, Daddy applied to medical school. He was attending classes during the day and working odd jobs at night and on weekends to pay the bills.

"I think Mommy thought once Daddy got his practice going he'd finally get rich and then they'd travel to Europe and see all those exotic places she'd always dreamed of. But I guess she got tired of waiting for him to pay off the bills and take some time off," she sighed.

"Do you know where she is now?" Dick asked gently. He'd never heard her talk about her mother before.

"I have no idea where she is," Lorinda answered, shaking her head. "Daddy and I haven't heard from her in years—not since the divorce. I guess she didn't want either of us any more," she added, wiping a tear from her eye.

"I'm so sorry," Dick whispered. It was hard to imagine his home without his mother—her apron smudged with flour, her hands covered in garden dirt, or her arms balancing the large wash basket on her way to the basement.

"Oh, it's all right, really," Lorinda shrugged. "I have Daddy—which is more than he ever had."

Despite all her wealth, Lorinda had missed so much in life, Dick thought. And—having been deserted by her mother—well, it was no wonder she was looking for her grandmother. If only there were some way to make it all up to her. "But don't you want to see other places?" he asked.

"Of course. There are so many places I'd like to go . . . ," Lorinda answered, looking into space.

"All right. Close your eyes," Dick ordered, waiting until she did as he asked. "Now, if you could go anywhere—right now—where would you go? Try to picture it."

"North Carolina," Lorinda smiled without hesitation—her eyes still closed.

"Ocean or mountains?" he continued—playing the game.

"Clint's Bend," Lorinda responded. "I don't know what it's near, and I can't really picture it," she added, opening her eyes. "It's the small town where my father was born. Daddy says he hasn't time to go back there, so I'd like to go for him and look up his family. Who knows? I might even find my grandmother—or an aunt or uncle."

"Your father really doesn't know anything about his family?" Dick asked. "How strange. I don't think I can remember a time when I wasn't surrounded by zillions of burly, blond Everetts."

"You're so lucky," Lorinda sighed. "I'd so love to have a big family with aunts and uncles and cousins. As far as I know, there are no more Lockridges anywhere. But I keep hoping . . ."

"I could take you to North Carolina," Dick offered suddenly.

"Really? Do you go through North Carolina on your way back to Ohio?" she asked excitedly.

"Well, it's easier to go through Atlanta and Tennessee," he admitted. "But I could go that way—if you wanted to go. In fact, we could go to North Carolina over Christmas break. Then, I could take you home with me and show you a White Christmas and let you see what it's like to be smothered by a clan of Vikings.

"My mother would love it. My brother Bob would challenge me to a duel over you. And my little sister Janet would follow you everywhere. She's always wanted a big sister. Say you'll come. We'd have plenty of time to look up your grandparents in North Carolina," Dick begged, looking into her eyes.

"I'd love that," Lorinda sighed. "But, then, Daddy would be alone for the holidays. Besides, it's the Season, and there will be so many parties and dances at the Club . . . ."

"You mean you're going to be dancing with other guys all vacation while I sit and listen to my little sister play Christmas carols with one finger on the piano and my grandmother and aunt sing off-key?" Dick asked. He wasn't sure he could bear to sit at home and think of her dancing with a bunch of society guys.

"You don't know what the Season is like in Fort Lauderdale," Lorinda explained. "These parties are very important to my father's work. There'll be lots of his colleagues and patients there. Besides, I'm sure he's already accepted for both of us, and it would be rude to cancel out now.

"There's really no one else but you, Dick. Surely you know that," she concluded, brushing his cheek with her fingers.

"Then I guess I have no choice but to wait for you," he smiled at last, grabbing her hand. "But I don't have to like it. And I'm giving notice right now, Lorinda Lockridge, that I intend to be the one to take you to North Carolina one day and help you to find your grandmother. So don't accept any other escort," he added, entwining his fingers in her silky hair and gently laying her back on the rough wool blanket.

CHAPTER TWENTY-TWO

FROM THIS DAY FORWARD

Even in the air-conditioned auto, the South Florida heat was oppressive. Looking across the back seat at his brother Bob's ruddy face, Dick laughed. He should have remembered to tell him he could change at the church, he thought as he watched Bob pull the starched, white collar and its accompanying bow tie away from his perspiring neck and wipe at the damp tendrils of pale-blond hair with his handkerchief.

Blinking in the bright sunlight as the limo drew to a stop, Bob looked through the window across the flat expanse of white sand—dotted with dark-green seagrape bushes, twisted coconut palms, and a myriad of brightly-colored blankets and scantily-clothed sun bathers. "So this is the famous Fort Lauderdale Beach," he sighed as he grabbed the door handle and emerged onto the busy street—hurriedly rounding the car and joining Dick on the sidewalk.

Jerking his chin toward a cluster of young women stretched out on the hot sand a few yards away, Bob studied his brother's face. "She must be some catch if you're willing to give all this up," he grinned—his deep-blue eyes alight.

"Just wait 'til you see her!" Dick answered, looking around on the busy A1A highway for any sign of the other limos hired for the wedding. The traffic in from the airport and hotel had been terrible. He hoped their parents and sister Janet would get here on time.

"Glad you two got here at last," Jim called, running from the wide double doors of the small, gray stone church and up the flagstone walk toward Dick and Bob.

"As luck would have it, my folks' plane was late. They're still at the hotel. We had no idea the traffic would be so bad," Dick answered, shaking his head.

"A1A's always like this," Jim laughed, waving his arm toward the two lines of swiftly-moving cars.

"Then it took ages to get into these 'monkey suits,'" Bob complained, pulling at his bow tie.

"Not my favorite attire either," Jim laughed, looking down at his own starched tuxedo shirt. "But I guess we have your brother's bride to thank for it. Cindy and I tried to convince her that bathing suits would be more appropriate in June, but she wouldn't listen.

"But how are you, Dick? Not getting cold feet yet, I hope," he added, clapping his roommate on the back.

"That's the last thing he's likely to get in this heat," Bob answered. "I'm Bob Everett," he added, holding out his hand to Jim.

"I'm sorry. I forgot you two haven't met," Dick apologized. "Bob, this is my roommate, Jim Lawrence."

"As long as you didn't forget to come today, you're forgiven," Jim smiled. "You can't imagine the frenzy Lorinda's in. She's been so afraid you wouldn't show. Obviously, she doesn't know you as well as I do. I told her it would take an act of Congress to keep you away, but you know Lorinda. She made me promise to let her know the minute you got here. And she's sent Cindy out every five minutes to check anyway."

"Well, we're here now—minus several pounds I know I've melted off since leaving the airport," Bob answered, pausing to pull out his handkerchief again and wipe his forehead. "As far as I'm concerned, the sooner we get this ceremony over with and I can get out of this straight jacket, the better I'll like it."

"At least Lorinda was thoughtful enough to find a church with air-conditioning. It's a lot cooler inside. Come on," Jim offered, leading the way through the two rows of seagrape bushes flanking the flagstone walk.

● ● ●

Do you think he'll notice?" Lorinda asked, twirling in front of the mirror and pausing a moment to tuck a loose sprig of baby's breath more tightly into the loose bun on the back of her neck.

"'Notice' is hardly the word," Cindy grinned. Leaning closer to the mirror herself to adjust the pale pink veil over her auburn curls, she caught Lorinda's eye in the mirror. "I'd say it's more like hitting him over the head. It's uncanny."

Taking the open locket into her hand, she looked from the locket to Lorinda and back again. "I swear, Lorinda, you're the spitting image of her," she added. Suddenly, she closed her eyes and seemed to shiver.

"Cindy, what's wrong?" Lorinda asked, grabbing her friend's arm to steady her. "Here, sit down. Are you all right?" she asked, concerned as she helped Cindy to the stool beside the dressing table.

"I don't know," Cindy answered, shaking her head. "It was just a spell, but it's gone now. I think my grandmother would have said 'someone was walking on my grave.' I guess it just sort of gave me the willies to see you looking so much like her—like seeing a ghost or something, I mean."

"Is it too much?" Lorinda questioned, looking into the mirror once more—where she met another pair of gold-flecked eyes.

"Your public is waiting, your highness," Phillip Lockridge announced, smiling at his daughter as he entered the door.

"Daddy," Lorinda beamed, forgetting Cindy for the moment. "You look terrific," she added appraisingly, looking over his broad-shouldered frame and carefully-combed dark-blond hair before standing on tiptoe to plant a kiss on his cheek.

She wouldn't allow herself to think about how much she would miss this first man in her life—not now. Not on her wedding day, she told herself as she blinked away a tear. But, as Dick had reminded her, they wouldn't be any farther away than she had been the past four years, since they would both be going back to the University of Florida for graduate school.

"And you, my darling, are an absolute vision," Philip grinned, cutting into her thoughts. "Dick's a very lucky young man. I'm sure there's not a man in the congregation who won't be envying him as you walk down that aisle.

"Now, what do you say? Are you ladies ready to get this show on the road?" he questioned, smiling at Cindy and offering his arm to Lorinda.

"Are you sure you're all right, Cindy?" Lorinda asked, turning as she laced her arm into her father's elbow.

"Never better," Cindy answered, jumping to her feet. "Guess it was just a little wedding jitters. Better to get them at your wedding than at mine," she joked as she led the procession out of the door.

• • •

BACKLIT BY THE late afternoon sun, Lorinda seemed to glow as she entered the wide double oak doors on her father's arm. Philip Lockridge—tall and regal with his deep golfer's tan—beamed as he peered at the assembled congregation, which was now on its feet. The gentle murmur running through the crowd showed its approval. Philip and his daughter made a striking pair.

Watching his bride as she drew closer, however, Dick gasped. Lorinda's deep tan had been hidden under a dusting of pale powder, and her long, dark-gold hair had been parted in the middle and swept back from her face into a loose bun at the back of her slender neck. A single drape of embroidered lace rested lightly over her head and swept across her bare shoulders, falling gently over the bouquet of white roses she carried.

Gone was the long-legged co-ed in shorts and tennis shoes. In her place was a reincarnation of the tiny young woman in her locket, which she wore as her only jewelry against the white Victorian lace wedding gown.

Knowing Lorinda was waiting for his reaction as she neared the altar, however, Dick smiled as he took her hand from her father's arm. "I see your grandmother made the wedding after all," he whispered, as they turned to face the minister.

● ● ●

So what do you think of Lorinda?" Cindy whispered, slipping up beside Dick as they waited to form the receiving line.

"Breathtaking, as usual," Dick smiled. "Although, I admit, it's a little disconcerting to think I may have married her grandmother."

"I swear when I saw her walking down that aisle, I really couldn't believe it," Jim called, walking up and putting his arm around Cindy. "She's the spitting image of that picture in her locket."

"Well, big brother, I think your Lorinda would look good in a flour sack," Bob answered, suddenly appearing at Dick's side. "So whoever she's dressed like must have been quite a looker as well. I see now why you were willing to pass up all those girls on the beach."

● ● ●

PHILIP, WHO WAS clearly enjoying the whole affair, stood beside Dick in the small, grassy, walled courtyard of the church as they both endured the final moments of the obligatory receiving line. As if sensing his new son-in-law's discomfort at having to converse with over a hundred people he had never met before, Philip had stayed by Dick's side for the past half hour. Reaching over every minute or two to clap him on the back, he had gaily introduced him to each of his fellow surgeons and the countless members of their Club, whose names and faces Dick knew he would never remember.

Both Lorinda and Dick had expected an outcry from Philip when they planned their wedding so soon after graduation. But having exacted a promise from Lorinda to continue medical school while Dick took a teaching assistantship and pursued his PhD. in English literature, he had given his blessing. Moreover, he had seemed genuinely pleased to welcome Dick into his small family by calling him "son" in front of all his friends and promising to teach him to play golf at the first opportunity.

Dick hoped he could—in some small way—live up to Philip's expectations. If he hadn't already grown to love this gregarious man, he decided he would have done so on the spot as he had watched his new father-in-law welcome the large, ruddy, blond Everett clan into his Fort Lauderdale society—as if a tribe of Vikings were common guests in the Lockridge household.

As the festivities continued, Dick could not help wondering what could ever have compelled Lorinda's mother to leave this cordial and compassionate man—not to mention their beautiful and talented daughter. He hoped someday to meet her.

Phillip had confided to Dick that he had hired a private investigator to try to find his ex-wife to tell her of the wedding, since he knew how much it would mean to Lorinda. After six months, however, they had found no trace. Dick knew how disappointed he had been that he could not give his daughter this one present she would have valued above all others.

Lorinda did not seem disappointed, however, Dick decided as he watched her hugging one of the guests and sharing a joke with her and her husband as they came through the line. Her mother had been absent so long that she would have seemed out of place had she shown up.

"I know the honeymoon is supposed to be a surprise for the bride," Philip whispered, as the line bogged down and they were alone for the moment. "But I can't help asking. Surely, you can tell her old dad where you're taking his little girl, can't you? After all, I might need to know in case of an emergency," he added, his clear hazel eyes holding Dick's steadily from behind his wire-rimmed glasses.

"Actually," Dick smiled, "it's the most perfect place I could take her. I know Lorinda will love it. I've planned a trip for the two of us to North Carolina. I know you've never had the time to go, and I've been promising for four years to take her up there to look up your family. She wants so much to find out about the first 'Lorinda.'"

"Son," Philip added, hesitating and swallowing hard before lowering his voice. "I love you as a son already, and I've gladly given you my little girl. I haven't asked anything of you except that you love my daughter and be good to her. But now I must ask something very important of you. Don't, I beg you, ever take Lorinda to Clint's Bend.

"I wish I could give you a good reason. But all I can say is that I know from my uncle that there's danger for her there. When I was just a boy, he made me promise never to search for my family.

"I never wanted to frighten Lorinda, so I've told her nothing of my background. The truth is—I know almost nothing myself. The uncle and aunt who raised me died when I was just fourteen—much too young to have voiced the questions I now have. And I'm not sure they would have answered them if I had asked.

"I made a life for myself—and for Lorinda—here in Fort Lauderdale. It's been a good one, and she's never lacked for anything I could provide. She's the only thing in my life that has ever truly belonged to me. Now she belongs to you as well. If you love her—and I know how much you do—promise me that you will help me protect her from whatever truth is out there. I'm afraid I must ask you to promise me that you will never take her to North Carolina to research her roots," he concluded.

"But North Carolina's the only place she's ever asked to go," Dick began, searching his father-in-law's earnest eyes for an answer. He was caught between two promises. He had promised Lorinda as well, and he couldn't bear to disappoint her.

"You both deserve the best," Philip interrupted, smiling. "A long drive after your graduation and all the wedding preparations would be hard on both of you. A cruise is what this doctor orders instead.

"You'll love the Caribbean," he continued, reaching into the inside pocket of his jacket. "A little wedding present—from me. I remember those lean graduate school days only too well," he smiled, handing Dick a large, white envelope before turning back to the next guest.

Dick swallowed hard as he looked at the envelope. He'd felt so guilty that he couldn't afford the type of honeymoon he would have liked to give Lorinda—or that she would have had if she had married one of the men from their country club. And now here was his chance. But, then, Lorinda had asked him so many times to take her to Clint's Bend. And he had promised . . . time and again.

He didn't like being caught by the promise Philip had exacted from him, but he couldn't go against his new father-in-law's wishes. After all, he and Lorinda still had the rest of their lives ahead of them. There would be plenty of time to research her roots.

Suddenly, though, he knew why Lorinda was so insistent on finding her grandmother. No one could resist a good mystery, and—whether or not he realized it—Philip had just whetted Dick's appetite as well.

CHAPTER TWENTY-THREE

A WHITE CHRISTMAS

Rough day?" Dick questioned, rolling a sheet of paper out of the typewriter and looking at his wife across the kitchen table as she entered the door. "I expected you home hours ago."

"Oh, Dick, it was awful," Lorinda blurted out, dropping her purse on the small table by the door and dropping onto the nearby sofa—her head buried in her hands. "You know . . . I don't know how Daddy manages. I'm not sure I'm cut out for medicine."

"Why not? You did so well last year, and I thought you were really enjoying the rotations this semester. With obstetrics . . . I mean, in your condition and with all those new babies being brought into the world . . . ," he added, standing and walking over to her.

"Dick, she didn't make it. She just . . . died—right there on the table," Lorinda interrupted, not bothering to wipe the tears flowing freely down her face as she looked up at her husband. "One minute she was just driving to the grocery store. She was so happy and expecting her first child. Then, suddenly, there was this other car . . . . Doctor Ballard and the rest of us tried so hard, but she had lost so much blood."

"Did the baby survive?" Dick asked, sitting down beside her and taking her hand.

"Poor little thing," she added, shaking her head. "He was several weeks premature, but Dr. Ballard thinks he'll make it. But for what? He's got no mother now, and his father is so broken up. He couldn't even bring himself to look at the baby—just sat there in the waiting room sobbing."

"I can understand that," Dick answered. "He's still reeling from the shock. But when he can reach out through his grief, that baby will be a lifeline for him. Look at the bond between you and your dad," he added with a smile.

"But I know how much a child needs his mother. At least I had mine for a few years. Daddy and I have never talked about it, but I know how much Mommy's leaving hurt both of us. And now that poor child . . ."

"At least he has one parent," Dick offered. "Look at your father. He had no parents, and look how he turned out."

"Oh, Dick," Lorinda said, raising her tear-stained face to look at him, "Do you think maybe Daddy's parents were killed in an accident? Could that be why the gypsy saw the blood?"

"It could be, I suppose. I'm not sure we'll ever know," Dick answered, shaking his head.

"I want to know," Lorinda said quietly. "I have to know. Now that we're going to have our own child, I want to know what happened to my grandmother.

"I've been reading so many books . . . . I mean, what if there's some disease I should know about?"

"Your father is so dead-set against this. He's told us so many times . . . ," Dick hedged.

"That's easy for him to say," Lorinda interrupted, "and he and Mommy were lucky I didn't ever have any medical problems. But they didn't have any more children, so we can't really be sure there isn't something . . ."

"I have an idea," Dick interrupted, laying Lorinda's hand down gently on the sofa and rising. Walking to the breakfast bar, he picked up an envelope and returned to the sofa.

"Letter from Mom," he smiled, waving the envelope in front of her. "She wants us to come up to Ohio for Christmas. I was going to say 'no,' but if we go to Ohio . . ."

"We can go to North Carolina on the way," Lorinda finished his sentence excitedly. "That would be so wonderful! Could we really go?"

"With luck, maybe I can show you your first White Christmas," Dick smiled at her sudden change of mind.

"I'd love it," Lorinda answered. "It would be such a change. The only white we've ever had for Christmas in Fort Lauderdale is sand! Daddy will miss us, but I'm sure he'll understand. After all, in my condition, I wouldn't be doing much dancing anyway," she smiled.

"Then, I'll write Mom right back. She'll be so excited. She's been after me for the past two years to bring you home for a visit. She really wants to introduce you to all her friends," Dick answered.

"Dick, I look like a beached whale," Lorinda laughed. "That's hardly the way to meet Dayton society."

"There's no society with my family," Dick assured her. "We play lots of 'Scrabble' and 'Monopoly,' sing carols, and make homemade taffy and cookies. If we're lucky, Dad might even make a little of his famous eggnog for guests who drop in. But that's about as social as it gets. So, what do you say?"

"I'd love it. Only . . . ," Lorinda paused, rubbing at her swollen midsection absently, "I'd have to ask Dr. Ballard. After all, I'll be seven months along by then. He may not want me to travel that far."

"My Uncle Eric is an obstetrician. He'll be just down the street—if you need him."

"Then, I'll ask Dr. Ballard at my appointment tomorrow. Won't it be fun to see your folks again and then to discover a whole new set of relatives in Clint's Bend? Do you know how many years I've begged Daddy to take me to North Carolina? He was always too busy. But I knew I could count on you," Lorinda smiled, throwing her arms around Dick's neck.

"Philip Lockridge. How will I explain this to him?" Dick wondered. Dick would be taking Philip's 'little girl' away—during the Season, and while she was expecting his first grandchild. And he would be taking her to the one place his father-in-law had begged him never to take her. He could still hear Philip's words as he looked into Lorinda's eyes—so like her father's.

But it meant so much to Lorinda. And, maybe when she found out the truth, it might help end her obsession with the first Lorinda. He was sure Philip would be happy about that. After all, what was the harm? Philip was forty-five years old. Whatever he was afraid of in North Carolina had happened so long ago. Probably none of his immediate relatives were still living in the same place. In fact, most of them probably were not still living at all. What harm could there be in letting Lorinda research old census records? She asked so little.

•   •   •

THE MORNING WAS cold and blustery—the sky a leaden gray. "Sorry we couldn't provide your white Christmas," Bob smiled as he walked Dick and Lorinda out to their car. But, judging by that sky, if you'd just stick around a while . . . ."

"No can do, little brother. We both need to get back to school, and I've promised Lorinda her visit to North Carolina on our way home," Dick answered, shaking his head.

"Then, keep a watch on the weather, and drive safely," Bob cautioned, glancing down at Lorinda's extended midsection. "I don't want that little nephew or niece or mine born in the back seat of your car in a blizzard—even if you do have the Everett cradle in the back seat!"

"That's why we're leaving early," Dick interrupted. "We're heading south to Knoxville. We should be able to outrun the snow," he added, loud enough for his parents, who were standing on the front porch, to hear.

"Dick, do you think it's wise to leave now?" his mother called hopefully, pulling the hood of her parka over her short, blond curls. It had been such a short visit. "Maybe you should stay until the storm is over . . . ."

"They'll be all right, Gloria," Dick's father, Alan, interrupted—his sparse, dark-blond hair standing on end in the biting wind as he wrapped his arms around his wife's shoulders. "They need to get ahead of the storm. A blizzard could delay them for days."

"Remember to call the minute the baby gets here. And you promised I could come down this summer to baby sit," ten-year-old Janet called, her long, blond pigtails flying behind her as she ran out of the door and stopped beside her parents on the steps.

"And we want lots of pictures," Gloria called loudly.

"We'll probably send so many you can paper your walls with them," Lorinda laughed as Dick held the car door for her. "Thanks so much for everything—all of you. It was a lovely Christmas. We'll call when we get home. And . . . don't worry. We'll be just fine."

As they backed from the driveway, Lorinda turned to wave, then grimaced and grabbed her abdomen as a sudden pain ripped through her.

"Something wrong?" Dick asked, looking at her in alarm.

"Just moved too suddenly. I'm all right now," she smiled, waving until they reached the end of the street.

"Maybe we should just go straight home. We have a two-day drive as it is. You're not feeling well, and the sky does look threatening," Dick offered, turning to look at Lorinda before pulling out into the intersection.

"Oh, no, Dick Everett. You're not getting out of this so easily," she answered. "I'm fine, and we won't have another chance to get to North Carolina for years."

"I know . . . . I know," Dick answered resignedly, following the signs to the nearby highway.

• • •

OH, MY GOSH, here it comes," Dick exclaimed several hours later as he turned on his wipers and attempted to clear the large, blowing snowflakes from his windshield.

"What's coming?" Lorinda asked sleepily, opening her eyes and lifting her head from the back of the seat.

"The snow," Dick answered irritably, pointing out the front window. "I was hoping we could outrun it."

"Oh, it's beautiful!" Lorinda called excitedly. "Look, Dick. Look at those big flakes! I never realized . . . I mean, all I've ever seen are paper snowflakes. Can we stop a minute? I might never get another chance . . ."

"We both might never have another chance if we get stuck out here," Dick grumbled, wiping the inside of his windshield with the back of his hand and leaning forward to peer through the flying snow. "And we're still miles from Lexington."

"Do you think we'll get out of the snow by then?" Lorinda questioned, looking out the window at the rapidly-whitening fields along the road.

"I wouldn't count on it. And, if it's this bad in Tennessee, there's no way we'll ever get over the mountains to Carolina. Those roads are hazardous in the best of summer weather. I'm surely not going to chance them in a blizzard," he answered.

"But, Dick, you promised," Lorinda pouted. "Couldn't we just find a hotel and wait until the snow ends?"

"I think that's exactly what we'll have to do, but with snow like this, I don't see the mountain passes being opened again for weeks," Dick said. "Why don't you watch the road for signs to Lexington and any hotels that might be advertised. With no chains, we can't go much further."

• • •

I CAN'T TELL you how lucky we were to find this room," Dick sighed, pushing the hotel door open with his shoulder and slinging the two heavy bags ahead of him into the room—where Lorinda was already seated on the bed. "They're already turning people away right and left in the lobby."

"Dick, do you remember Dave Mabrey?" Lorinda asked, ignoring her husband's statement.

"Who?" Dick asked, confused.

"Dave . . . Dave Mabrey. He was in my pre-med class."

"I don't see what . . . ," Dick answered, pulling off his coat and hanging it in the cut-out closet area at the entrance to the room before turning to his wife.

"He's in med school . . . here . . . at the University of Kentucky," Lorinda answered, pausing a moment to breathe heavily and grab her abdomen.

"Lorinda, what's wrong?" Dick called, noticing her actions and walking to the bed.

"I . . . I think maybe we might need him."

"Are you in labor?" Dick gasped. "I mean . . . With this snow the whole city is shut down right now. There's no way . . ."

"I'm not sure what's going on. It could just be false labor. That's pretty common in first pregnancies. But do you think you could look up his number and call him . . . just to be sure?" Lorinda asked, grimacing again and leaning back against the pillows—as Dick reached into the dresser and pulled out the telephone directory.

• • •

ALWAYS HOPED I'D see you two again," Dave Mabrey smiled, a wide grin covering his face as he walked into the hospital room. "But I never thought it would be like this," he added, pushing a stray lock of brown hair off his face and offering his hand to Dick before crossing to the bed.

"I . . . I didn't mean to be a burden," Lorinda called from the bed. "I know you have more important cases to look after right now."

"Well, I'll admit, it was tough finding a free ambulance. And you're lucky they were able to get you here. We've had several stuck. But you were right to call and get in here to let us check you out," Dave smiled, taking Lorinda's hand.

"Did you talk to the doctor?" Dick asked.

"I'll let him tell you in person. He'll be here when he's finished rounds. We've had several births already today. The low pressure, you know. But, basically, he thinks it's only false labor pains. I think he intends to send you back to the hotel now that your pains have stopped," Dave smiled.

"Then, once the snow has stopped, we can go on with our trip?" Lorinda asked excitedly.

"Only if that trip is straight to Gainesville—by the shortest route," Dave answered, shaking his head. "Lorinda, your travels may have brought on this bout. It's risky for you to drive any further than necessary. We'd probably ask you to stay here until you've delivered . . . . But, on the other hand, you still have several weeks, and I know how much you want to be back home. And, since Dr. Ballard at Shands has most of your records . . ."

"Don't worry." Dick interrupted. "I'm taking her right home— as soon as you folks say it's all right and the roads are clear. There'll be no side trips,' he added, not daring to look at Lorinda's face.

"Oops, there's my page. Guess visiting hour's over," Dave laughed. "But have me paged before you two leave. I'd like to say goodbye and hear what the doctor tells you," he added, pausing at the door to wave.

"Oh, Dick, I did so want to get to North Carolina and look up Daddy's family," Lorinda sighed, wiping a tear from her eye. "I'd hoped to give him a grandchild and a mother and father—or at least a cousin or two. But now . . ."

"It wasn't meant to be," Dick answered, shaking his head. "Maybe this was the Lord's way of keeping us from something we can't handle; although—I must say—the alternative hasn't been a whole lot better," he smiled.

"Dick, sometimes, I swear, you sound more like my father's child than I do!" Lorinda sneered.

"There's a reason your father never went back," Dick persisted. "Surely, he had the opportunity—if he'd wanted to go."

"I think he felt abandoned," Lorinda added, thoughtfully. "He probably was angry at the rest of his family for sending him away. That's why it's so important that I find them and tell him . . ."

"Right now, it's much more important that we get you home and get our baby here safely. And I'm not going to listen to any more arguments. You know what your father would say if we called him," Dick answered.

● ● ●

WELL, WHAT HAVE we here?" Most gorgeous baby I've ever seen. And I've seen lots of them, so I can't possibly be prejudiced," Philip Lockridge laughed—his smiling eyes above the green scrubs and mask he wore catching his daughter's eyes as he reached out to touch the tiny hand of the sleeping infant in her arms. "Couldn't wait to get him here, though, could you?"

"We're just lucky we were able to get back home. Last week, I thought we might be naming him 'Davy Crockett'!" Dick called from the green vinyl chair, which he had pulled up to the bed. "Luckily, Lorinda managed to hold on . . . . I'll tell you, though, I never want to go through a trip like that again."

"But what are you going to call him? 'Baby Everett' just doesn't have the right ring," Philip smiled.

"Daddy, I'd like for you to meet 'Philip Lockridge Everett,'" Lorinda beamed. "We named him for you, but we're going to call him 'Phil.' We'd planned it all along, but we didn't want to tell you in case he was a girl."

"Well, well . . . I couldn't be more proud," Philip smiled, obviously pleased, "even if his name is the only resemblance he bears to the Lockridges. With that white-blond hair, he's going to be every bit an Everett.

"But, Lorinda, how are you, Sweetheart?" he continued, pulling the mask down long enough to bend and kiss his daughter. "My Lord, you two had me worried to death! I had cleared my schedule for February so I could be here. But I couldn't believe it when you called, Dick."

"I told Lorinda we Everetts were an impatient lot," Dick laughed.

"Well, other than this," Philip smiled, briefly stroking the cornsilk hair on the sleeping child before pulling the worn desk chair around and taking a seat, "how was the trip?"

"Christmas was wonderful. There were so many of us that we opened presents until after noon!" Lorinda answered excitedly. "Of course, we always have fun at the Club, too. I don't mean that. But it was such fun being with a really large family. I missed that . . . . We both did, didn't we, Daddy? Wouldn't it have been fun to have lots of brothers and sisters and aunts and uncles and cousins around—like Dick?" she persisted.

"I never really gave it much thought. You were all I ever needed . . . until Dick and Little Phil, that is," Philip added. "Tripling my winnings in three years isn't bad, you know."

"Well, Dick and I have decided to have lots more grandbabies for you and start our own big family. That way, maybe we can make up a little for what you've missed," Lorinda smiled.

CHAPTER TWENTY-FOUR

UNEARTHING THE PAST

RALEIGH, NORTH CAROLINA, JUNE, 1999

DICK, I'M SO EXCITED!" Lorinda called, as she leaned toward the mirror in the spacious hotel room to secure a small diamond stud into her left ear and smooth her chin-length bob.

Catching her eye in the mirror as he entered from the bathroom, Dick smiled. It was hard to believe it had been almost forty years since they had first locked eyes that sunny morning by the lake. The tiny lines at the corners of her eyes and the few silver strands in her smooth, honey-colored hair had done little to diminish Lorinda's beauty—at least in his eyes. While her figure was no longer girlish, she still looked terrific in her new pink suit. It was a welcome change from the green hospital scrubs he so often saw her in. Dick raised an eyebrow to show his approval and was rewarded with one of her radiant smiles.

Examining his own image in the glass behind her, Dick only hoped she felt the same about him. His hair had darkened over the years, but he still had all of it—and very little gray. And, although his belt was on its last hole, he didn't think he looked too bad for a fifty-six year old.

"I adore Allison, don't you?" Lorinda asked suddenly, breaking into his thoughts and bringing him back to the present. "She and Phil are going to be so happy together. It's rather strange that our son's marrying a girl from North Carolina, isn't it?"

"Maybe we should have done that research you want to do before the wedding," Dick answered impishly. "You might find your family and the Roberts are related, and we'd have to cancel the wedding. Actually, though, I'm sorry it's taken so long to get you to North Carolina," he smiled, putting his hands on her shoulders and turning her to face him. "Believe it or not, I really had planned to take you earlier. I'm not sure where the years have gone."

"Oh, to your lecture tours and faculty meetings, to my patients, to Little Phil's soccer games and summer camps, to junior proms, and then to college," Lorinda smiled. "With all that going on, there hasn't been time for us for years. But that's all over now that Phil and Allison will be getting their own place. I'll miss them, but it'll be nice to have some time for ourselves at last. And after the wedding is over . . ."

"You want to go to Clint's Bend, right?" Dick teased, rolling his eyes in mock disgust. "Of all the romantic places the two of us could be going . . ."

"Dick, you promised," Lorinda faked a pout. After all these years, she still knew how to get to him.

Actually, they'd been through this several times since Phil and Allison had announced their wedding plans at Christmas. They were being married in Allison's home church in Raleigh, North Carolina, and Lorinda had begged to take a whole week after the wedding to do her research. For over thirty years Dick had kept his promise to Philip Lockridge and made excuse after excuse for never taking Lorinda to his hometown.

He had to admit to himself, however, that the mystery her father had opened for him on their own wedding day had continued to fester in his own mind—especially after Philip's sudden heart attack and death last year. There was now nothing in Clint's Bend that could hurt Philip, and he doubted anyone in the town had ever heard of Lorinda. So, despite his continued protests, he really was almost as anxious to visit the infamous town as Lorinda.

"Clint's Bend is only a two-hour drive from here," Lorinda continued—still pressing her point. It had occurred to Dick more than once that she should have followed her first love and gone from debate into law.

"As long as we're this close," she was going on at great rate, "it can't hurt to just go by there and see what we can find out. I could have gobs of relatives who still live there."

"Your father had every chance to go back to see for himself; yet, he never did. He must have had a good reason," Dick reminded her.

"Daddy was a workaholic. You know that. He was always too busy to look up his family," Lorinda smiled sadly. "Who knows? He might still be with us if he'd taken a little time off once in a while."

"But not one of those 'gobs of relatives' ever saw fit to look your father up, either," Dick countered.

"They don't know how much they missed. Daddy was such a wonderful man. I still miss him so very much . . . ," she added, reaching for a tissue and carefully wiping her eyes—to avoid mussing the mascara she seldom wore.

"I guess . . . I think if I could just find a little bit of him in Clint's Bend . . . Oh, you know what I mean, don't you?" she continued.

"You know, neither of us has any idea what went on in that town. I, for one, would prefer to leave well enough alone," Dick continued to protest—remembering his father-in-law's request.

"Well, there's nothing in Clint's Bend that can hurt Daddy now," Lorinda added sadly as a knock sounded at the door.

"How's it goin', Buckeye?" a heavy-set, white-haired man called jovially, grabbing Dick in a bear hug as soon as he opened the door and then holding him at arm's length to look at him more closely.

"Jim, my God, how long has it been?" Dick asked as he locked eyes with his old roommate.

"Long enough for 'tall, dark, and handsome' to go white," Jim laughed. "But look at you! You haven't changed a bit—hair's a little darker, but, hey, you could pass for one of your kid's frat brothers. And, Lorinda, good Lord, you look fabulous! You two been hangin' out in a spa or something?" he called, pulling her to him as she approached. "Wait 'til Cindy sees you! She's been stewing for the last month over whether to turn her hair auburn again."

"Should have done it," Cindy called from the doorway. "With our white hair, we look more like your grandparents."

"Cindy! My gosh, it's been forever," Lorinda squealed, rushing to hug her friend. "We were so excited when we heard you both were coming."

"Wouldn't have missed it," Jim answered. "After all, we got one Elliott to the altar. Had to be sure the next generation made it as well."

"Can you believe how long it's been?" Dick mused.

"Long enough to make Lorinda as old as that grandmother she was looking for," Jim teased.

"Did you ever find out any more about her?" Cindy asked.

"Not yet, but maybe next week," Lorinda offered, shaking her head.

"Lorinda wants to spend the next week searching for her family records. Want to stick around after the wedding and help us?" Dick offered.

"Wish we could," Cindy sighed. "It's been much too long since we've had any kind of vacation."

"Big case coming to trial next week, and Cindy's still got another week of teaching before school's out," Jim explained. "But be sure to let us know what you find out."

• • •

THE WEDDING WENT off perfectly. Allison was stunning in a floor-length, straight, white lace dress. Her dark-blond hair was caught up on the back of her head in a twist—into which her hairdresser had tucked small sprigs of baby's breath.

As Dick watched his new daughter-in-law waiting in the back of the church, he couldn't help remembering another wedding—on a June day in Florida so many years ago. In fact—except for her taller frame—she looked very much like Lorinda had that same day, and he found himself wondering at his own words uttered earlier in jest.

Suppose there was a connection with Lorinda's family? Maybe he should have let Lorinda research her roots earlier, he thought, looking over at her as she sat beside him in the front pew, wiping a tear—no, a flood of tears—from her eyes.

Phil looked quite handsome in his black tuxedo—his light blond hair slicked down for the occasion and his wide blue eyes locked on Allison as she entered the church. They seemed so young to Dick. But he and Lorinda had been just as young and in love, and they had made it. As the strains of the wedding march began and the crowd rose, Dick grasped Lorinda's hand and caught her eye before both of them turned to the back of the church. Dick had never felt so blessed.

• • •

THE RECEPTION WAS held at the Roberts' country club, which resembled a Southern plantation home—complete with marble columns. It was a grand affair in a large ballroom overlooking the distant golf course, where dozens of golf carts meandered slowly up the nearby hill toward the first tee box. As it was a warm day, the wide French doors at the back of the room had been thrown open. Beyond the doors lay a flagstone patio surrounded by white wooden trellises covered with climbing roses, which had outdone themselves for this occasion.

Lorinda and Dick were seated at the head table—beside two empty chairs meant for the bride and groom, who were at the moment making the rounds greeting all their friends.

They had met Pam Roberts and her husband John briefly the night before at the rehearsal dinner. Pam was a tall, slender, stunning redhead, who could have been Allison's sister instead of her mother. John was also tall with dark-brown hair, a terrific tan, and a physique kept young by his active life—in which Phil had said golf played a large part.

"Sorry now you never let Daddy teach you to play golf?" Lorinda whispered after Dick had turned down an invitation to join John and his two brothers for a golf date the next day.

"Guess I'll have to rely on Phil to teach me now," Dick laughed. "He hasn't managed to resist his father-in-law's passion as well as I did. In fact, he said the two of them have been out several times this last week."

As the band took a break and the noise level died down, John leaned over to Lorinda, who sat closest to him. "I understand from Phil that your family was from North Carolina."

"That's right," Lorinda nodded. "My father was from a small town called Clint's Bend. You've probably never heard of it. It's on the big bend in the Roanoke River. My father left there as an infant and grew up in Florida, though, so I know nothing about his family," she added.

"I had an aunt who lived in Clint's Bend," Pam spoke up. "It's a pretty town almost surrounded by the river. We used to go to visit her there each summer. I used to love the swimming hole and getting treats at the General Store. What was your father's name?"

"His name was 'Lockridge,'" Lorinda answered, brightening. "Did you know anyone by that name?"

"'Lockridge'? No, that name doesn't ring a bell," Pam frowned, trying to remember.

"Lockridge?" John questioned. "There was a Lockridge family who lived near us in Raleigh. They were all lawyers. In fact, my father went to school with one of the sons," he continued.

"Do any members of the family still live near here?" Lorinda asked excitedly.

"Old Mr. Lockridge is the only one left that I know of. He's in the Methodist Retirement Home now, I believe," John answered. "It's over on Hillsborough Road. I can give you directions if you'd like to try to see him while you're in town."

"Thank you," Dick smiled, entering the conversation. "That might be a perfect place to start. I promised Lorinda we'd do some research, and he might be able to help. Maybe he had relatives in Clint's Bend."

"'Lorinda,' that's such a lovely name," Pam smiled. "Is it a family name?"

"I was named for my father's mother," Lorinda nodded, as Dick cringed, expecting her to open her locket and insist the Roberts view "Grandma Lorinda." To his relief, however, she only smiled and answered, "That's why I'm so interested in finding out about her."

"Phil and I both love your name, too," Allison interrupted as she took the empty seat Phil had pulled out for her next to her father's. "In fact, we've already talked about it. We'd like to name a daughter after you some day."

"That's so flattering. I can't think of anything I'd like more than a granddaughter," Lorinda beamed. "And, when she's born, I'll give her my locket. Just think . . . three generations linked together." She'd always hoped to have a little girl someday, only her busy career hadn't allowed time for any more children.

"Are you sure you're ready to be a grandmother?" Dick teased. "Somehow neither you nor Pam bears any resemblance to the grandmothers I've known."

"We've been married only a little over two hours, and suddenly I'm going to be a father?" Phil broke in. "Let's take it one step at a time—if you don't mind—and get the wedding over with before you send me out to buy diapers," he laughed.

"Actually, Mom, the band's just getting ready to play again. I think it's traditional for Allison and me to start the dancing with you and John. Are you ready?"

"Better grab your chance before your mother needs a cane," Dick laughed.

● ● ●

DR. EVERETT, MR. Lockridge asked me to bring you up to the sun room to meet him. It's on the second floor. If you'll follow me, I'll show you the way and introduce you," the young dark-haired nurse smiled, motioning Lorinda and Dick across the wide marble floor toward the elevators at the back of the room.

An old gentleman with a shock of curly, white hair was seated on a tan vinyl bench facing the elevators—his cane resting against his leg. Standing as the elevator doors opened, he smiled. "It's been so long since I've had such a lovely visitor," he said, holding out his hands to Lorinda. "Please sit down," he offered, motioning to a matching bench set at right angles to his bench. "I understand you were a 'Lockridge,' too?" he asked as Lorinda and Dick seated themselves and turned to him.

"My father's name was 'Philip Lockridge,'" Lorinda nodded. "He came from Clint's Bend, North Carolina, but I know nothing of his family. You see, his uncle and aunt brought him to Florida when he was an infant. They died long before I was born, and my father never told me anything about the family. I'm not even sure he knew anything himself."

"Clint's Bend?" James Lockridge asked, running his fingers over the thin, white whiskers on his chin. "Named for the old Clinton Plantation right there on the bend in the Roanoke River. It was quite a place in its day, I hear. I had a cousin, Don Lockridge, who married a girl from there—name of 'Causey'," he said slowly, thinking back. Seems to me she was some kin to old man Clinton."

"Is your cousin still alive?" Lorinda whispered, her eyes catching Dick's for a moment before she looked back.

"Died right after his wedding," James Lockridge said, shaking his head sadly. "That's all I ever knew. Real tragedy. Nobody in the family would talk about it after it happened. He was buried outside Clint's Bend—in a cemetery behind a church overlooking the river. I do remember that. My uncle said it was a beautiful location, and it was what he would've wanted," the old man smiled. "Wish I could have helped you more."

"You've helped a lot," Lorinda responded, clasping the old man's hand. "You've given us a name to go on. That's what we've been looking for. And if he was my grandfather, that would explain why my father was taken to Florida. My poor grandmother—trying to raise a child alone!"

• • •

WHAT A PRETTY town," Lorinda called excitedly, peering through the windshield as they entered the small town of Weldon the next afternoon and turned east onto North Carolina Route 158. "It's all so old—so different from South Florida. I can't believe Daddy was born so close to here. What fun I would have had coming to visit my grandparents on vacations. . . ."

"There's the structure that made the town famous," Dick interrupted, leaning across Lorinda and pointing through the windshield.

"Where?" Lorinda asked, following his gaze.

"Over there. The 'Weldon-Wilmington Railroad,'" he answered as he slowed the car to look at the ancient concrete railroad trestle, which spanned the river—its years of weathered graffiti attesting to the many unknown lives that had come and gone in this quiet town. "I remember reading about it. It was one of the main communication links between the coast and the inland towns of the state during the Confederacy."

"What a gorgeous river," Lorinda remarked, craning her neck to look at the churning waters, which flowed into and out of a wide pool just beneath the bridge. A wide stretch of beach—dotted with automobiles, Sunday fishermen, and several families enjoying a picnic—followed the river until it disappeared at last behind a stand of tulip poplars, sweet gum, and oak trees.

"It must be the Roanoke River. We can't be far now," she added.

"Just a few more miles by my calculation," Dick nodded.

• • •

"WE'RE HERE!" LORINDA called a few minutes later as she pointed excitedly at a large wooden sign proclaiming "Clint's Bend" and listing the meeting times of local civic organizations. "Can you drive down the main street?"

"I think this is it," Dick laughed. "Looks like whatever there is of the town is straight ahead," he added as they rounded a curve and approached a row of one-level brick buildings ending in a T-intersection at the base of the courthouse steps.

"Look, Dick, there's a general store. I've never seen one of those before. I thought they went out with high button shoes," Lorinda laughed. "And what a beautiful old courthouse. Look at all the columns—and that long flight of marble steps. I'll bet it was here when Daddy was born. I wish it were open today. I can't wait to find all the records . . . ."

"Are you still sure you want to go through with this?" Dick asked, turning to her as he slowed for the stop sign. "I mean, your father was so adamant . . ."

"Have you ever seen a more peaceful town? I can't imagine what could ever have frightened Daddy about it," Lorinda answered. "It's a beautiful place."

"There's still something nagging at me that I can't explain, though," Dick continued, turning the wheel to the right to circle the courthouse. "Your experience at the fair and then your father's fear . . ." Despite the hot June day, he shuddered involuntarily as a chill overtook him. He couldn't help remembering what Philip had told him at their wedding.

"Honestly, Dick, what do you expect me to find after all these years?" Lorinda laughed. "Do you think there's someone gunning for me? You see the town. Can you imagine anything sinister ever taking place here?"

"You can laugh at me all you want to, but I tell you, whatever is waiting for us in Clint's Bend will change our lives. I'm sure of that," her husband concluded, turning to catch her eye as he slowed at the next corner.

● ● ●

HERE IT IS over here, Dick!" Lorinda shouted, excitedly. "Don Lockridge—born: December 14, 1896; died: February 4, 1921." The gray marble marker was stained with age and overgrown with foot-long grass, which Lorinda held out of the way as Dick approached. "February 4, 1921 . . . ," she puzzled. "That was my dad's birthday. He must have died the same day Daddy was born! How sad.

"I wonder what happened," she added. "Do you think he could have been killed hurrying to be with my grandmother?"

"I have no idea. Why don't we see if we can find your grandmother's grave. Maybe she was buried near him," Dick answered. "What did Mr. Lockridge say her maiden name was?" he puzzled as he began to brush the grass away and search around among the other markers.

"Causey," Lorinda reminded him as she, too, began to examine the other nearby markers. "It must have been 'Lorinda Causey.'"

"Here's a 'Clinton Causey,'" Dick called, stopping and peering down at a flat marker some distance away from Don Lockridge's grave. "He died on July 12, 1920."

"That must have been sometime after my grandmother and grandfather were married," Lorinda nodded, counting the nine months until the baby's birth on her fingers as she hurried over to look. "I wonder what relation he was?"

"He was older," Dick answered, bending down and examining the grass-covered stone. "Could have been Lorinda's father, since he was born in 1880."

"Look!" Lorinda called suddenly from beside him. "'Lorinda Lockridge'! Here she is. I've found my grandmother at last," she squealed excitedly as she fell on her knees and hurriedly began clearing the pine needles and grass from the base of the gray, upright stone. "It says she was born on January 10, 1905.

"My gosh," she called a moment later—her fingers working once again, "my grandmother was barely sixteen years old when my father was born! She was only a child herself. I can't believe it."

"People back then married a lot younger," her husband put in. "The girls probably didn't have any schooling beyond eighth grade. Then, they usually were ready for marriage . . ."

"Look, Dick, look when she died—February 5, 1921," she interrupted—tears standing in her eyes. "She died in childbirth—and only one day after my grandfather. So Daddy was orphaned when he was only one day old. What a tragedy. I wonder if Lorinda even got to see him? How terrible to bring a child into the world and never get to watch him grow up, or go to college, or get married."

"Remember, they didn't have the technology you doctors have today. Back then, countless women died in childbirth—and she was awfully young . . . ," Dick added.

"To have a baby—and to die," Lorinda muttered sadly, her fingers gently caressing the weathered, gray stone for a moment before she rose and brushed off the knees of her tan slacks.

"Come on," she called suddenly in a muffled voice. "It's too morbid hanging around here. It's as if . . . I mean . . . ," she shuddered involuntarily. Looking fleetingly around her, she walked quickly toward a large, gnarled oak tree beside the church—leaning against the bark with her face buried in her hands.

"You feel it now, too, don't you?" Dick whispered as he approached her side. He reached out for her hand and squeezed it. Her fingers were cold and unresponsive.

"Feel what?" she asked, turning to him—her liquid eyes filled with fear as she shook with yet another shudder.

"You felt it all those years ago at the fair. I saw it in your eyes when you left the fortune teller's booth. Your father knew it, too. I felt it at our wedding when he told me never to bring you here," Dick said. "There are just too many coincidences. There's something much deeper here than two accidental deaths—or a death in childbirth. The evil is all around us—even after all these years. We can both feel it . . . .

"Let me take you back to Raleigh, Lorinda, please," he pleaded with her as he pulled gently on her arm. "Then, let's go back home—where it's safe . . . ."

"No! I can't, Dick. I just can't!" Lorinda wailed suddenly, wrenching away from his grasp and wringing her hands in front of her. "I can't leave now. I have to know . . . . I have to find out what happened. Can't you understand? I've lived with this all my life. I've felt it since I was a little girl.

"Every time I asked Daddy to bring me back here to find my grandmother, I think I knew what I would find. But I can't stop now. I have to find out what happened. I owe my grandmother and Daddy that much," she added, the tears pouring down her face as she eluded her husband's outstretched hand and backed toward the wall of the weathered, white church.

CHAPTER TWENTY-FIVE

KISSIN' COUSINS

ONE WEDDING RECORD BOOK coming up," Dick announced as he pulled the monstrous volume from the rack in the tomb-like Records Room in the basement of the County Courthouse and slammed it onto the table—his hands subconsciously resting on top of the volume and holding it closed. "Lorinda, are you still sure you want to go through with this?" he called.

"The index lists 'Causey-Lockridge' as record number 497," Lorinda called from the high wooden table—ignoring his question as she ran her finger down the alphabetized column. Leaving the index open on the table, she walked across the room to peer over his shoulder.

Sighing audibly, Dick slowly opened the mold-mottled, red leather cover and flipped through the brittle, yellowed pages. The same painstakingly-neat penmanship was evident on each entry listing the name of the bride and her parents, the groom, and any witnesses to the wedding. He could feel Lorinda's excitement as she waited for him to find the right page.

Finally, laying the book flat, Dick pointed to the page listing entries number 490-499. "Causey-Lockridge," he announced as he found it.

"Take the information down for me, would you?" Lorinda asked excitedly, tucking a lock of hair behind each ear and putting on her reading glasses as she turned the book toward her to peruse the entry.

"Oh, no!" she uttered a moment later, as Dick looked up from the legal pad he was heading. "There must be some mistake!"

"What is it?" he asked, shoving the paper aside and peering over her shoulder this time.

"Look here—under 'date,'" Lorinda continued, pointing to the entry. "The date of Lorinda and Don Lockridge's marriage is February 4, 1921. That's the same day Don died—and only the day before my father was born . . . ."

"And your grandmother died," he added.

"What does that mean?" Lorinda continued, her eyes searching his from behind her glasses.

"I suppose it means they got married just in time to give your father a name," Dick whispered—trying to keep their conversation from the other two occupants of the room, who were busily plowing through land deed records.

"Surely, if they were in love and knew the baby was on the way, they would have gotten married sooner," Lorinda persisted. "I mean, people just didn't have babies out of wedlock in those days," she whispered back.

"You're kidding yourself," Dick smiled. "You're a doctor. You should know that. People have been having illegitimate children since the world began. It just wasn't accepted then like it is today."

"My father was not 'illegitimate,'" Lorinda hissed. "His parents were already married when he was born. He had a name."

"That's assuming Don Lockridge was his real father," Dick added.

"What do you mean by that?" Lorinda bristled.

"Just that, if your Lorinda was as beautiful as my Lorinda and then got herself in 'the family way,'" he added, smiling, "there might have been all variety of men willing to marry her—despite the parentage of her child."

"What am I dealing with here?" she asked, stepping back from the book and removing her glasses before meeting her husband's eyes—as if trying to distance herself from the facts on the page. She didn't want to hear them.

"I'm only trying to help," he shrugged. "You're looking for answers, and I don't suppose we're going to get many just setting up scenarios. Why don't you read me the rest of the information from the license. It's been seventy-eight years, but, there's a chance one of the witnesses might still be alive—or at least one of his—or her—relatives."

Replacing her glasses, she ran her finger back down the page to find the right license. "It was signed by 'Jake Causey' and 'Malene Causey,'" she answered. "Wonder who they were?"

"Malene was Lorinda's mother," Dick answered, pointing further down the page to the listing of the bride's parents.

"Was Jake her father, then?" Lorinda asked excitedly, pushing his finger away to look for herself.

Dick shook his head and continued to read: "It says her father was 'Clint Causey—deceased.'"

"The headstone in the cemetery," Lorinda whispered, looking up. "But he died only a few months before Lorinda did. Who do you suppose Jake was?"

"Tell you what," Dick offered. "It's getting late, and I'm hungry. What do you say we go get a burger and you can look at a telephone directory . . ."

"I suppose it's worth a try," Lorinda sighed, closing the volume.

"You might find a 'Causey' still living around here," Dick added as he took her arm and led her down the row of scarred tables, past the line of high, transom windows, and through the heavy door to the stairs beyond—breathing deeply only as they emerged once more into the sunlight.

● ● ●

SUCCESS!" LORINDA CALLED excitedly, running back to the table in the small diner and waving a small piece of paper as she slid quickly into the seat opposite her husband. "There was only one 'Causey' listed in the phone directory, but he's bound to be a relative, don't you think?"

"At least a distant one," Dick agreed. "Even if he's not directly related, this is a small town. He's sure to know something about your grandmother. Why not call him?"

"Now?" Lorinda questioned, looking at her watch. "Suppose he's not home . . . ?" Now that they were so close, she wasn't so sure.

"You'll never know unless you try," her husband smiled. He knew her too well.

"Well, if you think I should," she answered, looking at him for approval.

"Go ahead. You've got time while I order. I assume you want a hamburger—with the works—and a chocolate shake," he added, watching her nod. "If you find anyone home, see if we can come by for a visit right after lunch."

Lorinda looked back only once as she left the restaurant again. Dick watched from the window beside their table as she walked slowly to the telephone booth in the parking lot. She slipped on her glasses, put in her change, and spread out her small pad on the ledge under the telephone. She paused a moment. Then, he could see that she was talking.

After a moment, she began writing on her pad, pausing as if asking for clarification. Paydirt! Dick smiled to himself. Now, after all these years, they could finally solve her mystery. He just hoped she wouldn't be too disappointed at what she found.

• • •

GUESS WHAT?" LORINDA called as she slipped into the chair once more. "He's a cousin—'Ned Causey.' He says his father was 'Nate Causey.' He was Lorinda's younger brother. Ned still lives in the old family home. It's just outside of town—near the river. He has a wife and several children."

"Great news!" Dick agreed. Maybe now they could get on with things and get this over with. "When can we go to see him?"

"Right after lunch. He said he was home and would be waiting," she added solemnly, looking down at the paper placemat—printed with a green map of North Carolina.

"What's wrong?" Dick asked, reaching across the table to tip Lorinda's head up and look into her eyes. "After all your looking, you've finally found a relative . . . . I thought you wanted this."

"I did," she answered, her eyes brimming with tears. "Now I have a whole new set of relatives to meet . . . ."

"But . . . ," he added, waiting.

"Oh, I don't know," she continued, shaking her head and impatiently brushing away the tears which had spilled onto her cheeks. "I mean . . . Our own identities are so defined by our families—or whoever we think our families are . . . ," she began. "After all these years to find a whole new family I never knew existed . . . Oh, you understand what I'm trying to say, don't you?"

"I'm not sure. Don't you want to go through with this?" Dick asked, grasping her trembling hands. "If you don't want to go, we'll just call old Ned back up and tell him we have to go back home and don't have time to visit. It's as simple as that."

"I do want to meet him," Lorinda answered. "It's just that I'm not sure I'm ready to find a whole new family. I mean, I know my grandmother and grandfather are dead. But now there will be uncles and aunts and cousins and . . . What if they don't like me?"

"Lorinda, that's the silliest thing I ever heard," Dick interrupted. "What's not to like about you? You're beautiful and smart. You have a great career . . . .

"You're really worried about what they're going to tell you, aren't you? But you said you wanted to find out the truth. Everything that happened here occurred almost eighty years ago. Surely, neither you nor any of your relatives living today can be held to blame for whatever went on . . . ," he added, stopping as the waitress appeared carrying two juicy burgers with fries and two large shakes and placed them on the table.

CHAPTER TWENTY-SIX

THE END OF THE ROAD

HE SAID IT WAS number 100 Maple Avenue," Lorinda called, reading from the small scrap of paper in her hand as Dick drove slowly up Main Street—heading out of town. "It's over by the river. He said to turn at First Street. There's a sign just beyond the post office," she added, peering out the window.

"Go slowly . . . . It can't be far. Look, there it is: 'First Street,'" she read from the wooden sign at the intersection. "Turn right," she added as Dick slowed the car.

"Now, it's a farm—about two miles outside of town," she continued, reading from the notes in her hand.

"Maple Avenue," her husband called triumphantly a few moments later, pointing through the front window as he read the small, hand painted, wooden sign. "It must be that old, dilapidated Victorian—over there on the left at the end of the road," he pointed—seeing only two houses on the small dirt road. "You said he had a large family, and the other one's much too small."

"Oh, my gosh, Dick, it's falling apart!" Lorinda cried, leaning forward to peer over the dashboard as they turned right and started up the narrow dirt road. "To think that was really my family home . . . Dick, I'm not sure . . . ," she added, turning toward him as he pulled the car to a stop at the end of the road—alongside the sprawling, clapboard house with the gingerbread trim.

"We can't just leave now," he asserted. "They've surely seen us. You're the one who wanted to come. Remember? Come on. Let's just get this over with as quickly as we can," he added, unlatching his seat belt and climbing from the car.

As he circled the car to get her door, Lorinda continued to stare out of the driver's side window.

Strips of peeling white paint hung from the sides of the two-story Victorian home and from broken railings on the wide, wooden porch, which completely surrounded the front and right side of the house. Several spindly hydrangea bushes were trying desperately to cling to life in the dry earth beneath the porch.

The only other vegetation was a towering oak tree—hung with a rope swing—, which covered the left side of the house. Several fallen branches littered the bare dirt beneath it—partially concealing a collection of rusted toy cars and trucks lined up beneath the edge of the porch.

The house number was affixed to the gate post of a low, bare-wood picket fence, which ran only on one side—alongside Maple Avenue. Two battered bicycles lay on their sides beside the fence. A broken flagstone walk led from the gate to what appeared to be the back door.

"Lorinda?" a tall, thin man dressed in jeans and a plaid shirt called—hurrying from the kitchen door onto the porch as Lorinda stepped from the car. "I can't tell you how excited I am to meet you. I had no idea . . . I mean, to find a cousin you didn't even know existed . . . ," he began, running his fingers through coarse, collar-length sandy hair flecked with gray.

Studying Lorinda for a brief moment with bright-blue eyes, he suddenly grabbed her hands—his face breaking out in a wide grin.

"But it has to be true. Your resemblance to Aunt Lorinda's photo is uncanny! You look just like her!"

"Ned, this is my husband, Dick Everett," Lorinda called, pulling Dick up onto the porch beside her.

"Glad to meet you," Dick smiled at Ned, extending his hand. "You can't imagine how long Lorinda has looked forward to this meeting."

"My wife's in Weldon shopping this afternoon, but my daughter's fixing us some lemonade," Ned answered, a little embarrassed. "If you like, we can have it right here on the porch. It's a little cooler than in the house," he explained. "And probably a lot quieter, since my oldest son and all four of his children are visiting at the moment," he chuckled.

"We've been there," Dick laughed. "I know what you mean." They smiled conspiratorially.

"So, Lorinda, you were Philip's daughter?" Ned asked when Lorinda and Dick were seated in the worn wicker loveseat and he had taken the chair opposite them.

"I grew up in South Florida," she nodded, "but I never knew anything about his family. I don't think he did either. The only thing I knew was that he was raised for a time by his Uncle Jack and Aunt Carol. They both died, though, in some accident when he was in his teens," she added.

"They were my Uncle Jake and Aunt Carrie Sue," Ned nodded.

"So that's who Jake was!" Lorinda smiled, cutting her eyes at Dick. "No wonder I didn't recognize his name. What was Uncle Jake like?"

"I never knew him or Aunt Carrie Sue. They'd left town long before I was born. But Uncle Jake wrote to Granny for years—every time he went out of town. She'd forbidden him to let anyone know where he was living, you know. That's why they changed their names," Ned added, as Lorinda looked at Dick, puzzled.

"When I was very young," Ned went on, lost in his reverie, "I used to go with my dad when he brought Uncle Jake's letters to Granny. I remember that she always used to cry when she got one. My dad said Jake was always her favorite," he explained.

"Uncle Jake and Aunt Carrie Sue were both killed in the hurricane of 1935. I think a tree fell on their car . . . I can't remember the details. I do remember when Granny got the letter, though. It was from a close friend of Uncle Jake's. He'd asked his friend to mail it if anything ever happened to him. I don't think Granny ever got over it. She had a spell that same day, and she died about six months later," Ned concluded sadly.

"My dad was so worried about Granny that he didn't have time to do anything about your dad for a while. Then, after she died, he tried to contact the man who had written her to ask where Philip was. I was just a little tyke, but I remember him tellin' Mamma he wanted to bring your daddy back here. Said he'd promised Granny years ago to look after him."

"Did he contact Daddy?" Lorinda asked. "Daddy never mentioned hearing from any relatives."

"Apparently, the letter was returned unopened. Seemed the man had moved, and he'd left no forwarding address. I know Daddy agonized over it the rest of his life. Kept saying he wanted to go down to Florida and try to find Philip. But Mamma told him it was crazy and he'd probably spend all our money and still not be able to locate him. Couldn't tell where a teen-aged boy might have ended up."

"Daddy was put into a foster home for a while—until he finished high school," Lorinda nodded. "So I expect your mother was right. It would have been difficult to find him."

An uncomfortable silence followed for a minute. There was so much to say—and yet . . . the gap was so wide.

Finally Ned turned, relieved, as the kitchen door swung outward and a young girl of about sixteen with long, dark-gold hair exited. She was carrying a large tray with a lemonade pitcher and three full glasses, which she handed to each of them. "Nothing better than cold lemonade on a hot day," the girl responded with a smile, locking identical gold-green eyes with Lorinda, who started as if she had seen a ghost.

"Malene," Ned began, "this is my cousin Lorinda. Lorinda, this is my youngest daughter, Malene. She was named for your great-grandmother, 'Malene Causey.'"

"I'm pleased to meet you," the girl answered, reaching out a small hand tentatively. "But, Papa, I thought Annabelle was your only cousin," she inquired, puzzled, as she withdrew her hand and stood watching her father.

"No," Ned replied, slowly. "I had another cousin. His name was Philip Lockridge. He was Lori Beth's child. He left Clint's Bend long before I was born, though."

"Lori Beth?" Lorinda questioned. "Is that what she was called? I never knew," she smiled.

"Lori Beth . . . She's the one who was killed . . . ," Malene mused, trying to fit the pieces together.

"Killed?" Lorinda gasped. "I thought she died in childbirth. I saw her gravestone in the cemetery. She died the day after my father was born."

"That's true," Ned smiled sadly. "But that's only half the story. Actually, she and her bridegroom were gunned down on their wedding day—right in front of the church where she's buried. Although the sheriff tried his best, nobody ever found out who did it. Lori Beth lived only long enough for your father to be born."

"How awful!" Lorinda cried, tears standing in her eyes. "Why would anyone want to kill them?"

"It's a long story," Ned added, sitting back and stretching his arms over his head.

"Daddy, I was just going out. I'm taking my new CD over to Jennifer's, if it's all right with you," Malene interrupted, leaning down to brush her father's face with a kiss.

"Don't be long," he admonished. "Your mamma's gonna need some help with supper when she gets back."

"I promise," Malene answered, running back inside and slamming the kitchen door behind her.

"Now, where was I?" Ned asked. "Oh, yes. You see, Lori Beth was seeing a fellow called Willie Phelps. Seems they were pretty thick when he up and married her older sister, Leah Belle. I never heard directly, but I think it was a case of Willie having to marry Leah Belle—if you know what I mean," he continued, looking at Lorinda, who nodded.

"At any rate, Willie and Leah Belle had a little girl named Annabelle. Shortly after Annabelle's birth, Lori Beth found out she was going to have a baby, too."

"My father," Lorinda nodded. "His father was Don Lockridge. I saw his grave, and I found their marriage license at the courthouse."

"Lorinda," Dick said gently, putting his hand on her arm. "Why not let Ned finish?" he asked as she sat back once more and Ned continued—looking at a spider web on the peeling porch ceiling rather than at Lorinda.

"Apparently that's not what Granddaddy thought—at least according to my daddy's recollection," Ned answered, shaking his head. "Granddaddy was sure that Willie was the father of Lori Beth's baby, too. When he found out she was expecting, he went to the lumber yard Willie's daddy owned—just down the road," he continued, pointing back down First Street toward town. "He was looking for Willie—and carrying his old shotgun.

"When Granddaddy didn't find Willie there, he left. He had parked his wagon in front of the General Store and was heading up the courthouse steps when he was shot with a revolver—right through the back. He died on the spot," Ned concluded, returning his gaze to Lorinda.

"At the courthouse? Where we were today?" Lorinda gasped.

"It's the only one we've got," Ned nodded. "Anyway, the sheriff seemed to think Willie had done it, although no one saw the shooting, and no one ever found the gun.

"The trial was probably the biggest thing that's ever happened around here—before or since. Ask anybody in town. They'll tell you. Even folks who can hardly remember their names any more can remember where they were when that trial was taking place—and probably what everyone was wearing, too."

"Was Willie convicted?" Lorinda asked, wide-eyed.

"There just wasn't enough evidence, so the jury finally acquitted him," Ned answered, shaking his head. "Granddaddy's murder was never solved—although there are still folks in town who think Willie did it—despite the verdict. It made it pretty hard on him and his family over the years."

"But that's awful—if he really didn't do it," Lorinda added. "Didn't the sheriff have any other suspects?"

"During the trial, Granny received a letter," Ned went on, ignoring Lorinda and caught up in his tale. "It was all cut and pasted with magazine letters. It said Lori Beth and the baby both would die. She panicked and sent Lori Beth to her mother's to keep her safe.

"Don Lockridge, the lawyer who was prosecuting the case, had fallen in love with Lori Beth. When the trial was over, he asked Granny if he could marry her."

"Even though it wasn't his baby?" Lorinda asked.

"From all reports, Lori Beth was a real looker. Seems there were a lot of fellows around here who would have married her if she'd just said the word," Ned smiled.

Dick tried unsuccessfully to catch Lorinda's eye at this revelation, but she was glued to Ned's tale—her eyes wide with disbelief. Philip had been right. He never should have brought her here. She didn't need to hear all this. It had no bearing on her, Dick thought.

"But Granny said Don and Lori Beth were really in love and were planning to go to Raleigh to live," Ned continued. "That's where Don was from."

"We met one of his relatives in a nursing home there," Dick asserted, hoping somehow to turn the conversation. "'Lockridge' was the only name we had to go on. He's the one who told us Don had married a girl named 'Causey.' That's how we were able to find you."

"So what happened at the wedding? You said they were 'gunned down'?" Lorinda persisted, leaning forward in her chair. Dick shrugged. There was no way to stop it. She had waited too long, and—whether or not she wanted to hear it—he knew there was nothing to do but let Ned finish his story.

"Well, Granny was opposed to it, but Lori Beth wanted to get married in her own church—the one you passed on the way here— where the two of them were buried. As the two of them were leaving the church after the wedding, someone shot both of them as they stepped outside. Don died at the scene. Lori Beth was wounded pretty seriously, but she lived long enough to have your daddy."

"Didn't anyone see who shot them either?" Dick asked, in-credulous.

According to my daddy, only Granny, Uncle Jake, and he were there, and they were still inside the church. By the time anyone could get outside, there was no one anywhere around. The sheriff suspected Willie again, of course. He spent hours questioning him, from what I heard," Ned explained.

"But he couldn't prove those murders either?" Lorinda asked, aghast.

"Willie had a pretty good alibi. Old man Phelps swore he was at the lumber yard all morning—had his time card to prove it. Don and Lori Beth were shot with a revolver—just like Granddaddy had been. Nobody ever found either weapon, so the whole case would have been circumstantial," Ned sighed.

He paused to smile and wave as the young Malene slammed back through the screen door and ran down the porch steps—a small, padded case of compact discs tucked under her arm.

"Don died at the scene. They took Lori Beth to Doc Mason's in town. He kept her going 'til your daddy was born. But she'd lost too much blood, and . . ."

"But I don't understand why your Granny didn't take my daddy to raise," Lorinda interrupted, her eyes filling with tears. "It seems to me if she loved Lori Beth . . ."

"Daddy said he, Granny, and Uncle Jake were going to raise your daddy together," Ned nodded, pausing for a sip of lemonade. "Then, right after the funeral, Granny found another note saying the baby was next. She was afraid for his life, too.

"At the same time, Uncle Jake was in love with Willie's sister, Carrie Sue. Granny knew how much Jake loved Carrie Sue," he went on. "She also knew Carrie Sue's father would never let her marry Jake. So she gave Jake her wedding silver to pawn. She told him to get the minister to marry them and then to take Carrie Sue and the baby away somewhere where they could never be found.

"She asked him never to tell Philip any of what had happened. She was determined to give him as normal a childhood as possible. My daddy said she asked Jake only to tell him that he must never return to Clint's Bend," Ned concluded.

"So that's why he told me never to take you back," Dick said, turning to Lorinda.

"But that was so long ago. Surely there's no danger now," Lorinda added, looking back at Ned.

"I should think not," Ned answered, shaking his head. "Uncle Willie died over twenty years ago, and Daddy died about ten years ago. In fact, everyone who was alive at that time is now dead except my Aunt Leah Belle and her daughter Annabelle—who was an infant at the time. Annabelle's married and lives in Weldon. She never had any children."

"Aunt Leah Belle's still alive?" Lorinda asked, her mouth agape.

"She lives right across the driveway," Ned nodded toward the small bungalow across the narrow dirt road. "She's ninety-five years old now. She's rather deaf, and we have to shout for her to hear us. Sometimes she gets real confused about who we are and what year it is. But, you know, she's still as strong as a horse—carries her own wood into the house in the winter and shovels her walk.

"After Uncle Willie died, she had no money—and no friends, either. People never forgave Uncle Willie—even though he was acquitted. Daddy said the Phelpses never had any real friends after the trial. When Daddy inherited this house from Granny, he felt sorry for Aunt Leah Belle. He said it had been her family home too—at one time. So he had a small house built for her right across the drive—where the barn used to be," Ned continued.

"Little Malene does all her errands for her now and helps clean her house," he added. "She's such a sweet girl. She usually goes over to Aunt Leah Belle's before she goes out to see if she needs anything from town."

"I saw her run over there a moment ago," Dick nodded, as Lorinda and he turned to look at the small, yellow, one-story house with the blue trim and the crisp blue curtains at the window. A single, white wooden rocker sat on the porch, gently rocking from the thunder of Malene's heavy athletic shoes as she had rushed up the porch only moments before.

CHAPTER TWENTY-SEVEN

YOU CAN'T GO HOME

Curious to see Lorinda's great aunt, Dick continued to watch as a very elderly, thin, stooped woman with wispy, white hair spilling from a twist on top of her head pulled back the blue, cotton curtains from the kitchen window to peer out.

"Malene, child, who's that over on the porch with yer daddy?" she called loudly. Her voice echoed clearly across the narrow dirt road in the humid summer air.

Ned had brought out a family photo album and was now busily pointing out various relatives to Lorinda. Dick's attention, however, had been drawn to the drama unfolding across the street as he waited for Leah Belle's reaction when Malene told her who Lorinda was.

"Some relative of his and her husband," Malene answered loudly, shrugging nonchalantly as she bent down to plant a kiss on the paper-thin skin of the old lady's cheek and to tuck a thin lock back into her loose bun. "Aunt Leah Belle, you want me to give you another perm sometime?" she called—her love for the old woman apparent in her voice.

"What? Land sakes, no, chile," Leah Belle bellowed, her attention momentarily diverted from Lorinda—at whom she had been staring. "Ain't nobody gonna care how I look, an' I ain't gonna sit still fer all that fussin' again," she asserted, reaching up and refastening the lock Malene had just fixed.

"Who'd you say that was over there with yer daddy?" she asked again, pulling the curtain back further and peering more intently at Lorinda. "She looks real familiar."

Remembering Lorinda's uncanny resemblance to the original Lorinda, Dick wondered if Aunt Leah Belle would finally see it and know who she was. Ignoring Ned and Lorinda, who were still pouring over the family photo album, he turned his attention wholly to the elderly woman across the street, waiting for some sign of recognition.

"I don't think so," Malene added as she shook her head. "Daddy introduced her. He says she's his cousin, only they've never met before. Her name's 'Lorinda.'"

"Lorinda!" Leah Belle screamed, suddenly pulling the curtain completely aside and fixing her myopic eyes on Lorinda—just as Lorinda, hearing the outburst, looked across the street and caught her eye.

"Do you know her, Aunt Leah Belle?" Malene called, alarmed at her aunt's overreaction to the name.

"'Course I know her," Leah Belle answered angrily. "Always runnin' off an' leavin' me with all the work to do an' Pa yellin' at me. An', then, with her tryin' to take Willie away from me and little Annabelle. . . ."

"Aunt Leah Belle, you got things all mixed up again," Malene laughed. "She's never even been in town before."

"Oh, don't let her fool you none. She was here alright—long enough to cause all this trouble we been through. Then Mamma sent her away. They said she wasn't never comin' back, but I knew she couldn't stay away forever," Leah Belle added as she continued to stare across the narrow road.

"Malene, girl, I'm feelin' kinda tired," she said, turning suddenly from the window. "Think I'll go out on the porch an' set a spell," she called as she disappeared for a moment—only to reappear a second later at the open door of the bungalow.

"Want me to bring you your shawl?" Malene's voice drifted out of the opened door as she followed after the old woman. "Might get cool later."

"I won't need it," Leah Belle added, looking across the street again before turning to the young woman beside her. "But in the hall closet—way in the back, I think—," she added, pointing into the room behind her, "there's an old, quilted market bag. Could you bring it to me? It's got red an' blue squares on the sides. You'll see it," she continued. "It may be heavy, so lift it careful-like," she smiled as she walked out onto the porch and took a seat in the wooden rocker.

Interested, Dick continued to watch. Now, maybe Lorinda would finally find what she had been looking for all her life. It was amazing to find her great-aunt still alive. They'd certainly never even dared to hope . . . . Perhaps that bag she'd asked for was filled with old family photos she would share or some other pictures of the grandmother Lorinda so worshiped. At least, she should be able to tell her some stories of her grandmother as a young woman.

● ● ●

THANK YOU SO MUCH, Ned,—for everything." Dick heard Lorinda's voice at last and saw her smile as she rose from the love seat and placed her empty glass on the small wicker table.

"Wish you two would stay around long enough to meet Cassie," Ned answered, standing as well. "She should be home in just a little while."

"Maybe next time," Lorinda answered, shaking her head and looking across the field behind the house. "Looks like a storm's coming up, and we've got a long way to go back to the hotel."

Reluctantly following her lead, Dick stood as well. There was another story playing itself out across the driveway, and he wanted to see it to the end. Lorinda was right, however, about the storm. The sky behind the house was now leaden. If they didn't leave quickly, they'd be caught in it—and Ned didn't seem disposed to invite them in. If the inside of the house looked anything like the outside, Dick smiled to himself, he could understand why.

"I'm so happy to have met you. I wish we could have done this years ago," Ned smiled, grasping Lorinda's hands. "And I really wish I could have known your father. I heard so much about him as a child. This has been such a treat—although, I don't think I told you what you wanted to hear, did I?"

"The truth will out," Dick added, reaching out to shake Ned's hand as he stood. "I tried to warn Lorinda of what she might find, but she was insistent."

"At least I got to meet my relatives," Lorinda smiled. "It's been fun," she called, her voice breaking as she turned to go. Dick could tell the tears were welling up inside her. He understood what she was feeling.

The young woman Ned had described was not the grandmother she had hoped to find—the woman she had idolized all her life. He longed to go to her—to put his arm around her and tell her it was all right. It had all happened so long ago. But she had her pride. He had to leave her that, he decided as he watched her subconsciously wrap her fingers around her locket, take a wary look at the darkening sky, and hurry down the steps toward the car.

"I'm sorry if I disillusioned her," Ned confided as Dick also turned to go. "Lord knows it is a sordid story . . . . I didn't mean to hurt her. But she asked."

"It's not your fault. Lorinda wanted to know. She's been trying to find her grandmother since before I met her," Dick smiled wanly at Ned. "At least she has some answers now. She's strong. She'll deal with it," he concluded. He wasn't really sure she could handle it, but he couldn't tell Ned that. After all, he had only told her what she had asked to hear.

Dick took one last look across the street at Aunt Leah Belle, who was rocking silently in her chair—her eyes never leaving Lorinda. He wondered why no one had suggested that Lorinda meet her great aunt. He'd have thought that Ned . . . But perhaps it would have been too great a shock at her age. And maybe it was all for the best. He knew Lorinda could not have taken much more at that moment. And with the storm approaching . . . It wouldn't take much to get stuck on these dirt roads.

As he started down the stairs, Malene suddenly reappeared on the porch across the narrow lane. "This what you wanted, Aunt Leah Belle?" she asked, handing a brightly-colored cloth bag to the old woman in the rocker.

"That's it," Leah Belle smiled. "Been in that closet a long time," she added, loosening the drawstring at the top of the bag and peering inside.

"Gonna storm," Malene added, looking at the gathering clouds. "You'll need to get back inside . . . ," she continued, pausing to watch Lorinda approach the car. She seemed to be waiting for her to leave.

"Now, don't worry none about me, chile. I can git myself back inside when I'm good an' ready," Leah Belle added. "Go on an' git over to that friend o' yers house 'fore you drown," she continued, waving Malene away with her arm. As the young woman paused, the first peal of thunder rumbled across the adjoining field.

Watching for her father's nod, Malene bent to give the old woman a fleeting kiss before vanishing inside the house to retrieve her case.

Lorinda was already beside the car. Dick could see her wiping at the tears streaming from her eyes as she fished in her large purse for her keys.

As Dick reached the bottom of the steps, a loud explosion suddenly ripped the quiet country air and reverberated off the shingles of the old house. He'd had no idea the storm was that close, he thought as he jumped involuntarily. Suddenly, he saw Ned turn and bolt past him down the steps. Only then did Dick look up, horrified, to see Lorinda crumple silently—in slow motion—and come to rest at last in a small heap in the gray dust beside their car as the first large raindrops began to fall in earnest.

Rushing to Lorinda's side, Dick heard a wail ring out from across the driveway. Ned suddenly stopped in the road, looking from Lorinda to his daughter, who stood in the doorway of the tiny house screaming over the crumpled, lifeless body of an aged woman. An overturned, white wooden rocker lay on top of her, and an ancient revolver was clutched in her right hand—the barrel still smoking.

CHAPTER TWENTY-EIGHT

UNTO THE NEXT GENERATION

WAITING FOR LORINDA . . . IT was hard to remember a time when he hadn't been—with most of those times spent right here on the University of Florida campus. Waiting for the conclusion of rounds, an operation, a conference, a fund raiser . . . And waiting for the magical birth of their son, a young man who—after deciding to come into this world much earlier than expected—had actually proven no more disposed to punctuality than his beautiful mother. Dick Everett smiled to himself. It had seemed the longest day of his life—until the nurse had ushered him into the recovery room, where the delight in Lorinda's eyes as she presented Little Phil to him had made every second worthwhile.

He paused now to look across the suite's tiny sitting room at his son, who had always been the most important thing in his life—after Lorinda.

"She will be all right, won't she, Dad?" Phil asked from the sofa—his concerned gold-flecked, green eyes catching his father's as he picked up the telephone on the nearby table and glanced at the paper in his hand. "I mean . . . She's been in there for hours."

"You didn't spend your whole childhood with a doctor in the house not to know the hours these procedures can take," Dick answered, smiling wanly before glancing away. Not here. Not now. Here in this small hotel room above the campus student union, where every tree and building reminded him of Lorinda, he couldn't bear to look into Phil's eyes—so much like his mother's.

To Dick, Lorinda's eyes had always reminded him of that algae-covered lake down there—the golden flecks on the gray-green surface hiding the murky depths of sadness so far below. Seeing Phil's attention diverted as he dialed the number on the paper, Dick walked to the sliding glass door—his hand resting on the glass as he subconsciously traced the outline of the familiar lake on the clear surface. Then, glancing back over his shoulder and seeing Phil busily engaged in his phone conversation, he grasped the latch and slid the door open—stepping onto the narrow fourth-floor balcony and silently closing the door behind him.

Scanning the marshy, reed-enclosed lake beneath him a moment, Dick nodded as his eyes finally settled on a sunny spot on the opposite shore. "Albert understands. Don't you, old man?" he whispered to himself. "You think you're hidden so cleverly, but I see you watching me from across the lake. Only, maybe you're Albert, Junior—or even the third.

"How long do alligators live? I've never thought to ask," he continued, shaking his head. It had never seemed important before. Yet now it somehow seemed vital that this was really "his" Albert. How long had it been since they had first locked eyes? Forty years now—by his calculation. Yet, it seemed like only yesterday.

The carillon was ringing . . . There, right on cue. What time was it anyway? He'd lost all track of time. But it didn't matter, he decided, watching from his fourth-floor vantage point as the doors to the distant classroom buildings belched out students no larger than ants—their laughter and chatter wafting upward on the warm summer breeze. It was hard to remember ever having been that young—or carefree. But he had been. . . No, he still was that much in love, he smiled, catching sight of a young couple locked in a tight embrace under an oak tree beside the lake. Nothing had changed there.

Resting his elbows on the iron railing, Dick closed his eyes. But so much else had changed in his life. Perhaps it was finally time to deal with it. Surely, Phil would come for him when it was time. And he knew the wait would be worth it. It always had been.

He turned to watch his son through the picture window. Phil had hung up the phone now and turned on the television, but he didn't seem to be watching it. Dick knew he should go back inside to be with him. Despite the closeness between a father and son, however, there were some things they just couldn't share. Tears were one of them.

Yes, it was still there. Reaching into his pocket, Dick wound his fingers around the thin chain and slowly withdrew his hand. Catching the bright sunlight, the gold locket seemed to glow as Dick lifted it toward his face. A pale-pink fingernail swam before his eyes. The catch swung open, and those mesmerizing gold-green eyes smiled out at him. He caught a faint whiff of Chanel Number Five, and he smiled.

"She's been a part of me longer than you have now, my darling," Dick whispered. "And her legacy has cost each of us dearly. I haven't forgotten my promise. Please don't think I have. I've broken only one in my lifetime . . . . But maybe it's time now to break the second. I hope somehow you'll understand.

"This is where it all began," he continued, looking downward at the still, green waters below his balcony. "It seems fitting it should end here as well. Forgive me, Lorinda," he continued, looking upward at the cloudless, blue sky for a moment before balling the locket and chain into his fist. Then, reaching back over his shoulder, he threw with all his might.

The late afternoon sunlight bounced a fleeting, dark-gold beam of light into his eyes as the locket slowly drifted downward—disappearing at last into the murky depths of the gold-flecked, green water beneath him. A sudden movement from the opposite bank caught his eye as an ancient, gray-green creature slid slowly from the bank into the lake. Shaking his head at the intruder, Dick silently placed a finger to his lips. Old Albert wouldn't tell.

"Don't let him fool you!" a familiar voice rang in his ears—as a hand suddenly came to rest on his shoulder. He jumped, alarmed. The nails were short—and bare. The air smelled of English Leather aftershave, but the eyes were hers. Dick smiled as he turned to his son.

"The hospital just called," Phil offered, his face breaking into a smile. "It's time to go. Everything went perfectly the doctor said. Allison's in recovery, and the baby's fine."

With one final look at the placid lake below him, Dick turned. "And, now, my darling," he whispered to himself as he followed his son through the sliding glass doors, "it's time to meet the new 'Lorinda.'" Drawing a small, wrapped box from his pocket, he added, "I think she'll like my gift—a new silver locket with her own grandmother's photo inside."

Clarissa Thomasson was born and raised in Miami, Florida. She received her BA in English Literature from Duke University, and received her MA degree—also in English Literature—from the University of Florida.

After moving to the Washington, DC area with her husband and two daughters, Ms. Thomasson taught English literature, creative writing, and journalism in the Montgomery County, Maryland, public schools until her retirement in 1995. She now resides in Nags Head, North Carolina, where she is pursuing her writing career.

Lorinda's Legacy is Ms. Thomasson's third novel. Her first novel, *Defending Hillsborough*, was released in 1998, and her second, *Reconstructing Hillsborough*, was released in 1999.